"What a
my wor

"You resear

"My goal is to develop fusion power as an economically viable energy source. Two days ago, a representative from our government visited me at my lab in California. He requested that I continue my research under their supervision. All my results would be exclusive property of the Department of Defense. I turned them down."

"Surely you don't think the government is trying to kill you simply because you wouldn't work for them."

"No. They don't want my death. They want my work. And what better way to get it than to place someone, say a bodyguard, in a position where they had a reason to stay with me night and day? Even better, what if they sent a beautiful woman who would have unlimited opportunities to gather information?"

He could see the exact moment she understood his point. Twin spots of color bloomed in her cheeks—and he would bet it wasn't because he'd called her beautiful.

Her lips thinned. "You think I was sent here to spy on you."

Dear Reader,

This year may be winding down, but the excitement's as high as ever here at Silhouette Intimate Moments. National bestselling author Merline Lovelace starts the month off with a bang with *A Question of Intent,* the first of a wonderful new miniseries called TO PROTECT AND DEFEND. Look for the next book, *Full Throttle,* in Silhouette Desire in January 2004.

Because you've told us you like miniseries, we've got three more for you this month. Marie Ferrarella continues her family-based CAVANAUGH JUSTICE miniseries with *Crime and Passion.* Then we have two military options: *Strategic Engagement* features another of Catherine Mann's WINGMEN WARRIORS, while Ingrid Weaver shows she can *Aim for the Heart* with her newest EAGLE SQUADRON tale. We've got a couple of superb stand-alone novels for you, too: *Midnight Run,* in which a wrongly accused cop has only one option— the heroine!—to save his freedom, by reader favorite Linda Castillo, and Laura Gale's deeply moving debut, *The Tie That Binds,* about a reunited couple's fight to save their daughter's life.

Enjoy them all—and we'll see you again next month, for six more of the best and most exciting romances around.

Yours,

Leslie J. Wainger
Executive Editor

Please address questions and book requests to:
Silhouette Reader Service
U.S.: 3010 Walden Ave., P.O. Box 1325, Buffalo, NY 14269
Canadian: P.O. Box 609, Fort Erie, Ont. L2A 5X3

Aim for the Heart
INGRID WEAVER

INTIMATE MOMENTS™
Published by Silhouette Books
America's Publisher of Contemporary Romance

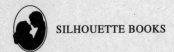 SILHOUETTE BOOKS

ISBN 0-373-27328-2

AIM FOR THE HEART

Copyright © 2003 by Ingrid Caris

Visit Silhouette at www.eHarlequin.com

Printed in U.S.A.

Books by Ingrid Weaver

Silhouette Intimate Moments

True Blue #570
True Lies #660
On the Way to a Wedding... #761
Engaging Sam #875
What the Baby Knew #939
Cinderella's Secret Agent #1076
Fugitive Hearts #1101
Under the King's Command #1184
**Eye of the Beholder* #1204
**Seven Days to Forever* #1216
**Aim for the Heart* #1258

Silhouette Special Edition

The Wolf and the Woman's Touch #1056

*Eagle Squadron

INGRID WEAVER

admits to being a sucker for old movies and books that can make her cry. A Romance Writers of America RITA® Award winner for Romantic Suspense and a national best-selling author, she enjoys creating stories that reflect the adventure of falling in love. When she and her husband aren't dealing with the debatable joys of living in an old farmhouse, you'll probably find Ingrid going on a knitting binge, rattling the windows with heavy metal or rambling through the woods in the back forty with her cats. You can visit Ingrid's Web site at http://www.ingridweaver.com.

This book is dedicated to Susan Litman and
Kim Nadelson, two extraordinary editors who
helped bring Eagle Squadron to life.
Thank you both for sharing the adventure.

Chapter 1

"Dr. Lemay, get down!"

The cry was muffled by the lap of water in the canal below him and the noise of traffic at his back. Hawk couldn't be certain he'd heard it. Curious, he pushed away from the stone wall that bordered the canal and turned around. The last rays of afternoon sunlight gilded the gabled windows and copper rooftops of Gamla Stan, Stockholm's Old Town, but the street level was already cloaked in dusk. Headlights bored through puffs of exhaust. Against the glow of shop windows on the other side of the road, pedestrians were swiftly moving shadows, their shoulders hunched against the breeze.

"Dr. Lemay!"

Hawk spotted her then. A woman was running along the sidewalk. He had a quick impression of blond hair and an athlete's stride before she disappeared behind a bus. As soon as the bus had passed, she leaped off the sidewalk and darted through the traffic toward him.

Tires screeched as a taxi braked to avoid her. There was a thud and the crunch of metal as a boxy delivery truck plowed into the taxi. It spun into the woman's path. Without breaking stride, she hurdled over the taxi's hood, slid down the front fender and kept running.

Hawk held up his palms and started forward. Was she suicidal or just plain crazy? "Stop!" he shouted. "Watch out!"

"Get *down!*" she repeated. She dodged past a station wagon and reached the curb just as Hawk did. She didn't stop. She launched herself through the air, hitting him square in the chest.

Hawk staggered backward at the impact. She wasn't a large woman but her momentum was too much to counteract. Off balance, he hit the sidewalk hard on his butt. His hands smacked the pavement behind him. His teeth clacked together, cutting off the oath he muttered.

Instead of apologizing, the woman threw her weight against his shoulders to knock him flat on his back. Before he could catch his breath, she spread-eagled herself on top of him. "Stay down," she ordered. "The shooter is on the second floor."

He lifted his head. "What—"

"Building across the street." She slapped her hand to his forehead and pushed his head back down. "The traffic will provide us some cover as long as you stay low. Keep still while I call for assistance."

"Ma'am—"

"Captain Sarah Fox," she said. "United States Army."

Army? Hawk twisted his head to look at her, but all he could see was her left ear and the curve of her cheek. She wasn't wearing a uniform. She wore a black wool coat. A silk scarf in a swirl of tropical colors was knotted at her throat. The fringe brushed his nose, bringing with it an aroma reminiscent of cinnamon.

She shifted, taking her hand from his head to reach into the pocket of her coat and withdraw a phone. With her forearm braced against his chest, she used her teeth to yank up the antenna, then thumbed a button. She spoke rapidly in what sounded like Swedish.

As a rule, Hawk didn't take this long to work things through. Sure, he liked to be confident of his facts before he drew any conclusions because he hated to be wrong, but he wasn't normally at a loss. He could blame it on jet lag, or on the shock of being tackled by a strange woman...or on the sensation of warm, spicy-smelling female draped over his body and silk tickling his nose.

With an effort he forced his brain into gear. She was an American; she said she was from the army. She knew his name. She said there was a shooter. She had spread herself over him as if she were trying to shelter him...

Damn! She was trying to shield him with her own body. The realization wiped everything else from his mind. Hawk clamped his arm around her back, hooked his leg over hers and rolled them both toward the stone wall he had been lounging against only seconds ago.

She grunted as his full weight settled on top of her. She shoved at his chest. "Dr. Lemay, you have to get off me. Your life is in danger."

"First of all, I don't believe the government's story," he said. "And second, even if I did, I don't consider my life worth more than yours."

"It's my job to protect you."

"I never hired you."

"This is hardly the time to debate my orders." She bucked beneath him, folding her arms in and her knees up.

With a move too quick to follow, she flipped him to his back, then scrambled over him to crouch at his side. Keeping herself between him and the street, she reached into her pocket once more. This time she withdrew a handgun.

The two-tone bleat of a siren sounded in the distance. Voices came from the street. The taxi driver was arguing with the driver of the delivery truck. More cars screeched to avoid them. A crowd was gathering.

But the woman appeared oblivious to the commotion she had caused. She sat back on one heel, bracing her elbow on her upraised knee to steady her gun. Her head moved from side to side as she scanned the area.

Hawk sat up behind her and followed her gaze. He saw plenty of faces turned toward them, but he couldn't see any threat. He moved close to the woman's shoulder. "Whatever you think you saw, ma'am—"

"Captain Sarah Fox," she said again. "United States Army. I would show you my identification but I'm occupied right now."

"I don't think anyone's shooting at me. If they were, we would both be dead."

"Which is why I knocked you down, sir. I saw a rifle."

"Where?"

"The dark-yellow brick building. Third window from the left, second floor above the antique store."

The truck that had hit the taxi blocked his view. Hawk leaned to the side and scrutinized the window she had described. It was a multipaned casement style, divided vertically by a black frame, identical to all the other windows in the quaint, centuries-old structure. One side had been cranked open, which was unusual, considering the chill in the air—it was November —but nothing was visible inside. "I don't see anything."

"Chances are he would have retreated when he realized he couldn't make his shot, but he could still be in the area." The siren grew louder. She raised her voice. "With the wall and the canal at our backs and the truck giving us cover in front, this is a good defensive position. It would be safest to stay where we are until the police get here."

Hawk moved his gaze from the open window where there might or might not have been a gunman and focused on the woman at his side.

She had twice identified herself as Captain Sarah Fox. Her military bearing, her physical agility and the ease with which she handled her firearm supported her claim. Yet she didn't look like a soldier. Her features were a study in classic softness, like something from a painting by Rembrandt. Wisps of hair the color of ripe wheat had pulled loose from the clip at the back of her head to tease her cheeks. The slim fingers that gripped her gun were delicately feminine. Her voice, even when it was barking orders, had a smoky timbre that evoked images of dimly lit bars rather than battlefields.

Hawk wasn't accustomed to following orders. He didn't have the temperament to obey blindly. He always preferred to work things through for himself.

But he was no fool. Although *he* didn't believe the government's story about a hired killer out to get him, this woman obviously did. What if he was wrong?

He might be willing to gamble his own life, but he had no right to gamble with hers.

The warm air hit Sarah like a fist the moment she entered the hotel lobby. Until now, the pain had been numbed by the cold. This was supposed to be light duty, an easy breather while the injury she'd suffered during her previous mission finished healing. It shouldn't have presented a problem, but she hadn't anticipated needing to tackle her subject within minutes of her arrival.

"Captain Fox, are you all right?"

She paused to glance at the man beside her. She didn't want to tilt her head, so her gaze only reached his chin. "That's what I should be asking you, Dr. Lemay." She began a careful visual sweep of the lobby. The marble-and-gilt old-world elegance of the King Gustav Hotel was illuminated by wall sconces. Great for atmosphere, not good for visibility. "I'll arrange for a doctor to check you over in case you got a concussion when you hit the sidewalk."

"I don't need a doctor. You're the one who seems to be in discomfort."

He was more observant than most people, she thought. That didn't surprise her, considering the number of degrees Hawkins Lemay had the right to string after his name. He was a Nobel laureate, a bona fide genius. He wouldn't be an easy man to deceive. "No, I'm fine. I regret having to knock you down, but it was necessary."

"Was it? I thought the police didn't find anything when they checked that building where you saw the gunman. They appeared to give us a ride to my hotel out of courtesy for your rank rather than out of a need for security."

Satisfied that the lobby didn't hold any immediate threat, Sarah started forward. "That's true, but I hadn't expected them to find any trace of the shooter. By all accounts, we're dealing with a professional."

"Could have been a mop handle."

"What?"

"The object you saw in the window. It could have been

some innocent cleaning crew at work instead of this alleged assassin.''

"Trust me, Dr. Lemay. I do have some experience with firearms and am able to recognize one.''

"It was dusk and you're probably jet-lagged like me.''

"I've been informed of your skepticism. We can discuss this further once you're somewhere safe.'' She gestured toward the front desk. "Let me pick up my bag first. I left it here when they told me you had gone for a walk.''

He put his palm on the small of her back as they moved toward the desk. It was a courtly gesture. It went along with the faint trace of the South that tinged his deep voice, a holdover from his early childhood. It also fit with the gallant way he'd tried to protect her out there on the sidewalk…even though he claimed not to believe her.

Sarah was accustomed to working with men as her equals. She couldn't remember the last time she'd been treated with gallantry. She had to admit it was a pleasant change, but she couldn't allow it to distract her attention.

She was here to protect him. Those were her orders. Work with the local authorities, organize security and take whatever measures were necessary to keep Hawkins Lemay alive while he attended the Stockholm Energy Conference. Once the conference ended, so did her mission.

She retrieved her suitcase from the desk clerk and turned toward the elevator.

Lemay took the suitcase from her grip before they had gone two steps. "Please, allow me.''

She decided not to argue with the courtesy—she preferred to keep both hands free, anyway. Besides, the weight of the gear in her suitcase was substantial. "Thank you.''

"How did you know where to look?'' he asked.

"I was scanning the buildings as I walked and spotted the glint from the sniper's scope."

"I meant how did you know where to look for me?"

"Your hobbies include fishing. Since Stockholm is built on islands, I deduced you would likely gravitate toward water so I chose the route that led to the nearest bridge."

"That's very astute reasoning, but how did you know about my hobbies?"

"I assembled a background file on you when I accepted this mission and I memorized it on the flight over." She stopped in front of the elevator. It was an old-fashioned model with frosted glass doors and a folding metal gate. The visibility it provided was an asset—Sarah could see at a glance it was empty.

"Background file?" Lemay asked as they stepped into the car.

"It's standard operating procedure, Dr. Lemay. Nothing personal. Unfortunately, it appears as if the shooter we encountered this afternoon has acquired information about your habits, as well." She closed the doors and slid the gate into position. She pressed the button for the fifth floor, which was the top story of the historic building that served as the hotel's main wing. The elevator started upward with a jerk. "As I said before, we can discuss this once we're somewhere more secure."

"Where are you staying?"

"Since I'm your bodyguard, I'll be staying with you."

"Wait a minute. I never agreed to this."

"It's the only way to do my duty properly. Until the conference is over, I'm your shadow. You don't go anywhere without me."

He hit the emergency stop button. The car shuddered as

it clunked to a halt between the second and third floors. "This has gone far enough."

"You have a two-room suite consisting of a bedroom and sitting room. I realize the rooms in the King Gustav are small by North American standards, but there should be adequate space for both of us."

"That's not the point."

"I'll bunk down in the sitting room. I've already arranged to have a cot sent up."

He set her suitcase on the floor and grasped her shoulders, turning her to face him. "I didn't agree to any of this. Who sent you? Let me talk to your commanding officer." He paused. "Captain?"

She had tried to keep her face expressionless but she hadn't been able to stop the wince when he'd touched her bruises. She shrugged off his grip and stepped back. "My C.O. for this mission is Major Mitchell Redinger. You can reach him at Fort Bragg. I'll give you his contact number once we're in your suite."

He leaned down to bring his face level with hers. "What's wrong? And don't tell me it's nothing."

There was no point lying—even someone who wasn't as intelligent as Lemay would be able to see she was in pain. "I took a round during my previous mission," she said. "My body armor stopped the bullet but the impact of the high-caliber round dislocated my left shoulder."

He returned his hand to her shoulder. He didn't touch her. He held his fingers a breath above her coat, then caught a stray lock of her hair and tucked it behind her ear.

The gesture was so unexpected, so…tender, it took Sarah a moment before she could continue. "There was some bruising so the joint is still somewhat sensitive," she said. "I assure you it won't interfere with my ability to do my duty."

He dropped his hand. "You hit me with your left shoulder when you knocked me down," he murmured. "You reinjured it because of me."

"My comfort is immaterial. My duty is to protect you."

"My God, you don't even know me."

He was wrong, she thought. She knew every fact about Hawkins Lemay that could be gathered by Army Intelligence. The background file she'd assembled had been impressively thick and contained far more than a list of his hobbies. And it had been a long flight.

His credentials as a scientist were beyond repute, his accomplishments in the field of particle physics were astounding. At only thirty-five, he was the world's leading expert on nuclear fusion, respected by his colleagues, courted by foreign governments and ambitious businessmen alike...and considered important enough by the American government to warrant personal protection. Major Redinger's orders had come straight from the Pentagon.

Still, there were things the file hadn't told her. She'd known Lemay was six foot two, 198 pounds, physically fit because of his daily jogging, but she hadn't known how gracefully he moved, or how long and tanned his fingers were, or how the battered, brown leather jacket he wore creaked subtly with his motions and smelled so deliciously of fresh air and man...

"You're the man I've been assigned to protect, Dr. Lemay," she said. "That's really all I need to know." She stretched past him to restart the elevator. It resumed its slow ascent with a jerk. Lemay reached out to steady her, but she ignored him and took a quick step sideways.

He picked up her suitcase. His voice was low and tense.

"I'm sorry I hurt you. Would it help to put ice on your shoulder?"

"No problem. I'll be fine."

"Who were you protecting that time?"

She kept her attention on the passing floors. "Excuse me?"

"When you were shot?"

"It was a hostage rescue. A seven-year-old boy."

"Since when does the Army do hostage rescue... Ah. I should have seen it." His voice took on a curl of interest. "Hostage rescue, bodyguard detail. You're no ordinary soldier, you're with Delta Force."

His insight didn't surprise her. After all, he was a genius. "Yes, sir. Here's our floor. Stay back until I check the corridor." She opened the gate with one hand and slipped her gun from her pocket with the other. She listened first, but she heard nothing from the hall. She held up her palm, motioning Lemay to remain where he was, then stepped out of the elevator. When she assured herself the way was clear, she glanced behind her.

She had half expected him to defy her order and follow her, but he was still standing by the elevator, her suitcase tucked under one arm as if it weighed nothing. His jacket gaped open, exposing a wrinkled denim shirt. The lighting in the corridor was as subdued as it had been in the lobby, yet the shadows couldn't hide the sharp glint in his gaze.

The striking blue eyes he'd inherited from Cynthia Hawkins, his New England mother. The midnight-black hair and strong bone structure had been passed down from Pascal Lemay, his Cajun father. Those were facts she had known since she'd memorized his face from the photograph in his background file.

But the photo hadn't shown that gleam in his eyes. It

was a glimpse of the power that dwelled behind the distinctive features, a hint of Dr. Hawkins Lemay's awesome intellect.

He held her gaze as he closed the distance between them. His big body moved with the careless ease of a predator, another fact that wasn't contained in his file. He paused in front of her, once more filling her senses with the scent of leather and man. ''Tell me the truth, Captain Fox,'' he said. ''What's the real reason you're here?''

Chapter 2

Hawk crossed his ankles and leaned against the door frame as he watched Captain Fox move through the bedroom. Like the rest of the suite she'd already been through, the bedroom was decorated predominantly in ivory and pale rose, with antique furniture that carried the dark patina of age. But the captain wasn't interested in the décor any more than he was. She'd claimed she was checking for bombs or booby traps, and she appeared to be doing a thorough job.

His belongings were still in his suitcase—he hadn't taken the time to unpack before he'd felt the need to go out for a walk—but even the suitcase hadn't escaped her scrutiny. She was sticking to her story, yet the more Hawk thought about it, the more he wondered whether he should trust her.

That wasn't anything new. He seldom trusted anyone. "Don't you find it odd that out of all the soldiers who could have been assigned to guard me, your Major Redinger chose an injured woman?''

She strode past the bed to the window, tested the lock, then closed the curtains. ''Not odd in the least, Dr. Lemay. I was the best person for the job.''

''Because you speak Swedish?''

''Yes, that was one of the factors in my favor.''

''What are some of the others?''

''I'm an excellent shot. And like many of the other soldiers of Delta Force, I've received bodyguard training from the Secret Service.'' She did a final survey of the bedroom and its adjoining bathroom, then walked past him to return to the suite's elegant sitting area. ''And as I already told you, my injury won't interfere with my ability to do my duty. The bulk of my work will involve coordinating security with the hotel and the local police.''

He pivoted to keep her in sight. Her inspection apparently complete, she unbuttoned her coat as she moved to the carved wooden wardrobe beside the suite's door. He was relieved to see that she didn't betray any difficulty moving her shoulder when she hung up her coat. While he still needed to be more certain of his facts before he could trust her, the pain he'd seen earlier when he'd grabbed her had been authentic, he was certain of that.

Her description of her injury had been curtly businesslike. She hadn't wanted his sympathy. Why? Was it because she was trying to be professional, or because she simply didn't like admitting vulnerability? Both, he decided. ''Is personal protection your specialty?'' he asked.

''My duties are varied, depending on the mission,'' she replied, taking her cell phone and her gun from her coat. She closed the wardrobe and turned to face him. ''But my specialty is intelligence.''

She wore a turtleneck sweater and tailored pants. Like

her coat, they were black. Unlike her coat, they didn't conceal her figure.

Hawk saw that her body was as feminine as her face, an appealing combination of slenderness and curves. Softness over strength, like the silk scarf at her neck that was a whimsical splash of color against the sober black of her clothes. Yet her appeal arose from more than her appearance. It was the fluid way she moved and the confident way she angled her chin. Although she wasn't tall, she had the kind of presence that gave the impression of height.

She slipped her phone into her pants pocket and reached behind her to tuck her gun into her waistband at the small of her back. The movement tightened her sweater over her breasts. Firm, temptingly rounded breasts that would fit perfectly into his palms…

Hawk lifted his gaze to her face.

She was staring straight at him, so she had to have noticed where he'd been looking. She seemed to have guessed what he'd been thinking, too. Yet she didn't shrink from his regard. She met it with the assurance of a woman who was at ease with her sexuality and saw no need to deny it.

Sarah Fox was an intriguing woman, a study in contradictions. She handled a gun as easily as a telephone. She had chosen a career in a male-dominated field, yet she was blatantly female.

What kind of woman would risk her life for a stranger? Or had she?

Damn, he'd lost his train of thought. What had they been talking about? "You said you work in intelligence?"

"Yes."

Pieces moved into place. An alternate explanation for her presence began to form. "It's finally starting to make sense."

"I don't understand."

"That's why the government chose to send you here."

"I told you why. While you are in Stockholm you are the target of an assassin."

"And when did you first learn about this assassination plot?"

"Yesterday morning."

"Yes, that's when I was informed, as well."

She shook her head. More strands of hair slid loose from her clip to brush the side of her face. "Dr. Lemay, why are you so skeptical? I would have thought that an intelligent man like you would have been grateful for our help."

"It's the timing that made me skeptical, Captain Fox. It's too convenient. The government 'discovered' this threat to my life less than twelve hours after I refused their offer."

"What offer?"

She sounded genuinely puzzled, he thought. Then again, what man would question anything she said in that smoky velvet voice of hers? He looked at the way her hair haloed her face, and he remembered the pleasure he'd felt when he'd held a lock between his fingers.

Was that another reason she'd been chosen for this mission?

The pleasure dissolved. He straightened up from the door frame and moved toward the sitting room window.

"Please, keep away from the window, Dr. Lemay. The curtains are closed, but the lamp casts your shadow on the fabric."

He still didn't have enough facts to form a definite conclusion, he reminded himself. He changed direction, crossing the room to the inlaid-walnut desk that held the suite's fax machine and one of the telephones. He steepled his fingers on the desk's glossy surface. "What do you know about my work, Captain Fox?"

"You research nuclear fusion."

"My goal is to develop fusion power as an economically viable energy source."

"Yes, I'm aware that you published a landmark paper on the subject several years ago, but you've kept your research confidential since then. That's what you plan to speak about before the closing ceremonies on Saturday, isn't it?"

"Correct." He lifted his gaze to the mirror that hung on the wall beside the desk so he could watch her reflection. "Two days ago a representative from our government visited me at my lab in California. He requested that I continue my research under their supervision. All my results would be the exclusive property of the Department of Defense."

She hesitated. "I wasn't aware of that."

"No?"

"No, sir. That information was not in any of the sources I accessed."

"Don't you find that odd?"

"Yes, it's definitely odd. A fact like that should have been made available to me. You said you refused?"

"Yes. I turned them down. I gave them nothing." He folded his arms over his chest and faced her. "Less than twelve hours later, they suddenly discovered someone wants to kill me. I find that odd, too."

"What does that have to do with—" Her breath hissed out. "Surely you don't think the government is trying to kill you simply because you wouldn't work for them."

"No. I don't think anyone's trying to kill me, especially not the government. They don't want my death, they want my work." He studied her face. "And what better way to get it than to place someone, say a bodyguard, in a position where they had a reason to stay with me night and day?''

''Dr. Lemay—''

''Even better, what if they sent a beautiful woman, one whose healing injury would arouse my sympathy? She would have unlimited opportunities to gather information. Not only about my work but about whom I associate with while I'm at this conference and what other offers I might receive.''

He watched her string the facts together. It didn't take her long. He could see the exact moment she understood his point. Twin spots of color bloomed in her cheeks— he'd bet it wasn't because he'd called her beautiful.

Her lips thinned. ''You think I was sent here to spy on you.''

''Were you?''

Her jaw flexed, as if she were clenching her teeth. ''My appearance, my sex and my physical condition are irrelevant. I am an officer in the United States Army. I am not a spy.''

''You're not regular Army, you're Delta Force. From what I've heard, you're all trained in unconventional warfare. Your stealth and secrecy are legendary. You don't play by the rules.''

''Sir—''

''In addition, you've admitted you're an intelligence specialist. You're trained to gather information.''

''Call my C.O.,'' she said. ''Major Redinger will confirm my orders. I am here to protect you.''

''But that's the problem. Would he be telling me the truth, or only confirming the cover story you agreed on?''

The color in her cheeks deepened. Her knuckles whitened as she balled her hands into fists. ''I didn't risk my life by running through four lanes of traffic for the sake of a cover story, Dr. Lemay. And I didn't knock you to the ground and add another bruise to my shoulder for show."

Her struggle to control her temper was so obvious, Hawk found he wanted to discard his logic and believe her. "There's another possibility. Perhaps you aren't yet aware of the true nature of your mission."

"I saved your life today, sir. That should be enough truth for both of us."

"Who wants to kill me?"

"We don't yet know."

"What evidence do you have the threat is real?"

"I can't give you details, but Delta's intelligence-gathering network is extensive. Our informants let us know when Americans abroad are in jeopardy."

"In other words, you have no hard proof, do you?"

"The only way I can prove beyond a doubt that I'm right is to let you be killed." She reached behind her for her gun, glared at him for an instant, then turned and ran lightly to the door.

Someone was knocking, Hawk realized belatedly. He'd been so focused on this woman he hadn't even noticed.

She pressed herself to the wall beside the door and called out in Swedish. A male voice replied. She took a long look through the peephole before opening the door as far as the security chain would allow. After a brief conversation, she replaced her gun at the small of her back, unhooked the chain and swung the door wide.

A thin blond teenager in the hotel's blue-and-gold bell-hop uniform wheeled a folding cot over the threshold. He smiled shyly at the captain, pocketed the tip she gave him and left.

Silence descended on the suite. Hawk looked from the cot to the black-clad woman who stood by the door. The flush in her cheeks slowly subsided. Her breathing steadied. She walked around the cot, inspecting it as carefully as she'd inspected everything else in the suite. By the time she had finished, she appeared to have her temper under control once again.

Hawk wondered whether she ever allowed herself to lose control completely. Then he found himself wondering what it would be like if she did.

She returned to where he stood, clasped her hands behind her back and braced her feet shoulder-width apart military fashion. She focused on a point somewhere behind him. "I will endeavor not to let your doubts about my honor or my integrity interfere with my duty, Dr. Lemay."

Hawk raked his hands through his hair. She had turned his argument around. He tried to tell himself his skepticism about the death threat business had a logical basis, but that didn't stop him from feeling like a jerk. "I didn't mean to question your honor, Captain Fox. I was questioning your orders." But even as he said the words, they sounded lame. "I apologize."

"No apology is necessary, sir. Regardless of what you believe, I intend to perform my duty until I am officially relieved."

"Captain—"

"This is nothing personal. If you object to the presence of a woman in your suite, I will station myself in the corridor outside your door."

He'd been wrong. Her control wasn't as total as he'd thought. Her pulse beat rapidly against the side of her neck. Her pupils had contracted to reveal flashes of gold in her green eyes. The elusive spice of her perfume mixed with the scent of hot skin.

Yet she'd been wrong, too. What was happening between them was definitely personal. It had been from the moment she had been willing to offer her life in order to save his.

Or had she?

He should send her away. Put an end to this charade here and now.

But what if he was wrong?

The question still couldn't be answered with any certainty. And if he did send her away, what avenue would the government try next? Wouldn't it be wiser to keep Captain Sarah Fox close until he learned what was really going on?

Hawk hated lies. His entire purpose as a scientist was to seek truth. So, not for one second did he believe the lie he'd just tried to tell himself.

His real reason for not sending this woman away had nothing to do with his work or his principles or whatever conspiracy might be playing out here. It was far more basic than that.

He didn't want her to leave. Right now what he really wanted was to lean over and place his lips on that delicate, vulnerable spot where her pulse beat at the side of her neck and draw her taste into his mouth the same way he was drawing her scent into his lungs. He wanted to slip his arms around her rigidly held body and press her close until she softened against him, until he saw pleasure instead of pain from his touch, until he discovered what other passions she keep reined beneath her impressive control...

"Dr. Lemay?"

He shoved his hands into his pockets and straightened up. "You can stay."

"Thank you, sir."

"And I'd prefer it if you call me Hawk."

"Sir?"

"Because I intend to call you Sarah."

* * *

Her bare sole brushed lightly across the carpet as Sarah slid her left foot back and made a quarter turn. She shifted her weight, bringing her right arm forward in a smooth arc. She concentrated on her breathing, trying to focus her energy on the ritual slow-motion movements of tai chi. She often used the exercises to relieve stress, but so far she was finding no ease for the tautness in her muscles.

She had thought Hawkins Lemay was gallant. A gentle intellectual. A man of high principles. She had been impressed by the accomplishments she'd discovered when she'd studied his background. She had been determined to keep him safe, not only because she'd been ordered to but because she had honestly admired him.

Yes, she'd admired him. Who wouldn't?

She hadn't guessed that within a few hours of meeting him she would want to do him bodily harm herself.

How dare he question her integrity? If she hadn't been on duty, if he hadn't been the subject of her mission, if she hadn't had the concept of personal honor drummed into her from the time she'd learned to talk, she would have…

What? Hauled back and slugged him?

That would have been dangerous. Not because he might strike back. He wouldn't. She had recognized the way he'd been looking at her, and it hadn't been violence that had been on his mind. Or hers, either, if she wanted to be truthful with herself. A large source of the tension that had sparked between them had been from something else entirely.

It had been sex.

Sarah wasn't naive, nor was she a prude. During the course of her missions with Major Redinger's team from Eagle Squadron, she regularly worked side by side with virile males in outstanding physical condition. She was accustomed to the effects of ambient testosterone. Most of the time she regarded the men as brothers, but a certain amount of low-key sexual awareness was inevitable. She'd never had a problem controlling it before. After all, it was only sex, not love. It was a normal, healthy physical response, nothing to be ashamed of and no big deal. She wasn't going to let it interfere with her purpose now.

Call me Hawk.

She gritted her teeth. She had to think of him as Dr. Hawkins Lemay, Nobel laureate, renowned physicist and the subject of her mission. Even if she were interested, that final fact made him off-limits.

No matter how good he smelled.

She pursed her lips and exhaled slowly, trying again to relax. Stretch to the side, bring the forearm vertical, circle with the palm. She settled into the familiar sequence. For the next ten minutes she moved around the antique chairs and the spindly-legged sofa in the center of the small sitting room, her body relaxing as it flowed through the routine with practiced ease.

A low trill sounded from the table that was in the midst of the furniture grouping. Sarah hopped over the back of the sofa and snatched up her cell phone before the second ring. "Fox here."

"I got your message, Captain. What's the situation?"

It was Mitchell Redinger's voice. Sarah shot a glance at the door of Hawk's bedroom to verify it was still closed, then curled one leg beneath her and sank into a corner of the sofa. "My flight was delayed, Major, so Lemay had arrived at the hotel before me. There has already been one attempt on his life."

"Report."

She gave her C.O. a summary of the afternoon's events,

including the names of the embassy official she'd contacted when she'd arrived and the police officer who had been first on the scene. She finished by relating the security measures she'd coordinated within the hotel.

"Nice work, Captain." There was a crackle of static. "Is Lemay cooperating?"

"Grudgingly, sir."

"I have confidence that you can handle the situation."

Sarah heard the note of dismissal in Redinger's tone and spoke quickly. "Was Lemay offered a government position two days ago?"

There was another burst of static. "Say again?"

"Dr. Lemay claims to have been approached by a defense department representative who was interested in his research."

"Yes, that is correct."

"Is it true Lemay refused?"

"Yes. Why do you ask?"

Sarah felt a momentary unease but she dismissed it. She probably hadn't been able to uncover this information while she had researched Hawk's background because the event had been too recent to be on record. The Major might not have thought to tell her about it because he hadn't considered it pertinent. "Just verifying my facts, sir," she replied.

After the call ended, Sarah frowned. Had she been infected by Hawk's paranoia, or had Major Redinger sounded more distant than usual?

She returned her phone to the table, propped her elbows on her knees and dropped her head into her hands. She wasn't going to let doubts infect her mind. Hawk didn't seem to trust anyone, but Sarah had always been able to trust the army. It was her family, the one constant in her life.

Do your duty like a good little soldier.

Her father's voice played in her memory. Even now, she felt her spine straighten in response. She pushed to her feet and did a circuit of the room, then opened her suitcase, took out a copy of the conference schedule, a floor plan of the hotel and a high-scale map of Stockholm. She carried them back to the sofa and sat down to study them.

The bedroom door clicked open. "The bathroom's all yours if you want it, Sarah."

"Thank you, Dr. Lemay," she said without turning around. "I'll order dinner from room service. Is there anything in particular you'd like?"

"That won't be necessary. How's your shoulder?"

She rotated it briefly, realizing the increased blood flow from her exercises had dimmed the ache. "It's much better. Thank you for your concern."

"Is that the conference schedule?" he asked, his voice growing closer.

She picked up the paper and twisted to hold it out to him. "Yes. Now that you're here, I'd like to go over tomorrow's and Saturday's events with..." Her words trailed off. She tried not to stare.

He was no longer wearing the wrinkled denim shirt and casual pants he'd arrived in. He was wearing a tuxedo. And judging by the superb fit, the suit wasn't any rental. Then again, he didn't need help from a tailor to make his shoulders look that wide or his chest that broad. The narrow satin stripe down the side of his trousers gleamed as he walked, emphasizing his long legs and the runner's muscles of his thighs.

"Are you sure you want to do that now?" he asked. He flipped up the collar of his shirt so he could loop his tie around his neck. The ends of the black tie dangled against his shirtfront as he reached over the back of the sofa to take the schedule from her hand. "The opening reception starts in half an hour."

She caught a whiff of soap. His jaw gleamed from a fresh shave. His hair was damp and combed straight back from his face, but he hadn't been able to tame it completely. Wayward curls brushed the back of his collar.

"Sarah? Is there a problem?"

She stood. "I'm not anticipating one, sir. The conference events that take place within the hotel are low risk. I've been in contact with the hotel security staff. They have experience overseeing international conferences like this one and are accustomed to working in cooperation with personal bodyguards. They will be monitoring the perimeter at all times and won't allow anyone into the venue without the proper ID."

He looked at her, his expression unreadable. "You appear to be very competent at your job."

"I do my best, sir."

"Have you changed your mind about being my shadow? If you'd prefer to remain here because of your shoulder—"

"No, I came prepared to accompany you to every event." She brushed the wrinkles from her pants, suddenly conscious of her appearance. She had removed her shoes and loosened her belt. Her sweater was rumpled and her hair was in tangles around her face. "I simply wasn't aware that you wanted to attend the reception."

He held her gaze for a long minute, then returned the schedule to her and walked to the mirror that hung on the wall beside the desk. He appeared to focus his attention on fastening his tie. "My mistake, Sarah. From now on I'll try to make you more aware of my wants."

It wasn't what he said so much as the way he said it that got to her. Or maybe anything he said when he was looking so damn sexy would make any normal, healthy woman imagine he was talking about more than business.

Hawkins Lemay in a tuxedo. The impact of that sure hadn't been in his file, either. Sarah allowed herself no more than a moment to absorb the view before she grabbed her shoes, picked up her suitcase and headed toward the bedroom. "I'll need twenty minutes to change into something more appropriate. Please don't open the door of the suite or go near any of the windows until I return."

The hotel ballroom had mirrored walls, making it appear larger than it was, multiplying the sparkle of the three enormous crystal chandeliers that hung suspended from the two-story ceiling and turning the crowd that milled on the marble floor into a series of endlessly repeating fragments of motion. White-gloved waiters wove among the guests to offer platters of hors d'oeuvres and flutes of champagne. A string quartet played on a dais in one corner, providing a refined background to conversations that hummed in several languages.

The reception was an elegant affair, an international gathering of the rich and powerful. Money, brains, political clout—everyone here was a player in the high-stakes world of energy production. Some supplied it, some came to bargain for it and some were willing to wage war for it. Some, like Hawk, were here to speak of alternatives to the status quo.

The Stockholm Energy Conference was supposed to be a forum for discussion, although Hawk knew the most significant discussions wouldn't be taking place at any of the public functions.

"Champagne, Sarah?" Hawk asked as he scooped a flute from a passing waiter.

"No, thank you, Dr. Lemay." She didn't look at him

as she answered. She kept her gaze moving in the same slow, methodical sweep she'd been using since they had arrived. A miniature radio receiver was nestled in her left ear, her link to the frequency that was being used by hotel security.

He put his free hand on the small of her back as they strolled along the edge of the room, but she didn't need to be guided. Although she seldom looked at him, she seemed aware of his every move and anticipated each shift of direction he made. He suspected he wouldn't be able to guide her, anyway. She didn't strike him as the kind of woman who could be pushed into doing anything she didn't want. He placed his hand on her, simply because he liked touching her.

True to her word, she had taken exactly twenty minutes to get ready for this black-tie evening. Any other woman likely would have protested the short notice, but not Sarah. She had risen to the challenge and the result was drawing the attention of every male they encountered.

Her dress was ice blue and glittered as she moved, giving a liquid sheen to her breasts and hips. Her arms and shoulders were covered, but she'd gathered her hair on top of her head, baring her neck and emphasizing the graceful curve of her throat. Her skirt was a wrap style, overlapping at her right hip. The panels parted with each step, displaying a teasing flash of her bare calf.

But Hawk didn't think she had dressed to entice anyone. The gown was a practical choice since the long sleeves would conceal her bruises. The slinky knit fabric would resist creasing, so it would travel well. It also would allow her ease of movement, as would the wrap skirt. The beaded evening bag that hung by a glittering chain from her good shoulder left her hands free. It wouldn't hold much more than her cell phone, but he didn't believe for a moment that she was unarmed. His gaze lingered on her leg. She probably had strapped her gun to her thigh.

He spread his fingers, enjoying the warmth that seeped through the dress from her skin. "Although you did mention that your appearance is irrelevant, I have to say you look lovely, Sarah."

"Thank you, sir."

"I take it that uniform you're wearing isn't typical Army issue."

"As a matter of fact, I acquired it for a previous mission. I was part of an advance reconnaissance team attending a reception at a dictator's palace."

"You were spying."

She walked a few steps in silence before she spoke again. "We were gathering intelligence so that the dictator's guards didn't slaughter the American students they were holding hostage there as well as the assault team sent to rescue them. You might call it spying, I call it saving lives."

"Was the mission successful?"

"Yes, Dr. Lemay."

"Please, call me Hawk."

"I'd prefer not to."

"If you plan to spend the next three days with me, what would it hurt?"

"Our relationship is strictly professional, Dr. Lemay. It would be best if we remain focused—" She paused, her back tensing beneath his palm. "There is a middle-aged bald man ten yards to our left who is observing you. Five-ten, around two hundred pounds, stands with his head pushed forward, favors his right knee. Do you know him?"

Hawk sipped his champagne as he glanced to his left, although Sarah's description had been accurate enough for

him to guess who it was without looking. "Fedor Yegdenovich. He's a physicist."

"A colleague of yours?"

"Unfortunately, no. He considers fusion research to be
a race, and he's determined Mother Russia will win."

"And the short, intense-looking man with him?"

"Earl Drucker," Hawk said. "Of the Texas Druckers.
His oil is running out and he wants to diversify into other
energy sources. The deal he proposed to me last month
was far richer than the government's. He offered me a
fortune in exchange for my research."

"You're a popular man, Dr. Lemay. Why didn't you
take his offer?"

"I'm not motivated by money." He returned his gaze
to Sarah. "But since you work in intelligence, you would
already know that."

She dipped her chin in agreement. "Yes, I'm aware of
your financial status. The income from the patents you
hold on your early discoveries amounts to several million
annually and has allowed you to fund your research yourself."

"Most women would be impressed by that."

"If I were interested in money, I would have requested
an assignment at the mint."

"Somehow I don't think that would have suited your
temperament."

"I'm also aware of the fact that you donate the majority
of your income to various charities, including veterans'
organizations."

"Damn, you really are good at your job, aren't you?"

"Yes." She met his gaze briefly before she resumed her
survey of the room. "Judging by your record of giving to
charities, you appear to have a social conscience and a
sense of patriotism. Which makes it difficult for me to

understand why you refused to accept the offer of our government."

"Ah. So you checked my story."

"Of course. No offense meant."

"No offense taken." He smiled. "After all, I checked your story, too. As much as I was able to, anyway."

Her gaze darted to his. "What do you mean?"

"What did you think I was doing while you were going through your tai chi routine? I went on-line with my laptop to do some background research of my own."

She raised her eyebrows. "And?"

"Your military record is impressive, Captain Fox. I take it your father influenced your career choice."

If he hadn't been watching so carefully, he wouldn't have seen the chink open up in her controlled expression. He glimpsed a tangle of emotions. Pride, longing, pain. He blinked and it was gone.

"Yes, I admired the general," she said. "It was natural to follow his example."

The general. Not Dad. Not Pops. A revealing choice of words, Hawk thought. "General Bartholomew Fox, hero of both the Korean and the Gulf Wars, would be a hard act to follow for anyone. Especially a daughter."

Another momentary chink. She looked away. "I have never shied away from a challenge, Dr. Lemay."

"Neither have I, Sarah." He stepped closer, running his palm up the back of her arm. "But I'm surprised you didn't try to talk me out of attending this reception. If I really am in danger, if the threat to my life is genuine, wouldn't it have been safer if we remained secluded in the suite?"

A light shudder followed his touch. "Would you have agreed if I'd asked?"

Hawk vividly remembered the way she had looked when

he'd first walked out of the bedroom, with her hair loose and her feet bare as she'd curled into the corner of the sofa. She had been even more appealing than she was now, because she hadn't quite managed to hide the spark of interest that had warmed her gaze as she'd watched him.

But would she have asked him to stay for the sake of her mission or for her? He dropped his hand. "Probably not," he replied.

"That's a courageous choice," she said. "As long as the risk is manageable, it's better not to give in to threats. The moment we let fear win, we've lost."

"What do you fear, Sarah?"

"Failure, Dr. Lemay."

It was an honest answer, Hawk decided. Both from the soldier and from the woman.

She pressed her index finger over the receiver in her left ear and stepped away to place herself slightly behind him. A hum of interest spread through the crowd.

Hawk glanced over his shoulder in time to see at least a dozen men in flowing djellabahs stride through the ballroom's main entrance. They moved as a group, maintaining a ring around the tall, bearded man who walked at their center.

Even though it had been fourteen years since they had last met, Hawk recognized Prince Jibril Ben Nour, the next in line for the throne of the oil-rich Persian Gulf nation of Moukim. The beard was new, but the long nose and the piercing black gaze hadn't changed. Nor had Jibril's aura of privilege—he moved with the sure-footed glide of a man who was unaccustomed to encountering obstacles in his path.

The prince and his entourage swept through the crowd without pausing to speak to anyone. They appeared to be heading straight for Hawk. This was what he'd anticipated.

Hawk placed his champagne glass on a nearby table and stepped forward to meet them.

Sarah quickly angled herself between Hawk and the approaching men. She pressed her back to his chest and nudged him backward, positioning him closer to one of the emergency exits that led out of the ballroom.

Hawk frowned. Under other circumstances, he would have welcomed the sensation of Sarah's body rubbing against his, but he knew what she was doing. She was trying to shield him, and he wouldn't allow it now any more than he'd allowed it this afternoon. He slipped his arm around her waist and drew her against his side.

"I don't like the look of this, Dr. Lemay." She curled her fingers around his wrist. "There are too many of them, and they're moving too fast. Their floor-length robes could conceal anything."

He moved his hand to her hip and held her in place. "Relax, Sarah. Nothing's going to happen."

She let go of his wrist and lowered her hand to her thigh. Her fingertips brushed the opening in her skirt. She didn't relax. Hawk could feel a change in the way she held herself, as if she were readying for action. Her breathing became deep and deliberate. Her weight shifted forward to the balls of her feet. The spicy-sweet scent of her perfume strengthened.

In the next instant they were engulfed in a swirl of white. A nasal voice issued a command. The prince's companions parted, then re-formed into a circle around them, blocking their view of the rest of the ballroom. One man grabbed Sarah by the waist and separated her from Hawk while two others caught Hawk's elbows. It happened so fast, he was being guided toward the exit before he realized he was moving.

There was a low grunt and a flurry of movement on

Hawk's left. Sarah spun away from the man who held her, anchored her fist in Jibril's robe and kicked the front panel of her skirt aside. A heartbeat later, her gun was in her hand, the barrel pressed beneath the prince's beard. "Call off your men," she ordered. "Now."

Chapter 3

The moment took on the slow-motion quality of hyper-awareness. Sarah's senses registered everything, from the whisper of settling fabric around her to the lilting strains of the Mozart bagatelle that still played in the ballroom. The receiver in her ear carried a low buzz of inquiry from the hotel security staff who were posted around the exits. They suspected there had been some kind of commotion, but they were unaware of its nature. A human wall draped in white screened their view.

She felt Prince Jibril stir. She knew very well that what she was doing could spark an international incident, but Hawk's safety was her prime concern. She repositioned her gun beneath the prince's ear and flicked her gaze across the men who surrounded them. She checked their eyes, searching for a sign that would give away their next move. She was outnumbered and outmuscled. She couldn't hope to overpower them. She had to play her advantage carefully. "Tell them to release Dr. Lemay, Your Highness."

"Madam, you are making a serious mistake," Jibril said.

The prince's voice was high-pitched for a tall man. His words carried an Oxford accent. Sarah couldn't tell whether it was fear or anger that tightened his tone. "If I am mistaken, I sincerely apologize," she said. "But please do as I say. I don't want to see anyone get hurt."

The moment dragged out. Sarah kept her breathing even, charging her blood with oxygen, preparing herself for any eventuality. Scenarios flashed through her head, none of them good. Without back-up, standoffs were risky. There were too many variables.

The prince gave a curt order in Arabic. From the corner of her vision, Sarah saw the men holding Hawk let go of his arms and step aside. He seemed uninjured, but she couldn't spare the time to study him. She kept her attention on the prince's bodyguards.

They were regarding her with stunned outrage, as if a chair or a hand towel had suddenly developed teeth and bit them.

"Sarah." Hawk's voice was a low rumble.

Although she still couldn't afford to look at him, she responded immediately. She had to let the prince's men know who was in authority. "Yes, sir?"

"It's all right. You can put away your weapon."

She tipped her gun toward the ceiling and took a step to the side, but she remained within easy reach of the prince, her muscles poised to react. This was the trickiest part, like dismounting from a tiger. "It appeared as if Prince Jibril's men were trying to abduct you, Dr. Lemay."

The prince gave a barking laugh. "Is that what this is

about? Abduct Hawkins? Oh, not at all. I gave orders to escort him from this noisy crowd so we could speak in private.'' He spread his hands wide in a gesture of appeasement. ''In their zeal to obey me, my men obviously gave the wrong impression.''

Sarah shifted her gaze to the prince. The man was smiling at Hawk, his teeth a white slash in his beard, his black gaze rock steady as he told the lie.

''You'll have to excuse Sarah, Jibril,'' Hawk said, brushing off his sleeves. He straightened his jacket. ''She has declared herself to be my bodyguard, and she tends to overreact.''

''An interesting choice, Hawkins. I see the years have not changed your eye for beauty.''

''Nor your appreciation of it. Sarah is very dedicated to her job.''

''And equally as prone to mistakes in her zeal as my palace guard. I do hope those dolts didn't alarm you.''

Sarah took another look at the men around them. They belonged to the Moukim palace guard? She had been in more trouble than she'd initially thought. These were commandos whose reputation as fighters compared to Eagle Squadron's best.

''I would like to invite you back to my yacht, Hawkins, so we can converse undisturbed,'' the prince continued. ''But I wouldn't want your rather, ah, impetuous pet to misunderstand my intentions again.''

''Sarah,'' Hawk said. ''Put your gun away. It isn't necessary.''

''Certainly, sir, as soon as Prince Jibril tells his guards to give us more space,'' she said, keeping her voice as neutral as possible. ''Just to be sure there isn't another misunderstanding.''

"Jibril?" Hawk asked. "Would you mind humoring her?"

"For you, my old friend, anything." The prince issued more orders. The men fell back two paces, opening the circle.

As soon as they moved, inquiries crackled over the radio. Sarah saw the hotel security personnel converging on them from the perimeter of the room. Nearby conversations tapered off as guests paused to follow their progress. Within seconds every face in the ballroom was turned toward them.

Satisfied that the several hundred reputable eyewitnesses were swinging the odds back in their favor, Sarah slipped her weapon into the holster on her right leg, twitched her skirt back into place and returned to Hawk's side.

The moment she was within his reach, Hawk grabbed her gun hand and tucked it into the crook of his elbow. When she tried to ease away, he pressed her fingers to his sleeve and trapped her wrist against his ribs. Beneath his jacket, his arm was corded steel.

She did a rapid survey of the area, momentarily concerned she had missed some other potential threat, but everything appeared clear. She tipped up her chin to look at him.

It was the first time she'd regarded him directly since the incident had begun. His lips were thinned and his jaw was clenched. The corner of one eye twitched. He dipped his head close to her ear. "This afternoon I wondered whether you were suicidal or just plain crazy," he muttered. "Now I know you're both. Don't move."

Before she could respond, Hawk released her and stepped forward to shake the prince's hand. "Jibril, it's good to see you."

The prince clasped Hawk's shoulder. "And you too, Hawkins. How long has it been? Ten years?"

"Fourteen." He drew back and grasped Jibril's arm. "You have my deepest apologies for the mix-up. This wasn't the greeting I would have hoped for."

"Think nothing of it, my friend. It was rather entertaining. A novel experience."

"You're gracious, as always, Jibril."

The first of the hotel security guards arrived then. Sarah still didn't like the situation, but she decided matters were under control, now that they were no longer hidden from view. Even a man as powerful as the Moukim crown prince wouldn't attempt anything overtly hostile in such a public place. She explained to the security staff that it was a false alarm and thanked them for their concern, yet she didn't relax for an instant.

The glares she was receiving from Jibril's palace guard were making the hair at the back of her neck tingle. By besting them, however fleetingly, she had not only hurt their male egos, she'd damaged their professional pride. She knew the military mind-set. This insult would not be forgotten.

But it was the emotions she saw when she met Hawk's gaze that could present a bigger problem.

The danger was far from over. It was only beginning.

Hawk paced across the sitting room, but the suite was too small. He yanked off his tie, balled it in his fist and threw it on the floor, then pivoted and paced to the door. What he really needed was a good, long run to clear his head. Work off the restlessness, the frustration, the fear.

Yes, fear. That was at the root of his anger.

Sarah could have been killed. Any one of Jibril's guards could have snapped that beautiful neck of hers with one blow. It was a miracle that she had escaped the situation unscathed.

She was an idiot. A madwoman. She'd risked her life unnecessarily because she'd thought she was saving his.

Again.

He hadn't anticipated this when he'd decided to keep her. He should have thought it through instead of being swayed by the chemistry that was going on between them. Whether the threat to his life was real or not, Sarah was managing to place herself in danger simply because she was so determined to do her job.

Whatever that was.

Damn! He turned away from the door and strode to the sofa. He couldn't go for a run. He had given Sarah his word that he would remain here. He wasn't going to add lies of his own to the mix. And who knew what Sarah would do if she came out of the bathroom and found him gone? Would she follow him? Or would she take advantage of the opportunity to hack into his computer?

He peeled off his jacket and looked at the bedroom doorway. Just how dedicated a soldier was she? Could she really have accosted Moukim royalty merely to reinforce her cover story? If so, she'd been a brilliant performer. A true method actor. She'd been completely convincing, from her fighter's stance to her coolly assessing gaze. And then there had been the way she'd kicked aside her skirt with no regard to modesty.

He dropped his jacket on the back of the sofa. He rubbed his face, forcing himself to take deep breaths. What was wrong with him? The standoff he'd witnessed tonight could have ended in tragedy if Jibril hadn't decided to defuse the situation, so how could Hawk think of Sarah's legs?

Yet the image of all that bare skin wouldn't go away.

It had been burned into his memory: delicate ankles, slender calves, taut thighs...with two wide bands of black elastic circling the right one to hold her holster in place. And before her skirt had settled, there had been a glimpse of pale peach lace where her thighs met.

Her underwear was peach-colored lace. Nothing practical or serviceable about that. It was the choice of the woman, not the soldier.

His gaze returned to the bedroom doorway. He heard the flush of the toilet, followed by the sound of running water. He was struck by the intimacy of their situation. Despite the background facts that both of them had dug up, they were still virtual strangers, yet Sarah showed no uneasiness about sharing accommodations with him.

Hawk's gaze dropped to the cot she had set up. She had placed it between the bedroom and the door of the suite, as if she intended to protect him even while she slept...or give the impression that she protected him.

"I'm finished now. Thank you for waiting."

He hadn't heard her approach. She was standing in the doorway. Her face was scrubbed clean of makeup, her hair was a cascade of loose curls around her shoulders. The dress she had worn tonight was draped over her arm in a fall of shimmering ice blue. In its place she wore an olive-green T-shirt and a pair of plaid flannel drawstring pants.

She wasn't dressed for seduction, she was dressed for bed. Yet the sight of her sent Hawk's pulse racing. Why was that? Was it the challenge she presented? Or was it because she seemed oblivious to the effect of her appearance? Her lack of vanity was as attractive as the self-assurance she displayed, her take-it-or-leave-it attitude. It arose from that confidence in her femininity he'd noticed the first time she had caught him looking at her body.

The anger he'd been struggling to control shifted. He no

longer wanted to grab her and shake her for putting herself in danger. He wanted to kiss her.

He clamped his hands on the back of the sofa. "Sarah, we have to talk."

"I agree, Dr. Lemay." She carried her dress to the wardrobe and hung it up beside her coat. Her breasts swayed beneath the T-shirt as she raised her arms. "We need to discuss some ground rules."

He dug his fingers into the upholstery. "Good. We can't have a repeat of what happened this evening."

"Exactly. In the future, I'll need to know the details of any meetings you arrange."

"Why? So you can report on them?"

"No, so I can assess the risk and suggest an alternate arrangement." She took a brush from the bottom of the wardrobe and went over to sit cross-legged in the center of her cot. "I'll fax a written apology to Prince Jibril tomorrow, but the incident could have been avoided if you had told me you had gone to the reception specifically to meet him."

She really didn't give an inch, he thought. And she was right—he had attended the reception in order to meet Jibril. "Sarah, the incident happened because you overreacted. You were jumping at another mop handle."

"The prince was trying to abduct you, sir."

"That's not true. You heard what he said."

"Precisely." She tipped her head sideways and ran the brush through her hair from the roots to the tips. "I heard and understood every word he said. I speak Arabic."

The revelation shouldn't have surprised him. She had already demonstrated her gift for languages. "And?"

"He lied to you. He didn't tell his men to escort you to a quieter place. He told them to keep you quiet and get you outside."

"The two versions sound close. You could have made a mistake with the translation."

She tipped her head the other way. A shadow of a frown creased her forehead. "I suppose that's possible, but I don't believe I did."

"So now, in addition to the plot to assassinate me, there is a plot to kidnap me? Better not embroider the story too much, Sarah. It's difficult enough to believe already. I'm just an ordinary man—"

"Bull."

He let go of the sofa and crossed his arms. "What happened to the 'Yes, sir. No, sir'?"

"You are not an ordinary man, Dr. Lemay. You're bright enough to realize the impact that your research into fusion energy could have on the balance of power in the world and even on the course of history, so don't insult my intelligence by pretending otherwise." She put down her brush and rotated her shoulder. "People and nations who rely on oil as the source of their income would not be pleased to have their way of life made obsolete. Neither would the big auto companies. Or the unions. Not to mention the various utility companies. I don't think the issue is who at this conference wants to stop you. It's who doesn't."

He realized her shoulder was probably bothering her again. He already knew she wouldn't accept his sympathy or any offer of help. Still, he wanted to demand she be more careful, he wanted to shout at her for being reckless enough to get hurt in the first place. He wanted to walk over there and help her finish brushing her hair. "Sarah…"

"And I wouldn't rule out your good friend Prince Jibril Ben Nour. The oil reserves of Moukim provide his wealth and his political power. How can you trust him when you don't trust me?''

''What makes you think I trust him?''

That made her pause. Her cheek moved, as if she were chewing it. ''You appeared to be friends.''

''We have a connection, but it's not as simple as friendship.''

''I wasn't aware of that.''

''Wasn't it in my file?''

Her gaze flicked over him. ''I've been discovering there are many things that weren't in your file.''

There was an intriguing undertone to her words. He crossed the room to stand at the foot of her cot. ''Such as?''

She took a deep breath before she would meet his gaze. ''Nothing that has any bearing on my duty. What is your connection to Jibril?''

''We met fourteen years ago. I was doing my doctorate at Stanford and he was representing his family in negotiations for a grant to the university.''

''Then your connection is financial.''

Hawk considered leaving it there, but for the sake of Sarah's safety, he couldn't. Unless she knew the truth, she might do something insane like taking on Jibril's commandos again. ''That's how it began,'' he said. ''We were friends once. Until we both fancied ourselves to be in love with the same woman.''

Her lips parted but she made no sound. The look of shock on her face should have been comical, but it didn't make Hawk feel like laughing. Didn't she believe it was possible for him to have once been in love?

Then again, he wasn't so sure of it himself. He unfastened his cuff links and turned away. ''It was a long time ago,'' he said.

The cot creaked. Sarah stood up and moved in front of him. "Fourteen years isn't that long. What happened?"

"Do you mean who won?"

She nodded. "That's one way to put it."

"Technically, neither of us. The lady died."

"Oh, God," Sarah whispered. "I'm sorry. I had no idea." She lifted her hand. For a moment it seemed as if she were going to touch him.

And once again Hawk wanted to kiss her. Not out of desire but to absorb the compassion he saw in her gaze.

He closed his fist over his cuff links, feeling the metal jab his palm. "I didn't tell you as a ploy to gain your sympathy, Sarah. I thought it would be safer for you if you understood that my relationship with Jibril has nothing to do with my work or his oil. The last time we saw each other we met to bury a person we both cared about."

She dropped her hand. "I appreciate your candor."

"You would have found out eventually. You *do* work in intelligence."

She cleared her throat, as if reminded of her job. "This does put a different spin on the situation."

"I don't believe the prince would have waited until now if he had wanted to kill me. If he was harboring some jealous grudge, he knows me well enough to have eliminated me anytime, so there isn't any reason for you to put yourself in the kind of danger you did tonight."

"I hope this means you realize my only concern is your safety."

He walked to the bedroom. "I haven't changed my mind, Sarah. I still don't fully trust you, and I think you're a menace to yourself and everyone around you." He paused in the doorway to look over his shoulder. "But you're one hell of an interesting woman and I don't intend to get rid of you yet."

Was there such a thing as too much knowledge? Sarah hadn't thought it was possible. In the course of her work, she was accustomed to using any method available to collect intelligence. Even the tiniest detail, like the location of an air vent or whether a guard was right- or left-handed, could mean the difference between the success or failure of a mission.

So why did she wish that Hawk hadn't told her he'd been in love?

"It would have been faster to walk," Hawk said.

Sarah acknowledged his grumbling with a nod but she didn't take her gaze off the traffic. The low angle of the morning sun glinted from the hood of the rental car, leaving spots in front of her eyes. She took one hand from the wheel to fumble on the seat beside her for her sunglasses. "Faster but more exposed. We still have plenty of time to reach the harbor, Dr. Lemay. I studied the city map before we left the hotel, and although this route isn't direct, it isn't predictable, either. That reduces the chance of encountering an ambush on the way to the pier where the prince's yacht is moored."

"Hold still." His leather jacket creaked as he leaned toward her. He set her aviator sunglasses into place on the bridge of her nose and looped the wire arms over her ears. "Is that better?"

"Yes. Thank you, sir."

He left his arm across the back of her seat, picking up a lock of her hair to rub it between his fingers. "I don't plan on staying long, Sarah. This is a courtesy meeting, that's all."

"I understand. I appreciate the way you kept me informed. I alerted the American Embassy so they will be aware of your movements."

"The embassy? Why?"

"It's just a precaution, since we're dealing with the future ruler of Moukim. Our diplomats will contact his diplomats so they will also know that our people are aware of our movements."

"Ah." He curled her hair around his thumb. "You're setting up more witnesses like you did with the bystanders in the ballroom."

"Exactly."

"Is there any chance you would be willing to stay in the car and wait for me?"

She clicked on her signal and turned her head to check the cross traffic. The movement also freed her hair from his grasp. "No, sir. None at all."

He drummed his fingers on the back of her seat. "I didn't think so."

"I'll stay out of the way as much as possible while you meet with Prince Jibril, but I won't guarantee anything. If I perceive a threat, I intend to act. I would rather make apologies than funeral arrangements."

He withdrew his arm.

She felt like thudding her forehead against the steering wheel. "Sorry, sir. That was insensitive of me."

"What?"

"The remark about funerals. Seeing the prince after all this time must be stirring some very unpleasant memories."

"Oh, for God's sake," he muttered. "Your sympathy is misplaced, Sarah."

She didn't think so. She knew men. That was one of the side effects of living in the midst of them all her life. She knew full well how whenever they were hurt their first instinct was to bury the pain. At times it seemed the stronger the man, the more determined he was to keep his feelings inside. Some of the toughest soldiers in Eagle

Squadron carried around emotional baggage that would cripple most people. They would rather face torture than open their hearts to anyone, especially a woman.

Yet Hawk hadn't really opened up anything, had he? He'd divulged only the bare facts that he'd deemed pertinent. For that Sarah was grateful. The information he'd given her would allow her to do her job better, because she now understood the source of the tension she'd sensed between Hawk and Jibril despite their cordial greeting.

Hawk had drawn a very clear line. It would be foolish to cross it. It would be grossly unprofessional. It would endanger her objectivity and thus her ability to perform her duty if she allowed herself to feel sympathy for him. Feeling sexually attracted to him was making it difficult enough to maintain her professional distance.

Two more days and this would be over. Then she wouldn't have to wonder what the woman had been like, or whether even after fourteen years Hawk was still mourning her the way Sarah still mourned Jackson...

Damn. Hawk's memories weren't the only ones that were getting stirred up here. She'd better get her head on straight before she let herself get distracted.

Her pulse thumped hard. She realized it had been three minutes since she had checked her rearview mirror for a tail. She pulled to the curb.

"What are you doing?" Hawk asked.

"Making sure we weren't followed." She twisted on the seat to get a better view of the vehicles that passed them. None seemed familiar, but that was no guarantee. Until she knew more about who the hired assassin was, she wouldn't know whether he worked alone or had a team to help him.

"Quicker to walk," Hawk muttered as he leaned against the door. His jacket creaked again. The warm air that wafted from the heater in the dashboard brought the teasing hint of leather and man.

Something else that he'd said the night before came back to her. *I still don't trust you...but you're one hell of an interesting woman.*

He'd already called her beautiful, but he'd also called her crazy and suicidal. She didn't take compliments on her appearance any more seriously than she took insults—they were superficial and didn't affect her one way or another. Yet to be called interesting by a man as intelligent and complex as Hawkins Lemay... Lord help her, now that affected her. It was even more hazardous to her objectivity than the sight of him in a tuxedo.

Sarah settled her sunglasses more firmly on her nose and put the car back into gear. She couldn't let this get personal. She was going to do her duty. That's what she knew best.

Chapter 4

Jibril's yacht was more like a cruise ship than a private vessel, dwarfing the other ships that were moored along the pier. It was at least two hundred feet long, with enough room for a swimming pool on the foredeck and a helicopter landing pad at the stern. Despite its size, it wasn't ungainly. Its cream-colored superstructure had a sleek, aerodynamically tapered design. Its black hull gleamed like the coat of a well-tended race horse, straining against the lines that reined it in. Hawk was sure the color choice was deliberate, evoking sand and oil. The very fact Jibril had chosen to use this mode of transport despite the lateness of the season was deliberate, too. It was an ostentatious display of wealth. It was a statement of power.

It also carried a much more subtle message, one that Hawk wasn't sure how to interpret. The prince had named his yacht *Faith*.

"This way, please."

The man who met Hawk and Sarah as they came onboard was dressed in the thick twill pants and navy blue wool jacket of a sailor. His nose was angled to one side like a prizefighter who'd lost too many matches. Hawk recognized him as one of the guards who had accompanied the prince to the hotel the night before, and judging by the tension he sensed in Sarah, she recognized the man, as well. The guard led them past the empty helicopter pad, across the deck and stopped beside a set of thickly varnished mahogany doors. He rapped twice on the panels.

Another guard in the guise of a sailor opened the doors to a luxuriously furnished salon. Warm air billowed outward with the scent of lemon wax. The man dipped his head in a polite bow to Hawk. "This way, please."

Hawk wondered whether it was the only English phrase the men knew. He also wondered whether Sarah was invisible. The men were ignoring her completely, treating her as she were nothing but a piece of furniture that happened to be trailing behind him. Yet as soon as he and Sarah entered the salon, all that changed.

One of the two men stepped in front of Sarah while his colleague moved behind her. "We ask you to surrender your weapon before you go farther," the first man said. He held out his hand. "We will return it when you leave."

To Hawk's relief, Sarah didn't argue. She unfastened her black coat, withdrew her gun and handed it butt first to Jibril's guard. She then slipped her coat from her shoulders. The black sweater and pants she wore wouldn't conceal much. Still, she spread her arms to the side and allowed the other guard to frisk her. Her face was impassive as his hands ran under her arms and down her hips. It was Hawk who made a sound of protest as the man slid his palms over the insides of her thighs.

Sarah looked at Hawk, her chin lifted with no loss of dignity. "This isn't a problem, sir. He's a soldier doing his job," she said. She moved her gaze to the man in front of her. "I understand that, as I hope he understands that I'm merely doing mine."

The search was concluded swiftly. Sarah folded her coat over her arm and fell into step behind him as Hawk was led deeper into the ship. They went through another set of mahogany doors, along a carpeted corridor and up a wide staircase bordered by gleaming brass rails. At the top was a sprawling room decorated entirely in white. Sunlight blazed through a bank of windows in one wall, reflecting from the marble tile floor and gleaming from the groupings of low silk-upholstered couches and glass-topped tables.

"Welcome, Hawkins!" A tall, thin shape moved toward them through the glare. "What do you think of my home away from home?"

"A very impressive toy, Jibril." Hawk paused to look at the prince as they shook hands. Jibril was wearing western clothing today, a neat tweed blazer and trousers with knife-edge creases. Except for the beard, he looked even more like the man he'd been fourteen years ago. "How's the fishing in the harbor?"

Jibril laughed. "That was one passion we didn't have in common, my friend. I see you are still accompanied by your lovely but impetuous bodyguard." He turned to Sarah with a condescending smile. "Your apology was brought to me earlier, Captain Fox. It was prettily worded. How could I not accept?"

She dipped her head. "Thank you, Your Highness."

Jibril gave an order to the guard with the crooked nose, then gestured toward the group of couches closest to the windows. "I have asked Ahmed to have coffee sent up for the two of us. Now tell me, Hawkins. What in the world have you done that has caused someone to put out a contract on your life?"

Of all the things Jibril might have said, this wasn't one that Hawk had anticipated. Hawk glanced at Sarah, but she wasn't looking at him. She had taken up a position near the window and was scanning the room. She gave no indication that she realized Jibril had just backed up her story, yet Hawk was certain that nothing got by her. "What have you heard?" Hawk asked.

Jibril gave a neat tug to his pant legs and seated himself in the center of the largest couch. He waited until Hawk had taken a seat on the couch across from him before he replied. "A man in my position has many sources of information, as I'm sure you know. I assume you heard of this threat, as well. Why else would you have acquired a bodyguard?"

Why else, indeed? There would be no reason for both Jibril and Sarah to tell the same lie. They likely wouldn't have had the opportunity to coordinate their stories, either. Therefore, Sarah must have been telling the truth all along.

Hawk was surprised by the spurt of satisfaction he felt. Somehow he would prefer to believe Sarah was honest, even if it meant his life really was in danger.

Hell, that was completely illogical. "You mentioned a contract."

"Yes. It is rumored to be substantial." Jibril shrugged his shoulders. "But that is all I know. Who would do such a thing?"

"Apparently, there are many candidates."

"There is a saying in my country—the way to judge a man's worth is by the caliber of his enemies. And you, my friend, appear to have angered some powerful people. It must be due to your work. Your research could be viewed as a threat by many."

"That would be the logical conclusion."

Jibril smiled. "Always the scientist. You haven't changed."

"Nor have you, Jibril."

A white-coated servant appeared at the top of the staircase, carrying a tray that held a silver coffee service. The guard called Ahmed took it from him, placed it on a low table and set it in front of Jibril, then backed away to stand across from the window, his alert posture echoing Sarah's.

Jibril poured a stream of steaming coffee into a china cup, set it on a saucer and offered it to Hawk. "You still prefer it black, yes?"

"You have a good memory," Hawk said, taking the coffee.

"And a long one," Jibril said, pouring a cup for himself. "How is your research progressing, Hawkins? Are you close to achieving your dream of fusion power? Have you made a breakthrough?"

Hawk sipped a mouthful of coffee, using the time to consider how to word his reply. "A breakthrough is inevitable."

"Then you haven't yet achieved it. I must admit I am relieved. I am not looking forward to being competitors again."

Hawk paused. "This is what I wanted to discuss when I arranged to meet you yesterday. If we work together, we can all win."

"How could that be? In any competition, there is room for only one winning side."

"Not if we share a common goal."

"We share nothing, Hawkins. If you succeed in giving the world this virtually limitless energy supply, I and my people will lose our way of life."

"Think of it more as a change, not a loss. Your oil brings you wealth, but it also is at the root of too much conflict. How much human suffering can be traced to inequities in resources? How many more wars will be fought over the control of those resources?'' Hawk placed the cup and saucer back on the table. ''And what will happen to your people and your way of life when your oil runs out?''

Jibril waved his hand. ''It will not happen in my generation.''

''It will happen eventually. Wouldn't it be better to prepare for the future now?''

''Those are noble sentiments, Hawkins. You still aspire to be the hero while I am consigned to the role of a less romantic but practical man.''

There had been an edge to Jibril's voice. Hawk again chose his words carefully. ''I disagree. My sentiments are practical.''

''Then, if that is the case, our first concern should be keeping you safe.'' The prince leaned forward, a deep frown line appearing above the bridge of his nose. ''You must move out of that hotel and stay here with me.''

From the corner of his eye, Hawk saw Sarah turn her head toward him. Although she remained silent, he could feel the force of her gaze. He could imagine the effort she was making to restrain herself from protesting. ''That's a generous offer,'' he began.

''I have many guest suites where you would be comfortable, Hawkins, but this yacht was built for my security as well as my enjoyment. These windows are bullet-proof. The superstructure was designed to the specifications of a tank and the triple hull makes us unsinkable. It is a floating fortress, equipped to defend all onboard. It will provide complete protection.''

''I appreciate your concern, Jibril, but I do have protection.''

''Pah.'' Jibril flicked his fingers toward Sarah in a dismissive gesture. "My men are superb fighters and are completely loyal. You of all people must know that women are not to be trusted."

The prince's words resounded in the sun-filled room like the sound of a slap. Unlike the other barbs that Jibril had sprinkled through the conversation, this one was too flagrant to let pass. Hawk rose to his feet.

Sarah was at his side immediately. "Sir?"

Hawk waited until he was certain he could control his voice, then looked at Jibril. "I came here willing to work together. I want to let the past rest in peace. But be assured I have as long a memory as you do, my friend. There are certain things one never forgets."

The hotel fitness room had been installed in the basement like an afterthought, a facility hastily provided for the modern health-conscious guest. It wasn't large, scarcely half the size of a basketball court. Like the ballroom, a wall of mirrors gave it the illusion of space, but there was nothing elegant about it. Exercise equipment crammed the floor: stair climbers, treadmills, weight benches and devices that mimicked the motions of cross-country skiing. The music that played from the speakers mounted near the ceiling wasn't the refined strains of a string quartet, it was the pounding rhythm of hard rock. If Sarah's phone hadn't been programmed to vibrate, she wouldn't have known it was ringing.

She activated the phone and pressed her hand over her other ear. "Fox here."

"Captain? Where are you?"

It was Major Redinger's voice. Sarah moved to find the best reception and angled the phone as close to her mouth as she could. "In the hotel gym, sir."

"Sounds like a rock concert."

"Sorry, Major. I'll speak up, but I can't leave the room until Dr. Lemay does."

"What's he doing there? The people at the embassy said he had scheduled a meeting with the prince of Moukim."

"It concluded early. Dr. Lemay is exercising." She watched a pair of women move toward the door. They had come in fifteen minutes ago to use the rowing machines, but they had spent most of the time studying Hawk. Sarah didn't think they represented a threat to his life—their interest was strictly feminine and completely understandable.

She returned her gaze to Hawk. He was using one of the treadmills. He had been running in place for the past forty-five minutes. His white sleeveless T-shirt was darkened with sweat, molding the contours of his shoulders and his chest and exposing his well-developed arms. Below his running shorts his legs moved rhythmically, his powerful thigh muscles rippling with each stride.

Even if she hadn't learned from his file that he was physically fit, she would have been able to guess by the way he moved in his clothes that he was in good shape. But she hadn't expected his body to be quite so…enticing. He didn't look like a man who made his living with his brain. He was six foot two of lean masculinity, a well-toned male in his prime.

Still, Sarah didn't believe he was running for the sake of exercise. Nor was he displaying his body in order to tempt anyone.

His tension had been palpable ever since they had left the prince. Hawk had said it was supposed to be a courtesy meeting, but it had been clear to Sarah that he'd had another agenda. He'd wanted to approach Jibril about fusion power. The reasons he'd given had been sound, yet beneath the surface politeness the conversation had been full of thinly veiled references to their shared past. Unpleasant memories had definitely been stirred up, yet they hadn't roused the feelings Sarah had expected. She hadn't seen grief in either of the men. She'd seen a mixture of anger and resentment.

It didn't take a genius to realize that Hawk was trying to run off his tension. She could see it in each stride he took, in the hardness of his muscles and the determination in his eyes. It must have taken years to build up a physique like his. How often did he need to work off his feelings? Just how intense had the competition been between Hawk and Jibril for the woman they had both loved?

Sarah tried to remind herself not to become personally involved, but the more she learned, the more she wanted to learn. There were so many facets to Hawk she was only beginning to discover....

"Captain, are you still there?"

"Yes, sir."

"Interpol will be faxing you their latest information sometime this evening. Review it ASAP. I'll check in with you later."

She returned her phone to her pocket. The two women had left the room while she'd been talking. Only the tall blond woman, who was the hotel fitness instructor, remained. Sarah was about to resume her post by the door when Hawk hit the switch to stop the treadmill.

He put his hands on his knees, taking a few seconds to catch his breath before he grabbed a towel and wiped his face. He was stretching to cool down when the fitness instructor drifted over and smiled. Sarah couldn't hear what she said, but whatever it was, Hawk shook his head. Two minutes later he walked to Sarah.

"I'm finished here," he said. "I'll shower in the suite."

Sarah waited until they had exited the gym and were in

the relative quiet of the basement corridor before she spoke. ''What did she want?''

''Olga? From what I could understand, she offered to show me the sauna.''

Yeah, I'll bet that's not all she offered to show you. Sarah grimaced at the petty thought. The hotel employee was merely being professional. Sarah should be, too. She did a visual sweep of the corridor. ''I'm glad you refused, sir. From a security standpoint, using the shower in your room is more prudent.''

''That's what I figured.'' He looped the towel behind his neck and put his palm on the door to the fire stairs. ''I'd like to take the stairs instead of the elevator so I can cool down. Is that a problem?''

''Not at all. Thanks for checking with me. Your cooperation makes my job much easier.''

''That's why I used the hamster wheel in the gym instead of going outside for a run.''

''That was sensible of you. I wouldn't want you to place yourself at risk.''

''It's you I'm more concerned about.''

''I'm not the target, sir.''

''That wouldn't make any difference if you decide to put yourself in the way of a bullet,'' he said, holding the door open for her.

She realized he was being gallant again. Not simply by holding the door for her, but by trying to protect her the same way he had when they had first met. Now that Jibril had verified the threat to his life, Hawk was being careful for Sarah's sake. He didn't want *her* in danger. That's what was behind his new cooperativeness.

You still aspire to be the hero. That's what Jibril had said. Yet, judging by the tone he'd used, he hadn't meant it as a compliment.

They ascended the first three flights in silence. Sarah listened for other footsteps in the stairwell but heard none. There was only the sound of Hawk's breathing…and the sharp scent of honest sweat and the tantalizing close-up view of his taut body moving only inches away from hers.

She admitted to herself she would have been watching him work out even if she hadn't been duty bound to keep an eye on him. It wasn't just because he had an appealing body—she was accustomed to being around men who had far more spectacular physiques. It was because of all those other aspects that made up this man. "Did it help?" she asked.

"What?"

"The workout. Did you outrun what was bothering you?"

"It's not a matter of outrunning it." He rounded the end of the banister on the fourth-floor landing and started up the final flight. "It's a matter of getting it back under control. But you'd know all about control, wouldn't you?"

"I'm not sure what you mean."

"I think you do." He reached the landing of the fifth floor and grasped the door handle.

She stretched past him and put her hand over his to keep him from opening it.

The moment she touched his skin, her awareness of him spiked. She looked at his bare arm, at the fine sprinkling of dark hair, the swell of muscle, and she had to fight the urge to caress it. Oh yes, she knew what he meant about control. "Better let me go first so I can check the corridor, sir."

He didn't move aside. His hand tensed beneath hers. "Sarah, I owe you an apology."

"For what?"

"For doubting your story about the assassin. I simply hadn't had enough facts to be sure of my conclusion."

"You explained your skepticism yesterday afternoon. It was understandable. I didn't take it personally."

He released the door handle and turned his hand over, enclosing her fingers within his. "Yes, you did. You wanted to punch me for insulting your honor."

She had to keep reminding herself how perceptive he was. "It was my honor that prevented me from punching you."

He shifted to face her. "Always the good soldier."

She looked at the way his T-shirt clung to the line of his collarbone. His jaw was clenched, the tendons at the side of his neck standing out to frame the vulnerable hollow at the base of his throat where his pulse beat. She felt her own pulse trip in response. "That's what I strive to be."

"What about the woman? The one who likes lace underwear."

"This topic isn't appropriate."

He lifted her hand and rubbed her knuckles across his lower lip. "Neither is the way you're looking at me."

Oh, damn. Did nothing escape him? She focused on the door behind him. "Dr. Lemay—"

He moved their joined hands behind her back and drew her closer. "Call me Hawk."

She could feel the heat roll off his body. His skin was still damp. His grip on her fingers tightened. His breathing was harsh and rapid, but she didn't think it was only due to his run or the climb up the stairs. "No, sir. I can't do that."

"Then we'll have to think of something you *can* do."

She moved her gaze to his face.

That was a mistake. She had already read his intentions

in his voice and his touch. Now she could see them in his expression. His eyes gleamed as he focused on her mouth.

She was skilled in hand-to-hand combat. She knew at least a dozen ways to get out of this hold, several of which would be relatively painless. The simplest of them all would be to tell Hawk to stop—she was positive that he wouldn't force himself on her or any woman.

Yet she did nothing as he lowered his head. She saw the kiss coming. Despite her years of training, despite her sense of honor, she stood there and let it happen.

His lips were warm and tasted of salt. They settled over hers gently at first, as tenderly as the way he would touch her hair. Pleasure flowed through her like a burst of unexpected sunshine. And then she made her second mistake. She kissed him back.

The gentleness turned to possession. He slipped his other arm around her, pressing her breasts to his chest. Even through her sweater she could feel the damp heat of his muscles. Her nipples hardened. She shuddered.

He slipped his tongue past her lips. With one bold sweep, he explored her mouth. She could feel his strength, the same determination she'd seen and admired for the past day. She swayed into him, aligning their bodies. She brought her free hand to the back of his head and held him steady as she stretched upward....

A door opened somewhere below them. The sound jerked Sarah back to her senses. With a whispered curse, she twisted out of Hawk's embrace and drew her gun, placing herself between him and the stairs.

The footsteps were difficult to hear over the pounding of her pulse, but they were retreating. Thank God. Her momentary lapse wasn't going to cost anything.

Damn! How could she have let this happen? Of all the stupid, self-indulgent, irresponsible things to do. No matter how attracted to him she was, it was no excuse for jeopardizing the mission and his life.

"I'm not going to apologize for that." Hawk's voice was rough. He stepped behind her. His teeth grazed her ear. "I think we both wanted it."

She tilted her head away. "Then I'll apologize, sir. As a soldier—"

"I wasn't kissing the soldier, Sarah. I was kissing the woman."

Chapter 5

The curtains were drawn against the evening darkness. The soft light from the lamps mellowed the ivory and rose tones of the suite, providing a hushed atmosphere. Hawk was alone with a fascinating woman, but the rush of his pulse had nothing to do with romance. He tilted the shade of the lamp on the desk to throw more light on the photograph he studied.

It was black and white with the telltale graininess that was the result of a telephoto lens. It had been transmitted by fax, which had added a further degree of blurriness. Still, the resolution was high enough to portray a distinctive face. It belonged to a white man in his late forties. He had close-cropped gray hair and a thick mustache. His deep-set eyes were spaced wide apart and were unusually pale.

Sarah gathered the rest of the pages that had printed out from the fax machine, tapped them on the desktop to square them up and started reading from the top one. "His name is Dieter Weltzer. He's a German national who has been linked to several terrorist groups but has no strong affiliations. He's a freelancer.''

Hawk tried to discern the expression in the black-and-white face, but he could find none. ''A freelance assassin who has been hired to kill me.''

''Yes. Prince Jibril's sources were correct. Weltzer doesn't work cheap. Interpol uncovered a deposit of a quarter million dollars that appeared in one of the accounts Weltzer uses.''

Hawk let out a low whistle. ''Who wants me dead that much?''

''That's the real question. Unfortunately, we still have no information on who hired him.''

Hawk dropped the photograph on the desk. It wasn't every day a man looked into the face of what could be his executioner. ''At least we know what he looks like.''

''Not necessarily. He could have shaved his mustache and be wearing a hairpiece. He could use tinted contacts or dark glasses to hide the color of his eyes.''

''He won't be able to disguise everything.''

''That's true. There are some aspects like the shape of his head and the proportion of his limbs that he can't change. All this information was distributed to the Swedish authorities, as well. They will be watching every point of entry and stepping up surveillance of this area.''

''He would probably be in the country already,'' Hawk said.

Sarah nodded and started on the next page. ''They say he has always worked alone, so he's very mobile. His preferred method of attack is using a long-range rifle and firing from a concealed vantage point.''

''Like yesterday beside the canal.''

''Yes.''

"You really did save my life."

She looked up to meet his gaze. "Yes, Dr. Lemay. That's my job."

There was no hint of triumph on her face, even though she was continuing to be proved right. Her strength of character moved him. It also maddened him. "Thank you, Sarah."

"Sir?"

"For saving my life." He caught her elbow. "But if you ever put yourself in danger for me like that again I'll lock you up."

"I intend to protect you however I see fit." She pulled her arm from his grasp. "I don't tell you how to do your job, so don't tell me how to do mine."

"Sarah—"

"And in the future, unless it's necessary during the course of this mission, I would prefer it if you tried not to touch me. I'll endeavor to do the same."

"It was only your arm."

"Yes, but I only touched your hand this afternoon and it led to a kiss. We were lucky that time. We can't afford to let things escalate again."

They had avoided the topic for the past four hours. He'd had his shower and worked on his speech; she'd retreated into her role of his bodyguard; but the topic couldn't be ignored forever.

Hawk knew she was right. He shouldn't grab her like this. Especially now that he was beginning to absorb the seriousness of the threat to him. Interpol had just faxed them the identity of his potential killer. They both had to stay alert, and he sure as hell couldn't do that if all he was thinking about was taking Sarah in his arms again.

His gaze dropped to her lips. His muscles clenched as he remembered the spicy sweet taste of her mouth, the feel of her tongue stroking his and her nipples hardening against his chest—

"Dr. Lemay."

He hadn't even realized he'd started to lean toward her. He straightened up and paced to the window.

"Sir, your shadow."

He changed direction so the lamp didn't cast his silhouette on the curtain. He detoured past the sofa, walked around her cot and reached the wardrobe. He braced his hands on either side of the wooden doors and took a deep breath. "All right. I agree that kissing you in the stairwell this afternoon wasn't wise. I could have put both of us in danger."

"I was equally responsible." She cleared her throat. "This kind of thing has been known to happen as a reaction to tension."

"What 'kind of thing'?"

"Sexual attraction, sir. It's a normal physiological reaction to the effects of adrenaline."

He looked at her over his shoulder. "Are you admitting you're sexually attracted to me?"

"You noticed it yourself, so I don't think there's any point denying it, and we don't have time to be coy."

There was that look again, the same one she'd given him when she'd seen him gazing at her breasts. Why did he find her take-it-or-leave-it self-confidence so alluring? "Does that mean you enjoyed our kiss?"

"Whether I did or not is irrelevant. We're both adults." She squared up the fax papers and set them back on the desk. "We know it didn't mean anything."

"It didn't?"

"As I've tried to explain, the incident arose from proximity and stress. It was an outlet for emotions. Neither of us should put any importance on it."

"So if I kiss you again, it wouldn't matter?"

"That's not what I said. The point I'm trying to make is that we don't have to let it be a problem. We can admit having impulses but we can still control them. We have more important concerns."

He turned to lean his back against the wardrobe. He folded his arms over his chest. "How many missions have you been on, Sarah?"

"I couldn't say exactly. I've been in the army for nine years."

"Have you had a problem with sexual attraction before?"

"No."

"Have you kissed someone you're supposed to protect?"

"Certainly not."

"Then what's different about this mission?"

"That's a good question."

"Could it be me?"

"I don't see why, Dr. Lemay. You're not my type."

"Oh? What's wrong with me?"

"It really doesn't have anything to do with you. I prefer military men."

"Ah. Like dear old Dad, the famous General Bartholomew Fox."

She stiffened. "No, like my fiancé, Captain Kyle Jackson."

Hawk was surprised by the sudden disappointment he felt. She wore no rings on her fingers, but he shouldn't have assumed she was free. He hadn't even stopped to consider the question. He should have. He couldn't be the only man who found Sarah Fox to be a fascinating woman.

And she wouldn't be the first woman to kiss another man while being promised to someone else.

"I've never met a man who could compare to Jackson," Sarah continued. "He was everything a soldier should be. He defined heroism. He was honorable and courageous."

"Was?"

"He was killed on a training mission in the Middle East five weeks before we would have been married."

He rubbed his forehead. "I'm sorry, Sarah."

"You see, I also know what it's like to lose someone you love, Dr. Lemay. I loved Jackson with all my heart and I haven't stopped. What we had was rare, a once-in-a-lifetime bond." She straightened her spine, as if responding to an unheard command to come to attention. "But that has no bearing on our current situation, except to reassure you that whatever attraction might arise between you and me is superficial and means nothing."

"Why do I have this urge to come over there and prove you wrong?"

She stared at him, her chin lifting. "It wasn't meant to be a challenge, sir."

"No, it wasn't. That's what makes it worse."

"Do you want Major Redinger to assign someone else to guard you? Because if you don't feel we can work together, I'll request to be replaced. I'm not going to let my pride stand in the way of this mission."

The sensible thing to do would be to take her up on her offer. That would keep her safe.

But what would her next mission be like? Rescuing a kidnapped child? Infiltrating a dictator's palace? Would she leave this assignment only to put herself in harm's way for someone else? As long as she stayed here, Hawk could do everything in his power to minimize the risk—

Damn. He couldn't even finish that lie. His reasons for wanting her to stay weren't any more rational now than they had been yesterday. He still wasn't ready to let her go. "I don't want anyone else, Sarah. I want you."

"Fine. Then we have to—"

Her words were cut off when a knock sounded on the suite door. A heavily accented voice called out. "Room service."

Hawk straightened up and pivoted toward the door. He was reaching for the knob when Sarah sprinted across the room to knock his hand aside.

"Move back," she whispered. She squeezed herself between him and the door. "Let me check this out."

He bracketed her waist with his hands. "I ordered dinner, Sarah."

She put her eye to the peephole. "It appears as if it's arrived. That's the same teenage bellhop who delivered my cot yesterday." She pointed to her left. "This seems safe, but please, stand there out of the way when I open the door. I wouldn't want to hit you by mistake if I need to move in a hurry."

He knew it wasn't the right time to argue or to indulge himself, but he was torn between giving her room to work and staying right where he was. What was it about the feel of her body pressed to his that made him want to keep her there? No, this wasn't rational at all. He spread his fingers, moving his hands to her hips.

She twisted her head to look back at him. He could see flecks of gold in her eyes. A rosy flush tinged her cheeks. Her lips were so close to his...

"If you don't move," she said through her teeth, "you'll force me to shove you with my bad shoulder."

It was the most effective thing she could have said. He immediately lifted his hands away and stepped to the side.

He would never want to see Sarah suffer because of him.

* * *

Sarah usually slept like a rock when she was out in the field. She knew the wisdom of grabbing rest whenever the opportunity arose. She could sleep through a landing in a troop transport on a short runway or sitting up against a tree with nothing but a poncho to protect her from the pouring rain. But as she lay on her cot that night, sleep wouldn't come.

She curled on her side, her gaze going to the strip of light that showed beneath the bedroom door. She wasn't the only one awake. Until half an hour ago, she'd heard the faint tap of Hawk's keyboard—he'd been working at his computer since they had said good-night. What could be so important that he would lose sleep over it?

Now, that was a stupid question. Everything about Hawk's work was important. That was why someone had paid a quarter million dollars to Dieter Weltzer to kill him.

She sighed and sat up, raking her hair back from her face. She probably should have asked the Major for a replacement when she'd checked in with him tonight. She was getting far too personally involved with this mission. She and Hawk seemed to have come to an understanding about that kiss, but now that the attraction between them was out in the open, it was even harder to ignore.

Then why had she mentioned Jackson? If she wanted to maintain an emotional distance from Hawk, why bring her fiancé into the conversation? All right, her love for Jackson was the reason she would never love anyone else, but what was happening between her and Hawk wasn't love. It wasn't anything like the comfortable certainty she'd felt with Jackson. No, as she'd known from the start, it was based on sex.

Well, perhaps it was a bit more than that. It could be called a crush—because of the background research she'd studied on the flight over, she'd already begun to admire the famous Dr. Lemay even before she'd met him face-to-face.

A crush. It seemed so…juvenile. She didn't think she'd had a crush on anyone before, even when she'd been a teenager. For one thing, she hadn't had the opportunity. The general's career had taken them to bases all over the world. The frequent moves had been stimulating, but they put an end to relationships before they had a chance to start. She'd become an expert in the art of packing. She'd also become skilled in the art of saying goodbye in a dozen languages. The friendships she'd made among the other Army brats were quick but fleeting. They all knew the routine, and they knew better than to make promises about keeping in touch.

That was why the love she'd shared with Jackson had been all the more precious. It had been the exception to the rule. They had been a perfect match. She'd known he was the right man from the moment the general had introduced them. She merely had to think of Jackson and other men paled in comparison.

So she could handle this. By this time tomorrow, it would all be over. That's what she had to keep reminding herself. Yes, only another twenty-four hours to go, and Hawk's scheduled activities would be over, the conference would have ended and they would all be able to go their separate ways and resume their normal lives.

Somehow that thought only made her wider awake.

She tossed back the blanket and got to her feet. She was always more at ease doing things and making herself useful. She did a circuit of the room, taking time to ensure the door was securely bolted and the window was locked, then went to the desk and picked up the photo of Weltzer.

Interpol said he was a sniper, but as long as Sarah and Hawk stayed inside the hotel, Weltzer wouldn't be able to set up any long-distance shots. What strategy would he try next? An ambush? Explosives? Not being able to use his preferred method of attack would put him at a disadvantage. Would Sarah be able to neutralize him before he did any damage? She would have to meet with the hotel security people again in the morning and coordinate a plan of action. If she didn't feel it was adequate, she would advise Hawk to cancel his appearances.

Would he agree? Probably not. He didn't seem to be the kind of man who gave up easily. About anything.

A thud came from the bedroom, like an object dropping to the carpet. The grill from an air vent? The lamp in front of the window? Even as she was going through the possibilities in her head, Sarah snatched her gun from beneath her pillow, ran to the bedroom door and swung it open.

She took in the scene at a glance. The curtain was motionless and still drawn closed; the air vent in the wall opposite the bathroom was still in place. The door of the tiny closet was open and held nothing but Hawk's clothes and a spare blanket. There was no intruder. No movement. Hawk was stretched out on top of the bedspread, his shoulders propped against the quilted satin headboard, his head lolling to the side. Sarah had an instant of gut-wrenching horror—had Weltzer gotten past her after all?—but then she heard the snore.

Hawk wasn't dead, he was sleeping.

Sarah breathed out slowly through her nose, trying to regain her calm. This wasn't good. The fear she'd felt just now wasn't because she'd thought she might have failed to do her job. It was because she didn't want Hawk hurt. Her concern was for the man, not the subject of her mission.

I wasn't kissing the soldier, Sarah. I was kissing the woman.

She waited another minute until her pulse had settled, then moved farther into the room—she still needed to determine the source of the noise she had heard. She could see nothing out of place until she rounded the bed. Hawk's laptop computer was lying on the carpet, propped open like a book standing on end. It must have slipped off his lap when he'd fallen asleep.

She flicked the safety on her gun, tipped it toward the ceiling and turned her attention to Hawk. Except for his shoes, he was still fully clothed. Scraps of paper with scribbled notes littered the bed around him. Several disks were stacked on the bedside table with the lamp. One of Hawk's hands rested on his stomach, rising and falling with his steady breathing. The other hand lay palm up at his side, his fingers curled. A pen lay just beyond his fingertips, as if it had rolled out of his grasp.

Finally, he looked more like the intellectual she knew he was. A dedicated scientist falling asleep at his work. Yes, this was how she should picture him. It was far better than remembering how he'd looked in the gym half-naked and glistening with sweat.

She gritted her teeth and returned her gaze to his computer. Should she pick it up, make sure it wasn't damaged? If she didn't move it, he might step on it when he got up. On the other hand, if she touched it, he might accuse her of trying to spy on him again. She didn't want to risk losing the cooperation she'd gained.

He wasn't a man who trusted easily. Why? Was it due to his intellect? Did that make him overanalyze every aspect of a situation?

Or was his distrust rooted more deeply than that? Why had Jibril said Hawk knew women couldn't be trusted?

Oh, great. She was doing it again. His hang-ups, his past, his emotions, none of those were her concern. Getting him through the next twenty-four hours was. She set her gun on the bedside table, walked to the closet and reached for the spare blanket that rested on the shelf over the bar.

The mattress creaked. "Sarah?"

She turned, the blanket clutched to her chest. "Dr. Lemay. I'm sorry if I woke you."

He blinked a few times. "Must have fallen asleep. What time is it?"

"Around one."

Paper crumpled as he sat forward. He yawned and rubbed his jaw, his palm rasping over the beginning of his beard. He looked at the blanket in her arms. "Are you cold?"

She hesitated, not wanting to admit the blanket had been intended for him.

"You're welcome to share the bed with me, if you like."

"No, thank you, sir. You snore."

His lips curved into a lazy smile. "I've never had any complaints before."

Had she thought this was a safe way to picture him? His eyes were half-closed, his big body still relaxed with sleep and that smile...

He had dimples. She hadn't seen them before. Beside those masculine lines that framed his mouth, two tiny indentations folded into his cheeks.

No, this wasn't safe at all. "Actually, I came in here because I heard a noise. I'm pretty sure it was your laptop hitting the floor."

His smile froze. The sleepiness disappeared from his face. He swore and leaned over the side of the mattress.

"It's probably okay," she said. "The carpet is thick."

He grabbed the computer and levered himself back on the bed. He set it on his outstretched legs and hit a few keys. The hard drive crackled. "Come on, come on," he muttered, peering at the screen. "Where is it?"

Sarah moved to the foot of the bed to watch him. "Did you lose something?"

Hawk studied the computer screen for a moment, then exhaled hard. "Still there. Damn, that was too close."

"Maybe you should try to get some rest. You can finish this in the morning. You don't have any meetings planned until eleven."

He took a disk from the night table and inserted it in the computer. "I canceled the morning meeting."

"The one with the representatives from Greenpeace?"

"Yes." He saved his work, closed the lid of his computer and set it aside. "I decided it isn't worth the risk. I'm also skipping the panel discussion with the University of Uppsala Theoretical Physics Department."

She couldn't completely hide her start of surprise. She'd known he was taking the threat to his life seriously now—ordering dinner from room service had illustrated that much—but he was being more cautious than she'd expected. "Does this mean you're canceling your speech, as well?"

"No, Sarah. Now that I can't count on Jibril, I have no choice but to go forward."

"What does the prince of Moukim have to do with your speech?"

Hawk picked up his discarded pen, regarding her in silence for a while. He seemed to be weighing something in his mind. Finally he clipped the pen in his shirt pocket and patted the mattress beside him. "Sit down. I'll tell you about it."

Sarah didn't move.

He lifted his eyebrows. "Worried you won't be able to keep your hands to yourself?"

She dropped the blanket near his feet and sat on the corner of the mattress opposite him. "I'm accustomed to enduring personal deprivations in the field, so I'll do my best to restrain myself, sir."

His lips twitched. "Better watch out. That's sounding like a challenge."

"You were going to tell me about Prince Jibril?"

His expression sobered. "Right. From what you said yesterday, you understand the significance of my research, and how fusion energy could change the power balance of the world. As a scientist I have a moral duty to take responsibility for what I develop. That's why I came to this conference. I had hoped to use my connection with Jibril to make the transition easier."

"The transition? You're talking about it as if fusion power is a sure thing."

Hawk pinched the bridge of his nose. He looked tired. "It's a matter of when, not if."

"I had no idea you were so close to a breakthrough."

"That's why I haven't published anything in years. I've done my best not to let anyone know until I can be sure my discoveries don't end up causing more harm than good."

"That's very admirable."

"In theory, anyway. I thought I'd approach Jibril because he's an influential man in OPEC. I realize there are other oil producers who aren't members of the organization, and as you pointed out yesterday, there are countless businesses and labor groups that will be impacted by my research, but Jibril was a good place to start. The biggest change has to be a change in attitude. If he had agreed to work with me, we could have phased in the change gradually. Moukim could have served as an example to OPEC of how an oil-based economy could profit from the new technology instead of resisting it.''

''Is that why you didn't want to work for the Defense Department?''

He nodded. ''Yes, that's why I turned down our government's offer. This discovery is too important to be left to the politicians or hoarded by one country. Fusion power should ease the tension between our culture and the rest of the world instead of aggravating it.''

''But Jibril wasn't in a mood to cooperate.''

''No. I hate being wrong, but seeing him was a mistake. We were friends once, but I had underestimated the importance he put on our past.''

''I'm sorry it didn't work out.''

He began gathering the notes that were scattered on the bed around him. ''So am I. It won't be easy to change attitudes with only words. I've rewritten this speech three times.''

She picked up a paper that was close to her hip and leaned forward to hand it to him. ''I hope I didn't antagonize the prince further by my conduct at the reception.''

He took the note and stacked it with the others. ''It had nothing to do with you, Sarah. I should have known it wouldn't work the second I saw his yacht.''

''Yes, I would imagine someone who was accustomed to that much wealth and power wouldn't want to see it threatened.''

''That's part of it, but it's not what I meant. Do you remember what the boat was called?''

She closed her eyes, taking a moment to recall the image of the black-and-sand-colored yacht. She zeroed in on the lettering at the stern. ''Yes.'' She returned her gaze to Hawk. ''It was called *Faith*.''

He tossed his notes beside his computer. ''So was she.''

Sarah didn't have to ask whom he meant. She knew by his tone. Faith must be the name of the woman he and Jibril had loved. And mourned.

Just when she thought she was getting a handle on her feelings, she got drawn in deeper. It must have been difficult for Hawk to approach Jibril in the first place. Seeing that name on the boat would have made it worse, yet he had gone through with the meeting, anyway, in the hopes of minimizing the problems that would arise from his research. She realized this scientist was as committed to his own concept of duty as she was to hers. She had to respect him for that.

He swung his legs off the bed and got to his feet. "Stay there for a minute."

"Where are you going?"

He strode to the bathroom. "Since we're both up, I'm going to run you a hot bath. The heat should be good for your shoulder." He paused in the doorway. "Take all the time you want. I'll work in the sitting room until you're done."

He might have teased her about getting into bed with him, but there was nothing suggestive about his words this time. It was clear to Sarah that Hawk's offer was made out of genuine consideration, not as a ploy to get her naked.

Obviously, the respect between them was mutual.

She cursed under her breath. On top of everything else, now she was starting to like him.

Chapter 6

"Stay close to Lemay and await further orders."

Sarah frowned, pressing her free hand over her ear, unsure she had heard Major Redinger correctly over the noise in the suite. A pair of Stockholm policemen stood near the door, talking with the head of hotel security. The official liaison from the American Embassy—a red-headed bulldog of a man named Pendleton—was hovering nearby with his own cell phone pressed to his ear. Until a few minutes ago, Hawk had been in the midst of them, using Pendleton as a translator as he went over the measures they had taken. Now he was sitting on the sofa, clicking at the keyboard of the computer on the coffee table in front of him.

It wasn't yet four in the afternoon, but full darkness had already fallen. The soft lighting from the lamps around the suite did nothing to dull the edge of tension in the atmosphere. It was almost show time. There was less than two hours to go before Hawk was scheduled to address the conference. If Weltzer was going to make a move, it would have to be soon.

So, why was the Major changing Sarah's orders? "Say again, sir?" she asked. "I'm having difficulty hearing you."

"Stand by." There was a pause. When Redinger spoke again, his words came through clearly. "Remain with Lemay," he said. "Coordinate his security. I'll want a full report at the close of the conference."

Sarah terminated the call and stored her phone in her suit jacket. She had misunderstood. Nothing had changed. Her duty was to keep Hawkins Lemay alive. Her anxiety was making her jumpy.

She couldn't afford that. She had to be calm. Put aside the incipient panic and concentrate on her duty.

She walked to the group by the door and had them review the precautions that had been put in place. Pendleton finished his phone call and joined them, offering assistance in the form of an armored limousine, but it wouldn't be necessary until Hawk was ready to leave for the airport since Hawk's speech and the closing ceremonies for the conference would take place in the hotel ballroom.

It wasn't complicated. The risk factor was more than acceptable. Because of the high-level diplomats who had been in attendance here for the past three days, the security both within the hotel and on the surrounding streets was already as tight as a drum.

Sarah had done exactly what was expected of her. She had determined what was needed, she had made use of the local authorities, she had even succeeded in gaining the cooperation of her subject. What should have been an easy breather of a mission was becoming precisely that. Easy.

Yet she couldn't remember feeling this nervous. Instead

of the low-level excitement that usually preceded action, she felt...dread.

Somehow she managed to finalize the arrangements with the police and the hotel staff, thanked the embassy man for his cooperation and ushered them from the suite. The moment she and Hawk were alone, her stomach knotted.

How could she decide the risk was acceptable? What if she was wrong, what if her anxiety caused her to slip up? What if the next time she saw Hawk lying motionless with his head lolling to the side he wasn't merely asleep?

"How are you holding up, Sarah?"

She checked the door lock, wiped her damp palms on her skirt and moved to the wardrobe. "Fine, thank you, sir. How about you?"

"Impatient to get this over with." He packed up his computer and stored it in the bedroom, then returned to cross the room to where she stood. He had dressed in a sober charcoal-gray suit and a tailored shirt for his appearance. The suit emphasized his height and his broad shoulders, the crisp white shirt brought out the piercing blue of his eyes. He looked distinguished and controlled...except for his loosened tie and the furrows that his fingers had left in his neatly combed hair.

Sarah had a sudden urge to smooth his hair, just as she'd wanted to spread the spare blanket over him the night before. But that wasn't what she was here for. That wouldn't help keep him alive. She opened the wardrobe and bent down to unlock her suitcase. "There are a few more details we need to take care of," she said.

"Pendleton from the embassy said the police were going to escort us from here to the ballroom."

"That's right. One officer is stationed in the corridor, the other at the stairwell."

Hawk moved past her to look through the peephole. "They seem very competent."

"They are. So is the rest of the force. The security cordon around the building is tight. There isn't much risk of Weltzer getting inside."

"Since the rest of the security is good, is there any chance you would be willing to stay in the suite and wait for me?"

The words were familiar. It was almost exactly what he had said yesterday when they'd been on their way to visit Jibril. She glanced at him over her shoulder. "No, sir. None at all. Any chance you'll change your mind and cancel your speech?"

"No, Sarah. None at all."

She withdrew the garments she had packed at the bottom of the suitcase and straightened up. "Fine," she said. She held up a pair of bulletproof vests. "Then you need to put on one of these."

He didn't make a move to take either one. "Only if you wear the other."

"Don't worry, I intend to. After my last mission, I have a lot of respect for body armor." She moved to where she had rolled her folded cot out of the way beside the wall and put one of the vests on top of it. "These vests aren't as bulky as the police-issue models but they're just as effective. You can wear it under your clothes. If you take off your shirt, I'll help you fit this one to your chest."

He slipped off his suit jacket. "Why do you put yourself through this, Sarah?"

"Why? It's my duty. I already explained that."

He draped his jacket over one corner of the folded cot. He laid his tie on top of it, then started unfastening the buttons on the front of his shirt. "I'm beginning to believe you really don't understand what an exceptional woman you are.''

"I'm just a soldier.''

"That's what I mean. You don't want to acknowledge there's another side to you. Why are you so determined to be tough?''

"Because I'm on duty and your life depends on it. Why are you so determined to risk your life to talk about a scientific theory?''

"Because it's the right thing to do.'' He finished unbuttoning his shirt and tugged the tails free from his pants. "And my work is my life.''

She rasped open the Velcro straps that held the sides of the vest together. "Well, the Army is my life. Is that so different?''

He held her gaze in silence for a while before he spoke again. "You have a point. It's not that different at all.''

"Then you should understand why I need to do my job.''

"Go ahead.'' He stripped off his shirt and dropped it on his other clothes. "I don't think I could stop you if I wanted to.''

She looked at his chest. He wore no undershirt. Although his belt was still fastened and the dark-gray pants that matched his jacket were neatly in place, he was bare from the waist up.

The contrast of his civilized clothes next to his naked skin was compelling. His pants rode low on his hips. A line of silky dark hair rose above his belt buckle to frame his navel. It continued upward over the washboard swells of his abdomen. Male strength was implicit in each rise of muscle. She remembered how solid his chest had felt when he'd held her in the stairwell.

And she thought how defenseless this expanse of taut skin would be to a bullet.

Her pulse thudded hard. She had to put her personal feelings aside. She had to do her duty. She rose on her tiptoes to slip the vest over his head, then straightened the front section over his chest. "Hold your arms out from your sides."

His muscles flexed as he did as she asked. She caught a whiff of soap and man. Her gaze strayed to the black hair that shadowed his armpit even as she reminded herself she shouldn't be looking at him like this. It was too...intimate. She focused on the vest, pressing the straps into place under his left arm. "This has to fit snugly to optimize the coverage," she said. "But I don't want it to restrict your breathing. Let me know if it's too tight."

"It's fine."

His voice sounded pinched. She moved to his right side to adjust the other set of straps, then slipped her fingers beneath the edge of the vest to check the fit.

His skin warmed to her touch. She slid her fingers along his ribs. The fit felt good. Both the vest and her hand. She pressed her palm to his stomach. She wanted to learn his texture, trace the contours of muscle and sinew, explore that masculine hollow under his arm and the dip of his navel and all the other hidden places—

He caught her hand.

She inhaled deeply, striving for calm. It only brought his scent more strongly to her tongue. "Almost done, sir."

He rubbed his thumb over her wrist. "Your pulse is racing."

"It's adrenaline, Dr. Lemay."

"A side effect of tension."

"Yes. That's all. It's a normal physical reaction."

"It doesn't mean anything?"

"No."

"Sarah."

She lifted her gaze to his face. She tried to see the dedicated scientist, the subject of her mission. Instead she saw the man who had drawn her a bath. "We won't let it be a problem, sir. We can't."

His eyes gleamed. "Do you want some help with your vest, Sarah?"

Oh, God. She could imagine it all too easily. To strip off her suit jacket and her blouse, to feel his hands on her skin... "That wouldn't be a good idea, sir. This isn't foreplay. It's business."

He released her hand and picked up his shirt. He dragged it on roughly. "He must have been one hell of a man."

"Who?"

"Your fiancé."

She retrieved the other vest, alarmed to see that her hands were shaking. "Yes, he was. He was without equal. Our love was perfect. I'll never forget him."

Hawk started fastening his buttons. The extra bulk of the vest drew the buttonholes taut. He swore as he tried to push the buttons through.

Sarah wanted to apologize. He had lost someone he'd loved, too. Was he thinking about Faith? What kind of pain did he keep inside?

She turned away so she wouldn't reach out to help him with his buttons. His life could depend on her ability to be objective. If she cared about him, she would make more of an effort to remember that.

If she cared about him? The thought jarred her. How had she gone from lust to liking to...caring? She walked toward the bedroom, intending to put on her own vest in private.

"Sarah?"

She paused. "Yes, Dr. Lemay?"

"Please be careful tonight."

She wasn't sure how she would have replied. He seemed to have a knack for putting her off balance. She'd never known anyone who could stir her emotions so quickly. Not even Jackson.

That thought jarred her even more. Before she could pursue it, a loud buzz split the air.

She whirled, looking for the source of the sound. It came from the small round grill that was set into the ceiling over the door of the suite.

Hawk was at her side immediately. "That's the fire alarm!" He caught her arm and turned her toward the door. "Come with me."

She dug in her heels. "No. I have to check this out first."

He stopped. His nostrils flared. "I can smell smoke."

Sarah sniffed. He was right. The acrid scent of smoke stung the back of her throat. It must have been building for several minutes. She should have noticed it before, but she'd been too wrapped up in Hawk to be aware of anything else.

Damn! She was going to endanger them both with her negligence. "I smell it, too," she said. "But it could be a ruse to get you outside."

"Sarah, it's an old building. If there's a fire, it would spread fast. We've got to get out."

She ran to the door and put her eye to the peephole. There was a white haze in the corridor. The two men from the Stockholm police were already directing the other guests from the floor toward the stairwell.

Sarah dropped her vest and dug into her jacket pocket for her phone. "Wet down some towels to put at the bottom of the door," she said, glancing back at Hawk. "We don't move until I verify this."

Hawk nodded once and disappeared into the bedroom. By the time he returned with an armful of dripping towels, she had the hotel manager on the phone. The alarm had changed to an intermittent drone, allowing her to hear the manager, as well as catch the sound of the approaching sirens. She put away her phone. "There's a small fire in the basement," she told Hawk. "They're evacuating the building as a precaution while they work to contain it."

He crouched to fit the towels over the crack beneath the door. "Do we stay or do we go?"

She realized he was leaving the choice up to her. It was her responsibility to assess the risk, and he was trusting her to make the right decision. If they stayed and the fire spread, they could be trapped in the suite. If they left, they could be walking into an ambush. She put her hand on Hawk's shoulder and leaned past him to check the peephole. The smoke in the air was thickening fast. The corridor had already emptied of people. She could see no one out there...

No one? She thumped her fist against the door and called out sharply. There was no reply. Where had the policemen gone? Had they gone to another floor to help direct the evacuation? They wouldn't have left Hawk and her without alerting them first, would they?

Hawk rose from his crouch. "Where are the cops?"

"I can't see them." She drew her gun and thumbed off the safety. "Something's wrong. This fire could be a setup."

"So we stay."

"Yes. Stand by an inside wall," she said, backing away from the door. "I'm going to call for—"

There was a crash. Not from the door, from the window.

Sarah spun toward the noise, locking her elbows to steady her gun.

The curtain billowed inward amid shards of glass and shredded fabric. The lamp on the desk shattered. So did the mirror beside it. Automatic weapon, Sarah thought immediately. Silenced, but still deadly. "Get down!" she yelled.

Instead of dropping where he was, Hawk dove toward her, hooked his arm around her waist and yanked her to the floor with him. Then he rolled her to her stomach and flattened himself on top of her back.

"Dr. Lemay, no!"

"I've got a vest." His voice was harsh in her ear. "You don't."

Bullets whizzed over their heads, thudding into the wall. Plaster and bits of wallpaper rained down around them. The table beside the sofa disintegrated into splinters. A second lamp exploded into shards of porcelain. Only the glow of city lights that came through the shredded curtain kept the room from total darkness.

Sarah didn't waste time trying to dislodge Hawk's weight. She didn't waste time telling him how small a percentage of his body the vest actually protected, either, especially in an indiscriminate barrage like this. As it turned out, his heroics had given her an advantage—from her prone position she had a clear line of sight beneath the sofa to the window.

Against the sky, she saw the dark silhouette of a lone man. There was no balcony. He must have rappelled from the roof. He was laying down his own cover fire. She had to act fast. His next probable move would be to swing through the window and finish the job.

Thanks to her training, Sarah's grip on her gun hadn't loosened when Hawk had tackled her—the butt was still

seated firmly in her hand. She dragged her arm forward to
bring the gun into firing position. With her cheek pressed
to the carpet, she closed one eye, aimed at the muzzle flash
from their assailant's weapon and squeezed off two shots.

What was left of the window crashed inward. A black-
clad figure swung over the sill.

Before his feet touched the floor, Sarah fired again.

The barrage of gunfire ceased. The man toppled sideways and fell heavily to the floor.

Sarah felt Hawk begin to push himself up. She reached
behind her with her free hand and grabbed hold of his hair.
She gave his head a light shake, hoping he would get her
message. She wanted to make sure the shooter was alone.

Hawk eased his weight onto his knees and elbows, cag-
ing her beneath him. He put his lips next to her ear. "Are
you all right?"

She nodded, straining to see through the gloom, but
there was no sign of anyone else. Cold air poured along
the floor. Flashes of red rimmed the broken window frame.
The red flashes were from emergency vehicles, she realized. The wail of the sirens had risen to a crescendo. The
fire alarm was still emitting its intermittent buzz.

With all the noise—and the evacuation that had emptied
the upper stories—it was doubtful that anyone would have
heard the commotion up here. Considering the confusion
in and around the hotel, no one on the street would have
looked up to see the man outside their window. Chances
were good that no one would be aware of the life-and-
death struggle that had just taken place.

The fire had to have been set as a diversion, Sarah
thought. It hadn't been meant to draw them out of the suite
but to corner them inside it. The whole thing had happened
incredibly fast. Although it had seemed like hours, not
more than two minutes could have elapsed since the first

shot. A split second hesitation either way and Hawk could have been killed.

The fear that Sarah had put aside surged over her without warning. Her fingers tightened in Hawk's hair. She wanted to hit him for wasting precious moments by trying to protect her. And she wanted to turn over, tug his head down to hers and kiss him until this fear washed away.

But there was no time to indulge in emotion. They weren't home free yet. She wriggled out from beneath Hawk and rolled into a crouch. "Stay down," she ordered, giving his shoulder a firm squeeze. Her senses stretched to the max, she moved out from behind the sofa.

It was an eerie scene. Shredded curtains and the ragged end of a rappelling rope fluttered in the breeze. Red light strobed over the shambles of the room and the body under the window. One of the sirens whined to a stop. Seconds later the buzz from the alarm ceased. Sarah wiggled her jaw to alleviate the ringing in her ears and steadied her weapon on their fallen assailant.

He hadn't moved from where he'd fallen. Was it Weltzer? It was too dark to see his face. This assault wasn't his style, but they hadn't left him any opportunity for his typical long-range shots.

Sarah was sure she'd hit him in the heart, yet she wasn't taking anything for granted. She spotted his rifle near the remnants of the lamp table. Without shifting her aim, she reached out with her left hand, picked up the rifle and slung the strap around her neck, slipping her arm through the loop. The hot barrel singed her wrist. She straightened up and dug her phone from her pocket. "Here, take this," she said, lobbing the phone behind her. "Call for help."

She heard the smack as Hawk caught it. His voice came from just over her shoulder. "What number?" he asked.

"Hit any of the first three speed-dial. They're programmed to the local emergency services."

There was a muted beep. "Busy," Hawk said. "Circuits must be jammed because of the fire." He touched her back. "Sarah?"

"Keep trying," she said. "And, please, don't crowd me. I need to be able to—"

Without any warning, the man on the floor arched forward and sprang to his feet.

The movement was so unexpected it took Sarah off guard. Had she shot wide before? Had he been faking? She fired instinctively, but he moved so fast her shot hit the baseboard where he'd been lying. She swung to follow him, firing again. This time she could see she didn't miss. The bullet struck his chest. She saw his body jerk with the impact. But he didn't stop.

Son of a bitch! she thought. Hawk wasn't the only one with body armor. She hadn't missed. Her first shots must have knocked the wind out of him.

Something metallic glinted from the man's hand. It was a thin-bladed knife. He sprang toward Hawk. Sarah kicked out and felt a burning pain in her thigh.

In the next instant Hawk yanked her off her feet and spun her away. Before she could regain her balance, he moved past her to pick up a leg of the broken table. He swung it at their attacker like a baseball bat.

"No!" she cried. "Stay back!"

The reply Hawk gave her was more of a growl than a word. His improvised club cracked against the man's skull, sending him reeling toward the gaping window. The red light from the street flashed across a familiar face, one with deep-set eyes that were so pale they looked colorless.

So it was Weltzer, Sarah thought, taking aim on a spot between the man's eyes.

Before she could fire, the back of Weltzer's legs hit the windowsill. His momentum carried him over the edge. He grabbed for the shredded curtains but they tore away. Then he grabbed for Hawk, one hand still brandishing the knife.

"No!" Sarah launched herself at Hawk and propelled him out of Weltzer's reach.

And just like that, the square of sky beyond the window was empty. There was a chilling instant of silence. It was followed by a scream. Then a crunching thud five stories below.

Sarah grasped the sill and looked outside. In the midst of the emergency vehicles that were gathered in front of the hotel, a dark form lay motionless on the cobblestones. People were already running toward him, but it was clear even from Sarah's vantage point that he was beyond help. This time Weltzer wouldn't be getting up again.

She felt Hawk's presence behind her. He ran his hand over her back, up her arm, into her hair. "Sarah."

There was a tremor in his voice. It made her shudder. She fought to hang on to her control. "We can't stand here," she said. "It's too exposed. We can't be sure there isn't someone else out there."

The broken table leg clattered to the floor. Hawk moved against her back, slipping his hands around her waist. He pressed his cheek to the top of her head. His breathing was as rapid as hers.

"Dr. Lemay."

He crossed his arms in front of her and lifted her from her feet. Holding her off the floor, he backed away from the window. Broken porcelain and slivers of wood crunched beneath his shoes. He stopped when he reached the center of the room. "Is this far enough?"

"Yes."

He set her back on her feet. He loosened his hold but

he didn't let her go. His arms encircled her as if she were fragile and feminine, as if she didn't have Weltzer's rifle slung from her shoulder or her own handgun still clutched in her fingers. As if they hadn't both just watched a man die. "Are you okay?" he asked.

"No problem. How about you?"

"Fine."

"The emergency personnel on the sidewalk will see which window he fell from," she said. "Help should arrive any minute. We'll stay put until they get here."

"I can't believe how fast... Sarah, are you sure you're all right?"

She dropped her head back against Hawk's shoulder, inhaling deeply, fighting to stem the horror that was curling inside her. Oh, she wanted to stay right where she was and soak in his warmth. She wanted to embrace the fact that they were both still alive and to hell with her duty. It was almost over, anyway.

Yes, it was almost over. And that was good.

So why did she feel like crying?

Hawk turned over his shirt in his hands and looked at the bullet hole in the side. He'd been hit when he'd tackled Sarah. It had been like getting punched in the side by a pile driver. The vest had stopped the shot, but his ribs hurt like hell. Sarah would know how that felt. It had happened to her on her previous mission.

"Lift your arms, please."

The paramedic spoke English. Hawk did as he said, allowing the man to probe the area of the bruise. Hawk ignored the discomfort and moved his gaze to Sarah.

They had been brought to the hotel manager's windowless ground-floor office while the police conducted their investigation. The interrogation of Sarah and Hawk had been brief—their assailant had been positively identified as Weltzer, and the evidence made it obvious what had happened. Still, Sarah had insisted on an armed escort before she had agreed to leave the bullet-riddled suite for this office. Only then had she requested medical help.

She was sitting on the edge of the manager's desk, her feet propped on the seat of a chair. Her skirt was hiked to her hips to allow the other paramedic to disinfect the wound on her thigh.

''Your ribs do not appear broken, Dr. Lemay.'' The first paramedic pulled off his gloves and stepped back from Hawk. ''An ice pack should reduce the swelling. Would you like something for the pain?''

Hawk shook his head as he lowered his arms. He wasn't sure he could trust his voice. He hadn't realized Sarah had been injured until they had left the suite and the light from the corridor had revealed the rip in her skirt and the blood on her thigh.

The sight of her blood had been like another pile-driver blow to his chest. The paramedics had said the cut wasn't deep enough to require stitches. Only the top layer of skin had been broken. Weltzer's blade had merely grazed her since his intended target had been Hawk.

This time she hadn't stepped in the way of a bullet, she'd stepped in the way of a knife. She had saved his life. Again. She had been hurt because of him.

Hawk heard fabric tear. He looked down and saw he had pushed his fist through his shirt.

The door to the office swung open. The corridor bustled with activity as firemen withdrew. The hotel staff had begun allowing people to return to their rooms several minutes ago. The damage from the fire had been minor and was confined to the basement. The conference events would continue. Life was resuming its normal routine, almost as if nothing had happened.

One of the hotel security guards entered and walked over to Sarah. He spoke for a few moments in Swedish, then left.

Sarah pressed her lips together briefly before she looked at Hawk. "They found the two police officers who had been stationed outside our room," she said. "They were on the roof near the place where Weltzer had fastened his rappelling rope. They had both been shot."

"How…" Hawk cleared his throat. His voice was so rough he didn't recognize it. "How are they?"

"Dead."

He felt a cry build in his chest. It was rage mixed with helplessness. And guilt. Remorse grew thick enough to choke him. "They were trying to protect me. Just like you."

"That was their job," she said. She waited until the paramedic finished smoothing a row of sterile adhesive strips over her thigh to close the wound before she spoke again. "They knew the risks. It's not your fault, so don't feel guilty."

It didn't surprise him that she knew what he was feeling. She was an intelligent, perceptive woman. Yet her sympathy didn't ease the guilt, it made it worse.

Sarah was hurt and two men were dead because of him. No, three men were dead. Weltzer had been scraped off the cobblestones because Hawk had knocked him through the window.

But he couldn't feel guilty over Weltzer. The man would have killed him and Sarah.

But Weltzer was only doing what he perceived as his job, too. Someone else had given the orders.

"I understand what you're going through, sir." Sarah

slid from the desk and twitched her bloodstained skirt into place. "Every soldier goes through it whenever there are casualties on a mission. It's healthy to feel regret, but don't feel you were solely responsible for what happened." Her voice softened. "We all choose our own paths in life. We can't control the choices other people make."

She was right. Hawk should know how useless it was to attempt to control other people. The policemen and Weltzer. Sarah. Faith. They had chosen their paths themselves and he hadn't been able to influence them.

What made him think he could influence Jibril or his country? Or the direction of history?

He'd been a fool. An arrogant fool. He'd thought he had a duty to make sure no one suffered because of his research, but people were already dying.

What good was a speech in the face of that? Nothing he said would have the power to influence every choice of every politician and bureaucrat and industrialist.

The truth was, Hawk *was* just an ordinary man.

He raked his hands through his hair. It had all seemed so clear two days ago.

Sarah said a few words to the paramedics as they packed up their gear, then moved to where Hawk stood. Hesitantly, as if she couldn't help herself, she reached up to smooth his hair. "Our belongings have been moved to another room in a different wing of the hotel. If you're ready, I'll ask the police officers in the corridor to escort us there."

Hawk shrugged on what was left of his shirt, then cupped Sarah's cheek in his palm. They had agreed not to touch each other unless it was necessary, but dammit, this was necessary. So was the way he'd held her in his arms until the police had arrived at the suite. He looked into her eyes, drinking in the familiar strength in her steady gaze. "I'm sorry you were hurt."

"I'll be all right. It was only a scratch." She wavered, as if she were fighting the urge to lean into his caress. She didn't lean in, yet she didn't pull away, either. "Your ribs are going to ache for a few days."

"They're not as bad as your shoulder must have been." He brushed his thumb across her temple. "Sarah, saying thank-you doesn't seem enough. You saved my life."

"All part of the job, sir."

He moved his hand to her throat, placing his fingers over the pulse beneath her ear. It was racing like his. He knew much of it was a reaction to their brush with death. An effect of tension.

But there had to be more to what he felt than circumstance. Something was happening between them, something he wished they had the time to explore. Because despite the scientific knowledge he held, he was just a man. And beneath her training and her duty, Sarah was just a woman.

Why couldn't everything be that simple?

Chapter 7

Sarah didn't know whether she wanted to praise Hawk's courage or weep over it. Weltzer was dead, but whoever had hired him was still out there. Until they discovered who it was, the threat wouldn't be over.

Yet Hawk had refused to cancel his appearance. He betrayed no fear as he rose from his seat at the front of the ballroom and approached the dais. A murmur spread through the crowd. News of the deliberately set fire and the attempt on Hawk's life had leaked to the media. Until now the conference hadn't received much coverage—the bulk of the business here had been done in private meetings—but arson and intrigue had changed that. Television crews were set up in front of the hotel and in the lobby. Although no cameras had been allowed into the ballroom, reporters with notepads and tape recorders were lining the walls and crowding the aisles in a way that Sarah found alarming.

They weren't worried about Hawk's safety. They were

hoping for a story. If the confusion that their presence
created allowed another attempt to be made on Hawk's
life, they wouldn't care. They would likely be pleased.
Blood would make better headlines than scientific theories.

Sarah shifted her position, dividing her attention between the necessity of scanning the room and her desire
to watch Hawk. He was holding up well for a civilian who
had been under fire. The bruise over his ribs had to be
painful but he hadn't uttered a word of complaint. His only
concern had been for her and for the families of the slain
police-officers.

The violence had hit him hard. That's because he was
a brilliant and sensitive man. Yet he was no coward. He
hadn't hesitated to fight at her side as fiercely as any of
the warriors she knew. The nightmare moments of
Weltzer's assault flashed through her mind, but she
blocked them out. For Hawk's sake she had to keep her
head clear.

But what about her heart? That wasn't clear at all.

Hawk shook hands with the conference chairman and
moved behind the podium. He'd cleaned himself up and
changed into a fresh suit. On the surface he looked calm,
but Sarah knew the calm was deceptive. She could see the
hardness in his jaw and the determined light in his eyes.
His knuckles paled as he gripped the edge of the lectern.

That's when Sarah realized he carried no notes. She was
momentarily puzzled—he'd spent half the night preparing
his speech and had been working on his computer right up
to the time they had been escorted from their new hotel
room to the ballroom—but the moment he started to talk
she realized this couldn't have been the speech he'd intended to give.

"Three men died here today," Hawk said. "They died
because someone wants to stop an idea." His voice was

steady, as strong as his grip on the lectern. A hush fell over the room. His gaze traveled across the audience. "I have dedicated the past decade and a half of my life to this idea. I believed it was my responsibility to guard it and nurture it slowly until the world was prepared to accept it. I wanted to stop the bloodshed that has been caused by the struggle for resources, not cause more."

Sarah felt a lump in her throat. She wanted to tell Hawk again he wasn't to blame. He'd only been doing what he saw as his duty. She understood that. Oh, yes, she understood duty all too well. She swallowed hard and continued her scan of the room.

"Three men died," Hawk repeated, "because I am only months away from perfecting the technology that promises the world a safe, affordable, environmentally sustainable source of energy."

The audience stirred, obviously surprised to learn Hawk was so close. Sarah focused on Jibril and the knots of OPEC representatives, observing their reactions. Predictably, they didn't look pleased. Neither did the balding Russian physicist, Yegdenovich. Earl Drucker, on the other hand, was sitting bolt upright with interest.

"I was concerned about the problems that would arise by introducing this knowledge too soon," Hawk said. "But today I realized that I was wrong. If I die, the knowledge that I'm guarding will die with me."

Scattered murmurs spread through the crowd. Sarah felt the nape of her neck prickle. What was Hawk trying to do? Paint a bigger bull's-eye on his back?

Hawk slapped his hands against the lectern. "It ends now. Here. Tonight. I don't have the wisdom or the right to decide how you will use my discoveries. I can't control your choices. Therefore, I have come before you to an-

nounce that twenty minutes ago I uploaded the entire body
of my work to the Internet.''

The murmurs grew. Several people rose from their
chairs. Sarah pressed her finger over the radio receiver in
her ear. The news crews in the lobby must be listening
through a live link. They were clamoring for the security
guards to let them inside.

''My research is now available free of charge on the
Web sites of every major university in the world,'' Hawk
continued, raising his voice to be heard above the crowd.
''It is up to others to complete what I have started. I sincerely wish you all success.'' He bowed crisply. ''Thank
you and good night.''

More people got to their feet as the import of Hawk's
words sank in. Looks of shock were giving way to amaze-
ment in some, distress in others. Jibril and the OPEC con-
tingent rose as a block and walked out of the room. The
diplomats who remained were gathering into huddles. Yegdenovich was slapping his neighbor on the back like an
elated schoolboy. Reporters sprinted for the exits or had
their cell phones out and were talking furiously.

Sarah moved her hand to her mouth, pressing her fingers
over her lips. Good God. Hawk had just given it away.
The Defense Department had wanted exclusive rights to
this research. A Texas oil tycoon had been prepared to pay
a fortune for it. Someone had been willing to kill Hawk
to stop its progress.

And now it was on the Internet where any kid with a
computer could find it.

This was incredible. After all Hawk's effort, all those
years of dedication and personal investment in his work,
he'd just...let it go. Did he realize what he'd done?

Hawk turned his head, his gaze skimming over the audience until he zeroed in on Sarah. The sadness in his expression took her breath away.

My work is my life.

For the second time that day, Sarah felt like crying.

Yes, she thought. He realized exactly what he'd done. Dr. Hawkins Lemay could have had a place in history as the man who made fusion power a reality. Instead he'd publicly invited others to complete what he'd started. He'd sacrificed his personal ambition to ensure his dream was shared with the world.

Near the front of the crowd, someone began to applaud. The sound spread. Anyone not already on their feet rose to join the rest of the audience. Cameramen and photographers pushed their way into the ballroom. The receiver in Sarah's ear flooded with chatter as the situation spiraled out of control.

She blinked to clear her vision and started toward the dais, threading her way through the people who were pressing forward. She had anticipated defending Hawk against one assassin attempting to kill him, not a crowd of hundreds vying to congratulate him.

Hawk acknowledged the ovation with another bow, shook hands with the dazed-looking conference chairman and left the podium. He met Sarah at the bottom of the stairs. Reporters shouted questions. Microphones were thrust toward his face. He ignored them all and kept his gaze on Sarah.

That's when she realized the rest of what he'd done. By publishing his research, he'd neutralized the threat to his life. No one had anything to gain by his death.

In all probability her mission was over.

And that was good. That was what she wanted.

Wasn't it?

* * *

Hawk picked up the bottle of aquavit and rotated it in his hands, noting the way the clear liquid clung to the glass, forming sheets of tears. It was excellent quality, courtesy of the Theoretical Physics Department of the University of Uppsala. It had been delivered within an hour of his speech. A case of vodka had arrived next, a token of appreciation from Fedor Yegdenovich and his friends at the University of Moscow. Several other institutions had wired flowers, but Hawk had refused to accept them. Somehow he didn't feel like celebrating. He'd had the hotel redirect the flowers to the local hospitals.

He splashed another drink into his glass, thumped the bottle down on the side table and leaned back on the sofa. Even though it was in a different wing of the hotel, this suite was almost identical to the last one, including the uncomfortable antique furniture. Hawk was still waiting for the aquavit to do its job—how long would it take before this tapestry-covered rack would feel comfortable? It was an interesting problem. Had anyone thought to research it?

How much alcohol did a healthy, thirty-five-year-old man weighing 198 pounds need to consume to deaden his synapses to the point where an antique sofa would feel like a hammock and it no longer hurt to think? Variables would include the rate of consumption, the stomach contents prior to consumption, the subject's fatigue level, the quality of the alcohol and, of course, the reason for it all.

Yes, that would be the crucial factor. That was why Hawk still felt stone-cold sober.

"It's as you anticipated." Sarah put down the telephone. "Interpol has just confirmed that the contract on your life has been lifted. They claim their source is reliable."

He nodded.

"I'm still waiting to hear back from Major Redinger.

He's in transit and can't be reached until he arrives at his destination, but I've been in touch with my colleagues in Intelligence. Delta's informants agree with Interpol. The danger appears to be over. By publicizing your research, you eliminated the motive to kill you.''

Hawk touched the rim of his glass to his lips. The way to drink aquavit was with one quick swallow. Swift and neat. Without time for hesitation or second thoughts.

Perhaps that was the best way to do anything. Like drinking. Or giving away a lifetime of work. Or knocking a man through a window to his death.

''The police are continuing to investigate. They're trying to trace the assault gear Weltzer used, as he didn't usually operate that way. They're hoping that will lead back to the person who hired him.'' Sarah walked to the low bench where she'd left her suitcase, her bare feet whispering over the carpet. She had taken off her shoes sometime before midnight. She had discarded her suit jacket and her vest hours before that. Yet even barefoot and disheveled, she had a poise that fascinated him, that he couldn't get enough of.

Hawk tipped back his head and tossed the aquavit down his throat.

''The switchboard is still screening your calls,'' Sarah said, flipping open the lid of her suitcase. ''The main desk has a stack of telegrams and faxes that have been accumulating through the evening. Do you want them sent up?''

''No. What are you doing?''

She smoothed the folds from the sweater that was on top of her clothes. ''I'm packing.''

He put his glass on the table beside the bottle and rose to his feet. ''Why?''

"Now that the conference is over and your life is no longer in danger, my mission is finished."

Of course, he knew that. It was over. Swift and neat, like the way to drink aquavit. By ensuring Sarah's safety, he had guaranteed her departure. He walked to the window. For an instant he remembered the other window, the gunfire, the destruction, the brutality. He set his jaw and flung the curtain aside.

The cold peace of a long Scandinavian night spread out before him. Lights glowed from the street level, but most of the windows in the buildings around them were dark. It was almost two in the morning. Ten hours had passed since the attempt on his life. Eight hours had gone by since he'd ensured it wouldn't happen again. It seemed longer. How could so much have happened in such a short time?

He braced his fist on the window frame. This was the first time he'd been free to stand here without danger. He should be rejoicing. Instead, he felt…empty. Adrift.

"The hotel security team will remain in place to keep the reporters out of range until you depart for the airport," Sarah continued. "Your flight leaves at three tomorrow afternoon."

"I've decided to stay here for a few days."

"Oh."

"Sarah?"

"Yes?"

He yanked the curtain back in place and turned to face her. "I'd like you to stay, too."

She slipped her hairbrush into the side of her suitcase. She didn't pretend to be surprised by his invitation. Hawk knew she was too honest for that. He wondered how he could have doubted her word before.

No, he knew why he'd doubted her. *Women can't be trusted.* That was a lesson he'd learned fourteen years ago.

But this was a time for looking ahead, not back. He'd made sure of that, hadn't he? He'd torched his bridges in public. He'd done it spectacularly. There was no going back.

Sarah closed her suitcase and snapped the latches. She glanced at the folded cot that had been left just inside the door. "The threat to your life appears to be over, but if you still feel you need a bodyguard—"

"I don't want you as my bodyguard. That's not why I asked you to stay."

"I realize this must be a very emotional time for you. I could try to find a counselor for you to talk to."

He strode across the room and took her hand. "I told you once before, Sarah. I don't want anyone else. I want you."

She didn't pull away. She looked at where his fingers enclosed hers.

"Stay with me, Sarah. At least for tonight."

She dipped her head. Fine strands of wheat-colored hair swung against her cheek. "I do understand how difficult it was for you to give away your research. I couldn't imagine letting go of something I'd dedicated my life to like that."

"Yes, I knew you would understand," he said. "That's one of the things we have in common. We've both built our lives around our work."

"I could see it was painful for you, but it was a brilliant choice."

"It was the only logical option. Duty is a fine concept, but there's no honor in supporting something that's wrong."

She was silent for a while, as if considering his words. She laid her other hand on top of his. "What are you going to do now?"

"I don't know yet. Find another project. Or maybe go fishing."

"You could always continue your fusion research."

"There are a dozen physicists who are probably already in their labs doing exactly that. I'm no longer needed."

"You would complete it before anyone else."

"Who completes it isn't important, as long as it gets done. That was the point."

She ran her fingertips over his knuckles. "Do you have any regrets?"

"Sure, I do. I wish no one had needed to die for me to figure out how arrogant I'd been to think I could control what the world did with my knowledge."

"I told you before, what happened tonight wasn't your fault. If anything, it was mine. I was in charge of the security."

"You saved my life."

"So did your vest when it stopped that bullet. You did a good job of saving yourself when you hit Weltzer."

The thought of how close it had been, how easily things could have gone differently, made him shudder. "Sarah, I don't really want to talk about that right now."

She laced her fingers with his. "Then what do you want to do, Hawk?"

The sound of her voice saying his name hit him like another shot of aquavit. Warmth unfolded inside him that wasn't due to the alcohol. "You called me Hawk."

"My mission is over," she said, as if that were explanation enough.

And it was. He knew her well enough by now to understand her sense of honor. She had done her duty. Now it was finished. She no longer needed to throw up a barrier of formality between them.

Yet her duty hadn't been the only barrier. There were

her feelings for a dead soldier, the perfect man, the perfect love.

But he didn't want to think right now any more than he wanted to talk. His life had irrevocably changed. This was the one aspect of it that didn't have to be complicated. He lifted his hand to her hair, brushing a stray lock behind her ear. "You're a beautiful woman, Sarah."

"Hawk—"

"In here," he said, laying his fingertips against her temple. "This is beautiful. Your mind. Your strength of will. I've admired your intelligence from the moment I met you."

Her lips curved. Just as he'd guessed, that was one compliment she was prepared to accept.

"And in here," he murmured, shifting closer. He placed his palm on the upper curve of her breast. "In your heart. Where you keep your compassion and your courage. This is beautiful, too."

"Thank you, Hawk."

He held her gaze, his palm over her heart. Her chest rose and fell with the soft rhythm of her breathing. Slowly the rhythm changed, turning ragged. Her eyes darkened, the flecks of gold hidden by expanding black. He looked down. Against the collar of her blouse, her pulse beat rapidly at the side of her neck. He rotated his hand. "Since you're no longer on duty, is there any reason why I shouldn't kiss you, Sarah?"

"There are dozens, Hawk. Do you want me to list them?"

He ran his thumb along the opening of her blouse, pressing it into the dip between her breasts. "Maybe that was the wrong question."

Her eyes half closed in pleasure. "Then what would be the right question?"

"That's simple."

"Mmm?"

"Do you want to kiss me?"

Sarah didn't want to reply. She knew if she did, there would be no going back.

But his touch felt right. It had been so long, so very long, since she'd allowed any man to touch her like this. Her body was thrumming with demands that hadn't stirred in years, not since Jackson.

She felt a rustling of guilt, but she tried to ignore it. She had no reason to feel she was being unfaithful. Her love would never change. What was happening between her and Hawk was entirely different from what she'd shared with Jackson. This was just physical, the normal reaction of a healthy woman to a sexually attractive man. She and Hawk had been straight about it from the start.

Hawk moved his hand to her throat and unfastened the top button of her blouse. "Sarah?"

She looked at his face. The naked need she saw in his eyes shook her. She thought again of what he'd been through tonight, how he'd fought beside her as readily as he'd taken her into his arms afterward. She thought of what he'd sacrificed by giving away his work. She had no choice but to reply honestly. "Yes, Hawk. I want to kiss you. Why else would I be standing here letting you touch me even though we both know it's nothing but adrenaline and circumstance—"

His lips settled over hers. Firmly. Possessively. Putting an end to the question.

Sarah was glad. Just for tonight she didn't want to be the good little soldier, doing the right thing, loving the right man.

No, this had nothing to do with love. It was sex. A crush. An infatuation.

Hawk opened three more buttons on the front of her blouse and slipped his hand inside. The slide of his palm against her skin made Sarah's nipples tingle. She leaned closer, her pulse throbbing in anticipation as he traced the lace edge of her bra.

The caress she'd expected didn't come. Instead he slid his hand upward, pulled her collar aside and bared her left shoulder.

She knew it wasn't a pleasant sight. The old bruise from the dislocation was mottled yellow and green. The bruise she'd added three days ago was deep purple. She reached for her collar.

He stopped her with a murmur. Then he lowered his head and brushed his lips across her bruises.

The action was so tender, so...Hawk, Sarah felt her eyes mist. She wasn't accustomed to tenderness. It stirred far more than the urges of her body. She thrust her fingers into his hair, guiding his head toward her breast.

Hawk dropped to his knees in front of her.

Sarah braced her hands on his shoulders. "Hawk," she whispered. "I didn't mean...I wasn't asking..."

"I know what you need, Sarah." He wrapped one arm behind her legs and pushed up her skirt. "What we both need."

She felt his breath on her thigh. Her stomach contracted at the intimacy. Even as she told herself it was too fast, too soon to allow this, her fingers clenched on his shirt, holding him there, wanting him to go on.

He rubbed his cheek along the inside of her thigh, then placed a kiss in the center of her taped wound.

A sob built in Sarah's throat. This wasn't what she'd expected, either. She'd wanted passion, simple and mindless. She thought that's what he needed, too. Instead, he was treating her as if she were delicate. Vulnerable. Soft. Weak.

But she was tough. She was strong. She didn't need this. She'd proved that, hadn't she? She was an equal to any man. She'd fought her battles and been what everyone counted on her to be.

He straightened up, bringing his mouth back to hers. He kissed her until she melted against him. She folded her arms around his neck as much to bring him closer as to keep herself from falling. She could feel the tension in his arms, in the hardened muscles of his thighs. She felt the firm length of his arousal pressed against her stomach.

All right, this was more like it. She wanted to be swept away so she didn't have to think about what she was doing. "Hawk, please," she whispered.

He undid the rest of her buttons and helped her strip off her blouse. But he wouldn't be hurried. He tipped up her chin and kissed his way down her throat, then paused to lick the hollow at the base. A sound of pleasure rumbled from his chest.

She reached behind her back to unhook her bra.

He caught her hands in his. "Let me."

She hadn't known it was possible to take so long to slide a hook from an eye, or that the simple act could be so enjoyable. With her hands held behind her and her back arched, she felt exposed, wanton and unbelievably aroused. She felt the stroke of Hawk's thumbs beside her spine, the slide of his lips on her shoulder then the scrape of his teeth beside the lace strap as he slowly eased it down her arm.

Yet this still wasn't quite what Sarah wanted. She wasn't able to stop thinking. She remembered each detail of her time with Hawk. The intense emotions she'd tried so hard to suppress were pouring out, swelling with every touch. Her senses became heightened. She was exquisitely aware of every kiss and caress. Her nipples were so hard they were throbbing. Hawk brushed his lips along the upper edge of her bra, up to her other shoulder and dragged down the remaining strap. Still holding her hands, he took a step back, pulled her arms to her sides and let the garment fall away on its own.

At the touch of cool air on her sensitized breasts she wanted to scream. When the cool air was replaced by the warmth of Hawk's breath, then the rasp of his tongue, the sound that came from her throat was closer to a moan. She yanked her hands free to grab his hair. "Hawk!"

He wouldn't be hurried at this, either. He kissed each breast so thoroughly, when he lifted his head she was trembling. He smiled, got back on his knees and reached for the zipper of her skirt.

That took longer, far longer, than undoing a simple hook. He lingered over every inch of skin he revealed as he found creative, maddening, wonderful ways to remove the rest of her clothes. By the time she was naked, her knees gave out. She couldn't wait. Not one more minute, not one more second.

Hawk clamped his hands on either side of her waist and guided her backward past the bench that held her suitcase. Her shoulders hit the wall beside the wardrobe. She heard the clink as he unfastened his belt and the grate as he lowered his zipper.

He cupped her buttocks and pulled her upward. "Sarah?"

"Yes, Hawk!" She hooked her legs around his hips and climbed onto him, too close to the edge for patience. "Oh, yes!"

She shattered the moment he entered her. The climax rippled through her body and seared through her brain. He wrapped his arms around her and braced his legs apart, holding her until her sobs quieted and she had caught her breath.

Oh, yes, she thought. This was good. Perfect. If it had continued any longer, she would have gone crazy. She smiled and started to lower her legs.

Hawk grasped her thighs, tilted his hips and began to move again.

It wasn't over. It was just beginning. She dug her nails into his shoulders and hung on as another wave of delight built. Just when she thought she couldn't take any more, he showed her that she could.

Sarah was shaking as Hawk carried her to the bedroom. She didn't let that stop her from stripping off his clothes and treating him to the same thorough caresses he'd given her. She reveled in the freedom to explore all the shadowed, intimate places so unique to a man. She learned his taste, his textures, the sounds he made. His pleasure became hers as his shudders evoked her own.

For the rest of the night they spoke without words, slaking their needs even as they discovered new ones. Sarah knew this was passion, but it wasn't simple. It was sex, but it wasn't mindless.

It was more than she had wanted. Much, much more.

Chapter 8

Sarah awoke to the aroma of coffee and the feel of sunshine on her back. She had a moment of disorientation. Sunshine? Why were the curtains open? Where were her clothes?

Warm breath feathered over her elbow. Beard stubble rasped along the underside of her arm.

The night before came back to her. The things they'd done. The things she'd felt. Oh, God. Now what?

She kept her eyes closed, giving herself time to think. It might have been fatigue. She'd been running on fumes for days now. So had Hawk. That might be why the sex had been so...

Her mind couldn't come up with the right word. Special? Magnificent? Incredible? Oh, yes, it was all that. Her body was weary but thoroughly sated. Alive. Tingling with well-being, as if she'd finished a marathon and gone on a chocolate binge.

"Good morning, Sarah."

The tone of his voice brought a wave of remembered heat. The tinge of the South that colored his words was more pronounced today. It reminded her of his gentleness and his gallantry.

Was that why the sex had been different? Was it because he was so unlike a soldier?

But he wasn't all that different, was he? He didn't lack courage, and his sense of personal honor was as strong as hers. His tenderness didn't mean he was weak.

"I know you're awake."

She'd already figured out he wouldn't be an easy man to fool. She opened her eyes.

Hawk was kneeling on the floor beside the bed, his arms folded on the mattress near her pillow. He was wearing one of the hotel's white terry cloth bathrobes. It gaped open over his chest as he propped his chin on his hands and brought his face level with hers. His black hair was tousled in finger-combed tufts, one lock falling over his forehead. The night's growth of beard darkened his jaw.

She had seen him the morning before. It had been unavoidable, considering the close quarters they shared. Yet she hadn't seen him this close. And it was lucky she hadn't seen him smiling like this or she never would have been able to keep her mind on her duty. She would have been too busy imagining the taste of his lips.

His smile spread to his dimples. Two tempting dips appeared beside the folds that bracketed his mouth. The skin beneath his eyes was smudged with weariness—evidence of the emotional extremes of the day before—yet the fine skin at the corners of his eyes was crinkling into laugh lines.

She didn't have to look any farther to wonder why the sex had been so incredible. Hawkins Lemay was an incredibly sexy man, that's all. She'd known that from her first whiff of him.

There was nothing else she could do. She looped her arm around the back of his neck, pulled his head to hers and kissed him.

The mattress dipped. Without breaking the kiss, Hawk opened his robe and stretched out beside her, then splayed his fingers over her buttocks and guided her hips against his.

Had she thought she was sated? The feel of him dissolved the last remnants of sleep. Her body responded instantly, its demands even more insistent than the night before. She moaned and hooked her foot behind his knee, parting her thighs.

They slid together easily, already attuned to the angle that would bring them the closest. She felt the world shrink as her senses filled with the slide of skin on skin and the liquid sound of sex.

He rolled her to her back, weaving their fingers together to stretch her arms above her head. His robe draped them both, wrapping her in his scent, the soft terry cloth brushing her ribs and hips as his chest moved over her breasts. He set a leisurely rhythm, a sweet hello, good-morning pace that built in waves as effortlessly as the sunshine that spilled over the bed. His fingers tightened on hers as the waves peaked, the mattress groaning with their shudders.

Sarah smiled, nestling beneath him as the echoes of the tremors faded.

He passed the tip of his tongue over her upper lip. ''You should do that more often.''

She rotated her hips and raised one eyebrow.

''I meant smile.'' He sucked lightly on her lower lip. ''Hungry?''

''Mmm. I thought I smelled coffee.''

"I ordered breakfast from room service. Coffee, fruit, yogurt, Danish pastry. Do you want to do it in bed?"

She raised her other eyebrow.

"I meant breakfast, but I'm open to suggestions." He chuckled. "Lucky for us I asked them to send up another box of condoms along with the pastries."

She pulled her hand from his grasp and smacked his chest. "And here I was wondering how I was going to face *you* this morning. How am I going to face that kid from room service?"

Hawk caught her hand and brought it to his lips, his expression suddenly serious. "Sarah, do you regret making love with me?"

She wanted to argue his choice of words. They hadn't made love. She knew what love was, and it wasn't this. But his eyes still held shadows of the need she'd seen the night before, and she didn't want to hurt him....

Sarah had a moment of panic.

She couldn't remember the color of Jackson's eyes.

Were they brown? Green? She closed her eyes and called up an image of Jackson. He was wearing battle dress uniform, his gear slung over his shoulder. The transport was loading. She had driven him to the airfield. He had already kissed her goodbye and was no longer looking at her.

"Sarah?" Hawk eased his weight to his knees. "What's wrong?"

She squeezed her eyes more tightly shut. Jackson wasn't looking at her because he was skilled at saying goodbye, too. He was like her, an army brat. He knew better than to drag things out.

Hazel. They were changeable hazel surrounded by spiky brown lashes. The panic receded. She blinked and opened her eyes.

Blue eyes framed by long black lashes bored into hers. Hawk let go of her hand and skimmed his palm over her shoulder and then down to her thigh. "Did I hurt you, Sarah? I'm sorry. I—"

"No, you didn't hurt me." She brushed her fingers over the hair on his chest. "And I don't have any regrets. It was great. What time is it?"

"Almost ten-thirty."

"Ten-thirty?" She drew up her legs and rolled to the side. "I should get going. Where's my phone?"

"Sarah, your mission is over." A thread of steel ran through his words. "Don't do this."

She swung her feet to the floor and looked around the bedroom. She spotted some of Hawk's clothes at the foot of the bed. Through the doorway she could see the edge of a linen-draped service cart. Her clothes would still be in the sitting room. Why hadn't she heard the door open when that service cart had been wheeled in? Had she remembered to switch her cell phone ringer back on? The Major should have called her by now. Had she slept through that, too?

But Hawk was right. Her mission was finished. The assassin was dead, the conference had ended, the threat was over. There wasn't any reason to feel this lump of failure in her gut.

Be a good little soldier.

She rubbed her eyes. No, not yet. Another hour, another few minutes. What would it hurt?

The bed creaked. There was a slide of skin on cotton. "You were thinking of him, weren't you?"

She dropped her hands and stood. "I was wondering why my C.O. hasn't contacted me yet."

"That's not who I meant." Hawk tied the belt of his

robe as he moved in front of her. "You were thinking of your fiancé. The man you loved."

Damn, he was too perceptive. She dragged the sheet off the bed and wrapped it around herself, tucking one corner between her breasts. She wasn't normally self-conscious about her body, but she suddenly felt too exposed. "Yes."

"Because you believe you still love him?"

"Drop it, Hawk."

"I'm sorry for your loss, Sarah, but I don't want to share you."

"Share me? I think you have the wrong idea. What happened here last night—"

"Was inevitable." He pushed a lock of hair behind her ear. "It was wonderful."

"It was sex, Hawk."

"It was more than that and you know it."

This was crazy, she thought. How could she talk about Jackson when she could feel the heat of another man between her legs, and the smell of the sex they'd greeted the morning with still hung in the air? Gathering the hem of the sheet so she wouldn't trip, she walked to the other room.

Cutlery clinked as she bumped into the room service cart. She glanced down at the breakfast Hawk had ordered. A small brown paper bag was tucked beside the white china coffeepot, no doubt the extra condoms he'd ordered. There also were pots of jam, fruit, cheese, yogurt, a basket of pastries and two plates. Across one of the plates lay a single long-stemmed red rose.

Sarah bit her lip as she looked at the rose. Drops of moisture clung to the leaves. The petals were furled on the brink of unfolding. Hawk must have ordered the flower along with the food and the condoms. The gesture was sweet, exactly the kind of thing she might expect from him, but didn't he realize she didn't need to be romanced? She didn't have room for it in her life. Jackson had never wasted their money on flowers. He'd known their love didn't require gestures like that.

She turned her back on the flower and the breakfast and bent down to gather her clothes.

"How long ago did he die, Sarah?"

Hawk's voice came from behind her. She didn't look back. She grabbed her skirt and her blouse, then glanced around to look for her underwear. "It will be four years next spring."

"Has there been anyone else since then?"

"No."

"That's a long time for such a passionate woman. Seems to me if you'd only wanted sex, you would have had it before now."

Damn his logic. "I don't want to talk about him, Hawk."

Hawk's bare feet moved into her vision. He dangled her bra from his hand. "Why? Because he was so perfect?"

"Yes, and because I don't want to hurt you." She snatched the bra from his hand and straightened up. She carried the wrinkled clothes to her suitcase, opened the lid and tossed them inside. "I had hoped you would understand what's going on between us."

"Explain it to me."

She picked up her blouse again, automatically smoothing it out so that it would pack better. "It's a mutual attraction that has been exaggerated by the situation. You were still feeling the aftereffects of yesterday's violence and you'd had a large amount to drink so…"

He caught her elbow and spun her to face him. "Is that really what you believe? That I was drunk and needy and you went to bed with me out of pity?"

She saw the hurt in his eyes. She never wanted this to happen. "Hawk, no, I didn't think that. Last night was special. For both of us. But you can't deny the circumstances were exceptional."

"What about this morning? What's your excuse for that?"

"I'm not making excuses, but I didn't make any promises, either. You asked me to stay for one night. I did. Let's leave it at that."

"Sarah."

She lifted her hand to his cheek. His jaw was hard. She trailed her fingertips along the edge. "I like you, Hawk, and over the past few days, I've grown to care about you. Otherwise, I wouldn't have slept with you. But that's all there is between us. That's all there can be."

He inhaled against her hand. He regarded her in silence, his gaze intense.

Sarah had seen that gleam before. He was figuring something out. Once again she was vividly aware of the power of his intellect. She felt even more exposed. She tugged the edge of the sheet a bit higher. "I really did believe you understood. You told me you were in love once, too."

"It wasn't the same."

"Wasn't it? Faith died fourteen years ago, but you're still unmarried. I know that much because it was in your file. You've dated but you haven't had any steady relationships."

"That's true but it's not the same."

"Of course, it is. You must still love her."

"You've got it wrong, Sarah. I'm not pining over some perfect love. I don't have any illusions about why I'm still single. I know why. It's because I haven't wanted to repeat my mistake."

"Your mistake?"

"Your fiancé died on a training mission five weeks before your wedding. Mine died on our wedding day when her car skidded through a guard rail."

She felt something turn over inside her. This was more than she'd guessed. Hawk hadn't given any hint his relationship with Faith had been that serious. He'd not only been in love, he'd been engaged. To lose someone on the very day you were supposed to start a life together...

She knew the pain he must have felt. Yes, she knew that feeling of emptiness, of loss, of the world falling in.

Hawk put his finger under her chin. "I can see the sympathy on your face, Sarah, but I told you before it's misplaced. This isn't like you and your Captain Jackson, so don't feel sorry for me."

"But—"

"Faith wasn't on her way to the church when the accident happened. She had left me waiting at the altar."

Sarah drew in her breath. "What?"

"She called me at the church to tell me she was on her way to elope with Jibril."

It took a moment for his words to sink in. Faith had jilted Hawk before she'd died? And she'd chosen Jibril?

Sarah's head reeled. She needed more time to think about this. She knew she'd just been handed a key to Hawk's...what? His past? His psyche? His heart?

But she didn't want his heart, did she?

And how could any woman have chosen Jibril over Hawk?

Each question led to another, yet many of the things that she'd wondered about were finally beginning to make sense. Hawk's initial difficulty with trusting her, his single-minded devotion to his work, those tension-filled meetings between Jibril and Hawk...

And how could any woman have chosen Jibril over Hawk? That question wouldn't go away.

"Oh, Hawk," she murmured. "How that must have hurt. It would be like losing her twice. You wouldn't even have the comfort of your memories."

"The memories were lies, Sarah." He cradled her face in his hands, stroking her temples with his thumbs. "What you and I did was honest."

Honest. Yes. No wonder he had said he didn't want to share her. Faith had chosen someone else. Sarah pressed her palms against his chest. More questions slid into her mind. "She died fourteen years ago. You started your research fourteen years ago."

"My work was all I had left. That's why I made it my life. It was the one thing I could trust." He kissed the bridge of her nose. "Come back to bed with me, Sarah. You were right. We don't need to talk about this now."

"You just gave your work away."

He nudged aside her hair and kissed her ear. With the tip of his tongue he traced a line down the side of her neck.

"You were using me to fill the void."

"Sarah..."

"You're using me, Hawk. That's why you're trying to make what happened between us into more than it was. You're trying to fill the void that was left when you gave away your research."

He grasped the edge of the sheet, tugged it aside and cupped her breasts in his hands. With a wordless murmur he bent forward to close his mouth over her nipple.

She fisted her hands in his hair. "Hawk."

He circled her nipple with his tongue, flicking and stroking, coaxing a response. His chest rumbled with another murmur as her body reacted quickly and unmistakably. He pressed closer and sucked hard.

Shards of pleasure flashed through her body. She knew he was doing this to end the conversation...but she hadn't wanted to have the conversation in the first place.

So what if he was using her? She was using him, too, wasn't she? Her grip on his hair turned into a caress.

Hawk wrapped his arms around her back and straightened up, bringing his face to hers. He took her mouth in a kiss that wasn't gentle.

Someone knocked at the door.

Hawk kicked away the sheet that was pooled around her ankles, lifted her up and backed her toward the bedroom.

The knocking continued.

Sarah broke off the kiss and looked past his shoulder. "Hawk, wait."

He rubbed the edge of his teeth over her collarbone. "They'll go away."

Her pulse was pounding. She struggled to focus. "No, I should check this out. The hotel security people should have stopped anyone from coming up unannounced."

"Sarah, it's over. We're safe."

There was a final hard rapping against the door. Someone called out from the corridor. "Captain Fox?"

At the sound of the familiar voice, Sarah returned to reality with a thump. She shoved at Hawk's chest. "Put me down. I have to answer."

He set her on her feet, brought her hand to his mouth and gently nipped the base of her thumb. "We'll send whoever it is away."

"We can't, Hawk. It's Major Redinger."

Hawk knew he was being studied. The Major was good at it, though. He hadn't interrogated him and he hadn't stared. He had asked politely after Hawk's health, congratulated him on the dramatic publication of his research and had confirmed that according to all available government sources, the threat to his life was over. Now he appeared content to stand by the window and look down at the street as he waited for Sarah, sipping coffee from the cup that he must know had been meant for her.

Hawk tightened the belt of his robe, crossed his arms and leaned one hip against the desk as he watched the Major. Mitchell Redinger could have posed for an Army recruiting poster. Even out of uniform, he had the classic bearing of an officer. He radiated reliability, from his square jaw and sharply honed features to the gold wedding ring on his left hand. Although he looked to be in his early forties, silver streaked the dark hair at his temples, giving him an air of mature authority. He was a man accustomed to command, someone whose orders would be obeyed not because of the rank he'd acquired but because of the respect he'd earned.

He would be a formidable adversary, Hawk decided, but it wasn't yet clear whether he was Hawk's.

Hawk glanced toward the bedroom door. The sound of running water still came from the bathroom. He had waited until Sarah had stepped into the shower before he'd answered the Major's knock. He'd wanted to give her the opportunity to compose herself—he knew how important it was to her to appear professional—but he realized the effort had been wasted. Redinger had scanned the suite as he'd entered, his gaze touching eloquently on the unused spare cot, the scattered clothes and Hawk's gaping bathrobe. Although his expression had remained impassive, he couldn't have failed to reach the obvious conclusion.

If it had been up to Hawk, he would have told the Major to come back later or, better yet, to butt out and leave them alone. He didn't want to share Sarah with the Army any more than he'd wanted to share her with her old love.

But Sarah had made her choice. The sound of the Major's voice had sent the woman who had trembled in Hawk's arms and matched his hunger stroke for stroke only minutes before into full retreat.

Only, the retreat had begun before that, hadn't it? Sarah had given him as much as she'd been willing to give. She had been honest. That was all he'd really asked of her.

Was she right? Were his feelings due to the emotions and the aquavit from the night before? He'd been empty and adrift. She had been there for him. There was no doubt the circumstances of the past few days had intensified the attraction. What he had felt for Faith had been an illusion, yet he'd known Faith for years. He'd known Sarah for three days, so how could he be certain about his judgment this time? Why was he pushing so hard?

Logically he knew he should gather more facts before reaching a conclusion, but as far as his body was concerned, his feelings were simple. He still wanted her. For another night, for another week, he didn't know where this would lead. He just knew he didn't want to let her go yet.

Which served to prove there had been nothing logical about his feelings for Sarah from the start. He returned his gaze to the Major.

Redinger was no longer looking out the window. He was looking at Hawk. He pushed Sarah's rose aside to place his coffee cup on her plate. "Captain Fox is an outstanding officer," he said.

"Yes, she is. She saved my life."

"I would expect no less. During each of her missions with my team from Eagle Squadron, she has performed her duty without fail. She has my respect as well as the respect of my men."

"Good. She deserves it."

"Although officially Captain Fox is assigned to one of Delta Force's support squadrons rather than an attack squadron, my men and I consider her to be one of our own, Dr. Lemay."

The Major's tone was too hard to be called polite. His gaze wasn't impassive, it was man-to-man steel. Hawk uncrossed his arms and pushed away from the desk. "I'm sure there's a point to this. If you'd like to make it before the outstanding officer we're discussing joins us, I'd suggest you do it soon."

Redinger nodded once. He walked around the room service cart, bent down to pick something off the floor beside the wall then moved to stand toe-to-toe with Hawk. He wasn't as tall as Hawk, but that didn't put him at a disadvantage. Strength was evident in the quiet way he held himself, his body exuding a power that arose from more than merely muscle. He held out his hand.

Hawk glanced down. A crumpled foil packet rested in the center of the Major's palm. It was an empty condom wrapper.

Hawk took the wrapper, put it in the pocket of his robe and returned his gaze to Redinger's. "I don't think that's any of your business."

"I disagree. Captain Fox may be an only child, but there are a dozen men who regard her as their sister. None of us would want to see her hurt."

Hawk scowled. "Then why the hell did you send her on an assignment like this one when she was already injured?"

"She was deemed fit for duty."

"She was in pain."

"She could have refused."

"Then you don't know her as well as you think you

do,'' Hawk said. ''Sarah has too much pride to back down from a challenge. She would never put her own welfare first. As her commanding officer, it should have been up to you to stop her.''

''You don't know Captain Fox at all if you think anyone could force her to do something she didn't want.'' His voice dropped. It wasn't soft. It was as ominous as the sound of distant thunder. ''And I believe you know I wasn't referring to her physical condition when I said we don't want her hurt.''

''Yes, I know. But she's been hurting for years and none of you self-appointed macho brothers of hers bothered to see it.''

''We all know about Captain Jackson.''

''Sarah's pain goes deeper than that. Jackson was a Band-Aid she tried to slap on top of it.''

Redinger didn't respond. He stared at Hawk in silence, this time studying him openly.

The sound of the shower shut off. Hawk gritted his teeth. He shouldn't take out his frustration with the situation on the Major. The man did seem to be genuinely concerned about Sarah. ''You are right about one thing,'' Hawk said. ''Sarah could never be forced into doing anything she didn't want.''

''I'll keep that in mind.'' Redinger took a step back. ''And I suggest, Dr. Lemay, that you do the same.''

Chapter 9

Despite the noon sunlight, patches of frost still silvered the grooves between the cobblestones where the buildings' shadows stretched into the street. A cold wind from the harbor brought the scent of damp stone and the tang of the Baltic. Pedestrians moved quickly along the sidewalk in front of the hotel, the vapor from their breath trailing in puffs behind them. Sarah slipped her hands into her coat pockets and quickened her stride to keep up with the Major. "I apologize for keeping you waiting, Major."

"Not a problem, Captain," Redinger said. "You were expecting me to return your phone call, not show up in person."

"I was told you were in transit, but I wasn't aware you were en route here."

"I had some business to take care of at the embassy. You don't mind if we walk while we talk, do you? I've been sitting in planes for the past twelve hours."

"Fine with me, sir. I've been cooped up for days and I could use the fresh air."

"You feel a need to clear your head, do you, Captain?"

His tone had sharpened. Sarah was pretty sure what had caused it. She glanced at him as they paused beside a lamppost at a cross street. He wouldn't meet her gaze. She had sensed the tension between Hawk and her C.O. as soon as she'd stepped out of the bathroom. Redinger was no fool. He must have read the signs. He would have figured out she'd slept with Hawk.

Sarah wasn't embarrassed. She wasn't ashamed, either. After all, she was a grown woman, and what she and Hawk had done in private was immaterial. It was over. It had no bearing on her duty. If the Major didn't bring it up, neither would she. "Yes, sir," she replied briskly. She put on her sunglasses so she wouldn't need to squint. "I always prefer to keep a clear head."

He dipped his chin in a curt nod. "Yes, you can be depended on for that. I'll listen to your report now."

They turned right at the next corner and started down an alley that led away from the harbor. For the next fifteen minutes they wove through the maze of narrow cobblestone streets of Old Town while Sarah related the events of the night before as they pertained to her mission. She answered the Major's questions, supplying more details as he requested them. By the time she was finished, their route had brought them to a street of small shops. Coffee bars and boutiques for the tourists were set into the ground floors of the weathered brick buildings.

Redinger slowed his steps. "Your father sends his regards," he said.

"How is the general?"

"Giving the boys at the Pentagon a run for their money. He has no patience for politicians."

"I hope he wasn't concerned when he heard the news about Weltzer's attack."

"No, he has the same confidence in your abilities as I do."

She realized she'd allowed her shoulders to hunch forward against the cold. She straightened her spine. "Thank you, sir."

"I've already spoken with Interpol and with Intelligence. Lemay took everyone by surprise with his announcement yesterday. By giving away his research, he made a name for himself in the media."

"He didn't do it for publicity. He did it to save lives."

"Primarily his own."

Sarah frowned. "From what I saw, he appeared more concerned about putting others into danger. Above all, he wanted to make sure his work gets completed, no matter what happens to him."

"Did you have any indication what he was planning?"

"No, sir. His decision came as a complete surprise to me."

"Has he been approached by anyone yet?"

"I'm not sure what you mean."

"To complete his work. Has anyone made him an offer?"

"Not to my knowledge. He went into seclusion immediately after the speech. He took no calls and saw no one."

"No one except you."

She pushed her sunglasses into place on her nose more firmly. "Releasing his life's work was a very emotional and difficult decision for him," she said. "He told me he's not interested in continuing."

"Do you believe him?"

"Absolutely. Dr. Lemay puts a high value on honesty."

"Are you sure he wouldn't complete it? Not even for his own country?"

"It wasn't a lack of patriotism that caused him to refuse the government's offer. He was thinking of the bigger picture. He doesn't want his work used as a political tool."

"Do you think it's possible he held back some of his research, that he didn't upload everything?"

"No," she said immediately. "He told me he used his laptop to access the mainframe of his computer in his lab in order to transfer all the files. I believe him."

"You sound very positive. Did you have a chance to see his notes or watch him while he did the file transfer?"

She looked at the Major. "Why are you asking me these questions, sir? You told me my mission was to protect him, that's all."

Redinger walked several paces in silence. "I simply wanted a complete report, Captain, as is customary when a mission has concluded."

Sarah continued to watch him, noting the tight lines around his mouth. She remembered how he'd seemed distant on the phone. She'd thought it might have been due to the poor reception, but there was no mistaking his discomfort now. "Is there a problem, Major?"

"That depends on you." He guided her toward the recessed entrance of a small bookstore. The sign on the door said it was closed on Sundays, but the alcove between the angled windows provided some degree of shelter from the cold breeze. "The team will be arriving in Dartmoor three days from now," he said. "We'll be going on a joint training exercise with the British SAS."

"Will I be participating?"

"I expect you to, Sarah. You're part of the team. I trust three days will be enough."

"I'm not sure I understand. Enough for what?"

"After our last mission, you were adamant about giving Sergeant O'Toole at least a five-day leave."

"I still don't—"

"To finish his personal business with Miss Locke."

He was referring to Flynn O'Toole and Abbie Locke, Sarah realized. Abbie was a civilian schoolteacher who had been involved with the team from Eagle Squadron during their previous mission. The sparks between her and Sergeant O'Toole had been obvious to everyone. That's why Sarah had barely waited for her shoulder to be popped back into its socket before she had called the Major from the hospital in order to smooth the way for Flynn's leave. She had believed Flynn and Abbie deserved some time in private.

"You're losing me, Major. What does O'Toole's leave have to do with me?"

"I'm assuming three days will be sufficient for you and Dr. Lemay, or will you be requesting more?"

Understanding came suddenly. There was a simple explanation for the Major's discomfort. It was the same as the reason for the sharpness in his tone when they'd left the hotel. She had assumed he was going to let the issue pass, but apparently he wanted to pursue the subject of her involvement with Hawk after all.

Sarah moved her gaze to the store's window display, a colorful pyramid of travel books. "I won't be requesting a leave, Major. The situation between Dr. Lemay and me is not like that of Flynn and Abbie."

"I'm not judging you, Captain. We both know these things happen during the heat of the moment."

"Yes, and the psych training we've had teaches us how meaningless these adrenaline-based relationships are."

"I got the impression that Lemay doesn't agree."

"My God. You actually spoke with him about this?"

Redinger didn't reply.

Sarah shifted her gaze so she could look at his reflection in the window. "No disrespect meant, sir, but I wasn't on duty when I slept with Lemay, so it really isn't any of the Army's concern what I do on my own time. You had no business interrogating him."

"Don't worry about Dr. Lemay. For a scientist he handled himself well. I'm not talking as your C.O. now, Sarah, I'm talking as your friend."

She turned, taking a closer look at the man in front of her. She had always admired Mitchell Redinger's dedication to the service. He was a superb officer, never expecting his men to do anything he wouldn't be prepared to do himself. He was tough yet fair, a natural leader. He seemed to accept the fact that the demands of leadership prevented him from befriending those under his command. That was probably why Sarah had seldom seen him smile.

It was just a small tilt at the corners of his mouth. It softened his face. It made him look...younger. Sarah's irritation faded. "I appreciate your concern," she said. "But I don't need more time. I'm eager to get back to work."

"Officially the exercise doesn't start for three days."

"I'm sure I'll find something to do if I get to England early."

"I won't expect you early." He hesitated. "Sergeant O'Toole made full use of the leave you arranged for him."

She cleared her throat. "I'm surprised Flynn provided everyone the details."

Redinger's smile turned lopsided. "Not those details. You were already on your way here when they returned to Bragg so you wouldn't have heard. O'Toole and Abbie are engaged now."

Engaged? The adamantly single, ridiculously handsome Flynn O'Toole engaged? He certainly hadn't wasted any time, but then, that's the way Flynn was. "Good for them. I hope they're two of the lucky ones and that everything works out."

"When I left the base, Sergeant Marek and his fiancée were talking about amending their wedding plans to make it a double ceremony."

At the thought of the scarred, noble Rafe Marek, another of her friends from Eagle Squadron, Sarah relaxed with a sigh. Rafe had met and fallen in love with Glenna Hastings on a mission months ago. Despite Sarah's initial protectiveness of her friend Rafe, she had eventually come to the conclusion that Glenna was perfect for him. The entire team had gone on the raid that had reunited the two lovers. "They're two more of the lucky ones," she said. "I wish them every happiness."

"We all do. It's rare to find the right person." The Major's voice softened. "It only happens once in a lifetime."

"Yes, I know."

"But sometimes the right person is difficult to recognize."

"Well, that's not a problem for me. I already did recognize him." She returned her gaze to the travel books. There was a photo of a beach and palm trees on one of them. What language would they use to say goodbye there? "Hawk is a good man," she said. "But he's not Jackson."

Hawk was standing alone on an arching stone footbridge that spanned a narrow section of canal when Sarah spotted him. He was wearing his leather jacket and a wrinkled pair of khakis, his head bare, his hair ruffled by the wind. His arms were crossed on top of the waist-high wall that ran along the side of the bridge. His gaze was on the water.

It was a different bridge, and the street she was on was

only a cobbled lane along the edge of the canal, not a main thoroughfare, but his pose was almost identical to the first time she had seen him. For a moment it seemed as if time were folding in on itself. How could so much have happened? How could it already be over?

But she knew how to do this. It was something she'd been trained in long before she'd put on a uniform. She crossed the lane and walked to his side. "Nice spot," she said.

He turned his head to look at her. "I didn't feel like sitting around in the room alone."

"How did you get past the reporters?"

"There aren't that many of them left. That kid from room service showed me how to get out the back way." He glanced past her shoulder. "Where's Major Redinger?"

"He left."

"He knew about us. I hope it didn't cause you any problems."

"No, the Major understands what happened." She squared her shoulders. "He told me the team is assembling for a training mission."

"Does that include you?"

"Yes. I wanted to say goodbye, Hawk."

"I'd like to come with you."

She started. "You can't."

"Why not? I don't have anywhere else to be. As a matter of fact, I'm currently unemployed."

If there had been any trace of self-pity in his voice, it would have made this easier for her. Instead, Sarah heard a tinge of humor. She found herself remembering the smile he'd greeted her with this morning despite the sadness she'd seen the night before. "Hawk, I won't be on my own time. I'll be on a training exercise."

"Then I'll wait for you at your base until you're finished."

"Hawk…"

"Even soldiers go home eventually, don't they?"

"Yes, but—"

"We need more time, Sarah. We need to figure out what's going on between us."

"We've been over that already."

He reached out, eased off her sunglasses and slipped them into her coat pocket. He leaned forward, his gaze warming hers. "As I recall, we started to discuss it but you never got the chance to reply after I sucked your nipple into my mouth. I'm sorry we were interrupted before we could finish the conversation."

A jab of awareness tightened her body. How could he arouse her so easily? A look, a few soft words, and she could almost forget where they were and what she had come to say. Almost. "Let's not drag this out, okay?"

"Drag what out?"

"Saying goodbye. Last night was great, but that's all it was. One night."

"Why did you really make love with me, Sarah?"

He'd spoken quietly. His voice was almost lost in the sound of the water and the wind. Yet she felt his words slice through her resolve. "Because we both wanted to," she replied. "It's as simple as that. I never wanted to hurt you. I made it clear from the start there's no future for us. You know I'll always love Jackson."

"You weren't thinking about him when you came apart in my arms."

"Leave it alone, Hawk."

"You called my name, not his."

"Hawk—"

"Did you ever call him by his first name?"

"What?"

"Captain Kyle Jackson. Whenever you mention him, you call him Jackson, not Kyle. Why?"

She stepped back from him. "I came to say goodbye, Hawk. I wanted to part on good terms. I didn't come to get ambushed."

"You call your father General, not Dad. Why?"

She turned and started walking toward the other end of the bridge.

He caught up to her in two strides. "Do you want to know what I think?"

"No."

"You do that because you need your distance, especially from the people you love. That's why you're in such a panic to leave me."

"You have an inflated opinion of the sex we shared. Who said anything about love?"

"Sarah—"

"And how dare you question the way I refer to my fiancé and my father? One night in bed doesn't give you the right to talk to me like this."

"The timetable was your idea." He grasped her arm. "Is that why you limited it to one night?"

She stopped walking and brought up her elbow, giving it a quick twist to break his hold. "You're treating me as if I'm a puzzle for you to solve. I'm not."

"But you are. You're a woman full of contradictions and you fascinate me."

"So I'm your new project, is that it? This is what I said before. Now that you gave away your other project, you're using me to fill the void."

"Sarah—"

"Instead of pushing me, why don't you ask yourself why you're refusing to let me go?"

"I told you. We need more time."

"How much is me and how much is your own past?"

"What do you mean?"

"You're dwelling on my love for Jackson as if you're in competition with him, as if you don't want to lose me, but I was never yours in the first place. Maybe what happened with Faith is mixed up in this as much as what happened with Jackson."

He stepped back.

"In the beginning, you didn't want to trust me," she continued. "I understand now why you'd have a problem trusting women. I'm sorry for the pain you went through when you learned about your fiancée's betrayal, but I'm not her anymore than you're Jackson. Winning me isn't going to make up for losing her."

"I know that, Sarah."

"Then trust what I'm telling you now. We had one night, Hawk. It's over. I don't know how much clearer I can make it. Let's say goodbye and get on with our lives."

"I can't stand by and watch you leave."

She made a cutting motion with her hand. "Then don't watch, okay? It's easier that way. Turn away. Make it clean and quick. Good memories and no regrets. That's how it's done."

"How what's done?"

"Saying goodbye."

"You're trembling."

"It's cold."

"You're scared. What are you scared of?"

"Scared? Like hell."

He touched his fingertip to the corner of her eye, then rubbed his thumb against the moisture that coated his glove.

"The wind is making my eyes water."

"You don't have to be tough with me, Sarah. You don't have to prove anything. Haven't you realized that by now?"

Damn him. He was being tender again, his voice as gentle as when he'd kissed her bruises. How could he stir her emotions so easily? What was it about him that made her lose control?

She had to leave. She should have left sooner. She retrieved her sunglasses from her pocket and put them back on. So she wouldn't have to squint. So the wind didn't get in her eyes. So no one would see her cry because she was trying so hard to be a good little soldier or no one would love her…

She turned and walked the rest of the way to the end of the bridge.

Hawk's footsteps pounded behind her. He grasped her shoulder. "Sarah, upsetting you is the last thing I wanted to do."

She blinked at the tears that continued to fill her eyes. She hated them. They were a sign of weakness. She saw the dark bulk of a van approaching and waited for it to go by.

"Sarah, please."

"Go away, Hawk. Just go away and don't follow me. I don't want to see you again."

"Sarah."

"You're making me sorry that I ever slept with you. The sex wasn't even that good. I've had the best. Jackson was a perfect soldier and an incredible lover and you aren't even my type."

He lifted his hand away.

Sarah bit her lip to keep her sob inside. She knew how he valued honesty. She knew why he valued honesty. She prayed that he didn't realize how big a lie she had just told.

The van had stopped to let her cross. She stepped off the curb.

Her vision was blurred. It was the sounds that alerted her. A scuff of shoes on the sidewalk. A cracking thud. She whirled to look behind her.

Hawk was no longer there. Two large, broad-shouldered men were dragging him toward the back of the van that was idling in the lane.

He wasn't putting up a struggle. He hung limply between them, his head sagging forward. A bright patch of crimson coated his hair.

It took a vital second for Sarah to register the scene. Her mind couldn't seem to grasp what she saw. Neither could her heart. This couldn't be happening. The danger was supposed to be over. She was leaving. Hawk was…

Hawk was bleeding. He was unconscious. He was being tossed into the back of that vehicle while she was standing here indulging her emotions and being weak and letting down her guard…

She didn't realize she had said his name until she felt the raw pain in her throat from the force of her scream.

Tires squealed. Sarah threw herself at the back of the van as it passed her and grabbed for the door handle.

They hadn't had the chance to close the door completely. It burst open, swinging her over the pavement. She hooked one leg around the edge.

Tires screeched again. The van careened off the lane into the first alleyway past the bridge. Sarah felt herself fall.

And then she felt nothing.

Chapter 10

Hawk awoke to darkness and agony in his skull. The pain was everywhere, a red haze that was sucking him back down to unconsciousness. It carried him along, washing over him while he fought to gather his strength.

The last thing he remembered he'd been standing on the sidewalk watching Sarah wait for some van to pass....

Had they been hit by the van? Where was Sarah? Was she all right? He had to find out. He couldn't let the pain take him. He concentrated, forcing his mind to keep working.

He was lying on his side. His cheek was pressed against something cold and metallic. He smelled...fuel. It was richer than gasoline. All around him was noise, a steady *thwup-thwup* drone that rose from the metal floor beneath him and rattled his teeth.

He blinked and raised his head. The darkness wasn't complete. There was a faint glow from somewhere behind him. He could see outlines of objects on the floor, the dull gleam of a curving metal wall….

The floor suddenly tilted. He tried to bring his hands forward to steady himself, but he couldn't move his arms. His cheekbone smashed against metal. Pain exploded. He clenched his jaw, struggling to stay awake, to stay rational.

But this didn't make sense. Where was he? What had happened? This was too real for a nightmare.

The floor tilted the other way. Hawk slid backward a few inches until his shoulders struck a thin strut of metal that was attached to the wall. He groaned involuntarily. The sound didn't get past his lips. A wide band of tape covered his mouth.

He breathed hard through his nose and tried to lie still, tried to gather more data. His mouth was taped. He couldn't move his arms because his wrists were bound behind him so tightly his hands were numb. He couldn't feel his fingers—they were useless. His ankles were bound, too. He was on the floor of some kind of moving vehicle, a large one that sounded like…a helicopter.

This was no accident. He was being abducted.

Why? Who? There hadn't been any warning. Sarah had believed the danger was over—

Sarah. Was she all right? Where was she?

She had been walking away, leaving him.

Where was she now? She'd been so determined to get away from him. He hoped she had. He didn't want her hurt.

But she'd been crying. He'd made her cry. What was wrong with him that he made a woman like her cry?

The floor tilted again. Hawk had no way to stop himself from sliding forward. He tucked in his chin, trying to prepare for whatever he would strike this time.

It wasn't a metal wall. It was something soft and warm that smelled faintly of spice....

His heart froze. He would know that scent anywhere. Sarah. She was here after all. Dammit, she was here. And she wasn't moving.

The terror that seized him was stronger than the pain. He rolled to his knees, bracing his thighs apart to steady himself against the movement of the helicopter. He strained to peer through the shadows. He could see nothing but a vague outline, so he curled forward until he felt the wool of her coat against his forehead.

He inched closer to her, using his nose and his cheek to feel his way along her body. He felt a button graze his temple and realized she was lying on her back. He pressed his ear to her chest, trying to feel movement, praying he would hear a heartbeat, but the vibration and the noise from the aircraft was too much.

He knew he wouldn't be able to help her, no matter what he found. That didn't stop him. He had to know. He worked his way up her chest to her throat. He felt the tickle of her scarf. Her arms were stretched over her head, her head lolled limply between them. Tape covered her mouth.

That was good, wasn't it? If she was bound and gagged she must be alive...or at least she had been alive when she'd been brought here....

Sarah! The wordless cry was strangled in his throat. He rubbed his forehead along the edge of the tape that covered her mouth until his temple brushed her nose. He closed his eyes and concentrated.

Please, God. Not again. Don't take another woman from me....

Warm air feathered over his eyelid. Hawk held himself as motionless as possible, hoping it hadn't been his imagination.

There. He felt it again. A puff of air. She was breathing.

Hawk realized afterward he must have blacked out then. When he awoke next, he was still on his knees, doubled over with his forehead pressed to Sarah's side. He sat up. His head ached but it didn't take him as long to get control of the pain this time. The light had strengthened. Sarah was still unconscious only now there was enough light for him to see she was breathing.

Her wrists were tied to the wall above her head with what looked like a cargo strap. A similar strap stretched from the other wall to hold her ankles. That was why she hadn't been thrown by the motions of the helicopter. Someone had wanted to make sure she was immobilized so she couldn't fight. Her coat hung open. She must have been searched and disarmed, too.

Hawk felt a burst of rage. Who had done this to her? And why?

But he knew why. It was because of him. She was here and she was hurt because of him. Why couldn't he have let her go?

Was she right? Was his refusal to let her go tangled up with Faith and his past? Were his feelings for Sarah an illusion, too?

They felt damn real to him now.

Yet Sarah had made her wishes perfectly clear. If he'd said goodbye quick and clean, the way she'd wanted him to, she wouldn't be here. He wouldn't have made her cry. She wouldn't have felt forced to lash out at him in return.

You're making me sorry that I ever slept with you. The sex wasn't even that good.

Hell, maybe he had been deluding himself the same way he had before. Maybe he would never be able to compare to the perfect Kyle Jackson. It no longer mattered. He didn't care if Sarah hated him when she woke up. As long as she did wake up.

He pressed his face to her neck, drawing in her warmth and her scent. He felt the steady beat of her pulse against the delicate skin beneath her ear.

He could feel her pulse. Only then did he realize that the vibration of the engine had stopped. So had the noise. They could no longer be airborne, yet he still had the sensation of movement.

He sat up and looked around. They were in the cargo area in the rear of the helicopter. Crates were strapped to the bare metal walls around them. Light seeped in from the front of the aircraft where a curtain was pushed aside to reveal the cockpit. The light wasn't from the sun. It was from an array of floodlights that glared beyond the windshield.

They must have landed while he'd been unconscious, Hawk thought. But why was the floor pitching?

There was a clunk from outside the fuselage. An outline appeared in the wall. A door slid open.

Hawk squinted against the glare of light, trying to focus on the figure who stood in the opening. It was a tall, slender man. Hawk couldn't see his face, but there was something familiar about him....

"Those dolts. I told them to bring you to me undamaged. I do hope your brain is still functioning."

At the sound of the familiar voice, Hawk stared in disbelief.

Prince Jibril Ben Nour pinched the neat crease in his pant legs and climbed through the doorway into the helicopter. He waited for two of his guards to take up positions beside him, then approached to stand over Hawk. "You should have died when you were supposed to, Hawkins. It would have saved us so much trouble." He propped his

hands on his hips and leaned down. His grin flashed white
in his beard. "But then, for a genius you've never been
that smart."

Sarah had experienced worse pain before, so the dull
ache that suffused her body was manageable. She let it
flow around her like a river, carrying her forward until she
could angle her way across the current to the calm near
the shore.

"Sarah?"

The voice seemed to come from a long way off. She let
it guide her. Somehow she was certain if she reached it
she would be safe, she could stop fighting...

"Sarah, wake up."

Warm fingertips brushed her cheek. She recognized the
touch. She moved her head to follow it.

"That's it, Sarah. You can do it."

She cracked open her eyelids.

She was lying on a bed in a strange room. Hawk's face
filled her vision. He was sitting on the edge of the mattress,
leaning over her. A bruise purpled his cheek beneath a dark
growth of whiskers.

She lifted her hand to lay her palm over his bruise. "Are
you all right? What happened?"

He closed his eyes and turned his head to press his
mouth to her hand. His nostrils flared. He breathed deeply
for a moment before he looked at her once more. "I'm
sorry, Sarah."

Her memory stirred. She remembered the van, the men
dragging Hawk, the blood on his hair...

Relief crashed over her. Thank God. He was alive. He
was safe after all. Her hand shook as she slid it to his
head. She sifted her fingers carefully through his hair. She
found a lump on his skull and traced it with her fingertips.

There was a crusted scab—the wound she had seen was dry and healing. He should be okay.

But it had been close. Too close.

She blinked back a surge of tears. "I saw them take you. I tried to stop them. I think I fell off the van."

He skimmed his fingertips along her temple, her cheek, the corner of her mouth. "You'll be all right. They told me nothing's broken. You hit the back of your head and were knocked out. You have some bruises and a few scrapes but they're already starting to heal. How are you feeling?"

"Groggy."

"It's going to take some more time for the drugs to wear off. You've been out for almost two days."

She struggled to focus. Drugs? The pain wasn't that bad. He'd said she wasn't seriously hurt. But two days? She lifted her head to look past his shoulder.

The room they were in was decorated in white, but it didn't look like a hospital room. It was too large and luxurious. This bed was too big. Instead of medical equipment, there were white padded armchairs and heavy glass tables along the walls. At one end of the room she saw a thickly varnished mahogany door that was slightly open to reveal a marble-tiled bathroom. At the side of the room she saw windows that were…round. She could see nothing beyond the glass but a gray mass of clouds.

She looked down at herself. She was still wearing the same black pants and turtleneck she'd put on before she'd left the hotel. There was a rip over one knee. None of this added up. Either it was the drugs, or something was definitely wrong. "Where are we, Hawk?" she asked.

"This is our room." He straightened up. He smiled. It looked strained. "You must be thirsty. Would you like some water?"

She nodded.

He slipped his arm behind her back and helped her to sit up, then poured her a glass of water from a pitcher on the bedside table. He watched her while she drank. "There's some aspirin if you want something for the pain. Those bruises must be sore."

"No, I'm okay. Nothing a soak in a hot bath won't fix. I can't believe I was out for two days."

"Are you hungry? I'll tell them to bring some food."

"Is this another hotel?"

He took the glass from her hand and set it back on the table. "No."

She looked at the glass. The liquid that was left in the bottom of it continued to move well after he had set it down. She lifted her gaze to one of the windows. The grayness outside appeared to be moving, too. She felt her stomach roll. "Hawk? What kind of drugs was I given?"

"Tranquilizers."

"Tranks? Not painkillers?" She rubbed her forehead as if she could rub away the haziness. "What happened while I was out? And how did you get away from those men I saw at the bridge?"

"I didn't, Sarah."

Her hand fell to her side. "What?"

"I'm sorry. There's no easy way to tell you this."

"Then just tell me. Don't make it worse by dragging it out."

Beneath the bruise and the bristling beard stubble, his cheek twitched. "We've been abducted," he said. "We were brought by helicopter to Jibril's yacht."

For an instant her brain was too sluggish to grasp what she had just heard. It was like that moment at the bridge when she'd seen Hawk injured and bleeding.

Her heart started to pound. No. Oh, no.

It still wasn't over.

She did another survey of the room, forcing herself to absorb the facts. They were onboard the *Faith*. That explained the movement and the windows that looked like portholes. "Those were Jibril's men in the van?"

"Yes."

"Why would he do this? It couldn't be for ransom. This boat alone must be worth close to a billion."

"I don't know what he wants yet."

"Why not?"

"I haven't seen him since we were brought here. I think he's waiting until we're out to sea. Or maybe making me wait is a ploy to unnerve me. That might be why they were keeping you sedated." He paused. "Sarah, Jibril admitted he was the one who tried to have me killed."

"What? Then why…"

"Why are we still alive? I don't know for sure." He lifted his palm to her shoulder, then eased a lock of hair behind her ear. "I'm sorry you were drawn into this. It's likely me he wants. I never wanted to see you get hurt, but I seem to keep doing it, anyway."

"It's not your fault, Hawk."

He hesitated, then swore under his breath, slipped his hands beneath her and lifted her onto his lap. Pressing his cheek to the top of her head, he held her to his chest as if she were something precious.

This was how he always held her, as if she were fragile and feminine and didn't have to be what she was supposed to be…

That was when she remembered the rest of what had happened before Hawk had been dragged into the van. The harsh things he had said. The hurtful things she had said. The tears.

Oh, God. She should have been paying more attention.

She should have been more aware of her surroundings. Instead she'd let her feelings jeopardize her judgment. She had failed. She and Hawk were in more danger than ever.

How could he be holding her like this after the way they had parted?

And how could she let him?

Sarah pushed out of his embrace and got to her feet. The room wobbled.

Hawk caught her arms to steady her. "Take it easy, Sarah. Give yourself some time."

We need more time, Sarah. We need to figure out what's going on between us.

She pulled away, wiping her eyes against her sleeve. Damn these tears. Damn these feelings. "We don't have time. We have to make a plan. We have to escape."

"We will. I promise you."

I didn't make any promises.

No, she wouldn't think about what had happened the last time he'd held her in his arms. She had to keep a clear head. His life as well as her own could depend on her ability to be objective.

She leaned over to brace her hands on her knees, taking deep inhalations, hoping the rush of blood to her brain would help wash away the haziness from the drugs and this horrible, persistent urge to cry. "What time is it?"

"I don't know. They took my watch. Early afternoon."

"You said we've been here two days. That makes it Tuesday."

He laid his hand on her back, rubbing gently. "People will be looking for us by now."

"Not for me. I wasn't due to report until Wednesday, and even then the Major might assume…" Her words trailed off, but she completed the thought, anyway. When she didn't show up for the training exercise in Dartmoor,

Redinger might assume she had decided to take the extra few days leave he'd offered her. He might even decide to cut her some slack and not immediately put her down as AWOL for not confirming it. He hadn't understood that what had happened between her and Hawk was over.

And it was over. It had to be. She dug her fingers into her thighs. "Hawk, please don't touch me."

His fingers tensed. "Sarah."

"I mean it. Keep away from me. I was groggy when I woke up, but now we don't have time for this."

He lifted his hand.

She straightened up and moved to the door. She tried the handle but it wouldn't turn. It was a simple tumbler lock, not a big obstacle with the right tool. "Where does this lead?" she asked.

"A narrow corridor. There are other similar doors along it. We're on the first level below deck."

She pressed her ear to the door. She heard the sound of men's voices speaking Arabic. The words were too faint to make out. "How many guards have you seen?"

"At least two dozen, but I haven't seen much of the ship."

She ran her fingers along the door frame, then started moving slowly along the wall, inspecting the baseboards and the furniture. "Do you know their schedule?"

"I haven't noticed one. I did observe they seem to work in pairs. What are you doing?"

"Checking for surveillance devices. There probably aren't any, since if there were, those guards I heard in the hall would have known that I'm awake and taken up positions closer to the door, but I want to be sure." She continued her inspection, studying the lamps, the light fixtures, the edges of the portholes, every corner of the room. She thought of spots where she would plant transmitters

or cameras and went over it again. A wave of dizziness
struck her as she reached the bathroom. She closed her
eyes and grabbed the door frame.

"Sarah!"

"I'm fine. No problem. It's just the tranks wearing off."
When she opened her eyes she saw he was right beside
her, his arms outstretched, ready to catch her.

But he wasn't touching her. Just as she'd asked.

Good. That was good. She didn't have the energy to
fight him. She regarded the bathroom.

It was almost as large as the bedroom. There were chairs
in here, too, and glass shelves stacked with plush white
towels. The white marble floor rose in steps to form a huge
scallop-shaped tub. The faucets were gold. So were the
soap dishes.

Hawk had said there were other doors along the corridor. Did they all lead to quarters like these? Probably. She
didn't think Jibril would have given the best to his prisoners. This was likely one of the smaller rooms—the ones
she'd glimpsed when she and Hawk had been brought onboard last week had been elegant to the point of deca-
dence. She could only imagine the conspicuous luxury in
the rest of the ship.

It was obscene. A prison was still a prison.

"Tell me what to look for," Hawk said. "I'd like to
help."

She pushed away from the door frame and headed for
the pair of marble basins that were set into a long, low
counter. "Look for anything that doesn't belong, like small
wires, buttons or chips. Jibril would likely be able to afford
the best."

Hawk was a fast learner, Sarah thought. He must have
been watching what she had done before. He went through
the bathroom as meticulously as she had gone through the

other room, moving the chairs, peering into the air vents and beneath the fixtures, using his fingertips to feel for the ends of wires.

She watched him as he worked. His hands were large, his fingers long and square, yet he had a sensitive touch. Not that his hands were soft—his grip was as solid as any man's she'd known. He was able to control his strength. Although he could pick her up as if she weighed nothing, those long, sensitive fingers of his had moved over her body as tenderly as a summer breeze....

No. She couldn't think about that. She had to concentrate. She had to set her priorities, keep her mind on her mission.

She looked away from Hawk and checked the items that were arranged on the counter. There were crystal bottles of bath oil, a gold-plated brush and comb set, rolled hand towels as soft as velvet. More luxuries for the prisoners. Either Jibril was deliberately taunting them, or he was too confident of his power over them to consider the possibility that a shard of crystal could be used as a knife.

She regarded the mirror that was fixed to the wall over the sinks. She checked the edges and the supports first before she leaned closer and peered at the glass. She tried looking from a different angle, but she didn't spot any telltale shadow from behind it. If she wanted to be sure it didn't conceal a camera, she could always break it, but it seemed as if her first guess was correct. The rooms were clean. More signs that Jibril was underestimating them? She pulled back, her focus shifting. She finally noticed her reflection.

She had never been vain about her looks—she knew they were superficial—yet what she saw made her slap her palms against the sink to keep from falling. It wasn't the tangled hair that bothered her, or the puffy circles under her eyes and the lines of strain around her lips.

It was the despair in her gaze.

Who was she fooling? How could they escape? Even if they could get out of this room, there was nowhere for them to go. They were outnumbered and outgunned, surrounded by miles of frigid water, at the mercy of a bastard who decorated a prison cell with gold and marble.

She had to be strong.

But how could she be strong when she was locked in here with the one man who made her weak, who made her feel like crying and throwing herself into his arms and wanting sweet promises and, yes, roses on her breakfast plate….

She jumped at the movement in the mirror. It was Hawk. He had come up behind her again, his hands held out as if he were going to hug her just as she wanted. No, she couldn't want it. "Don't," she said.

He met her gaze in the mirror. Slowly he pulled back his hands. "Sarah, I'm sorry for what I said before, when we were at the bridge."

"This is hardly the time—"

"No, I want to clear the air. I've had two days to think about it, and you were right. I had no business badgering you about Jackson the way I did."

"None of that matters. What's done is done. Forget it."

"I'm sorry I upset you. I was wrong to push you so hard, but—"

"So don't start doing it again, okay?"

He shoved his hands in his pockets. "If that's what you want."

"Yes, that's what I want. As far as I'm concerned, our relationship ended two days ago. This is no longer personal. I'm back on duty."

"Sarah…"

"That's how it has to be, Hawk. We'll work together to get out of here but that's all. We have to concentrate on surviving."

"We will."

He sounded so certain. Oh, how she wanted to cling to him, feel the sharp pleasure of his lips on her body and forget who they were and where they were….

She straightened her spine. "Yes, of course, we will."

He continued to look at her, his gaze taking on a familiar intense gleam.

He knew, she realized. He knew she was scared and she was hanging on by a thread. That was the real reason he'd backed off.

She looked down, letting her hair swing forward to shield her face. "Give me a few minutes alone, Hawk."

He stepped back. He said nothing more. She heard his footsteps on the marble floor, then the sound of running water.

Damn the man. He wasn't leaving, he was drawing her another bath.

Chapter 11

Moisture drizzled down the wall of windows, casting a gray pall over the room where Jibril had received Hawk and Sarah the week before. Nothing was visible beyond the ship's bow except clouds, water and the creeping wall of dusk. The long swells that rolled over the surface of the sea would have tossed around a smaller vessel, but the heavy *Faith* powered forward like a tank through sand dunes.

Hawk estimated they would be approaching the Atlantic by now. Storms could blow up with little warning at this time of year. Two people adrift in a lifeboat without a radio or supplies wouldn't have much chance of survival. There would be even less chance of survival in the water—they would succumb to hypothermia within minutes.

That was assuming they could get past the Moukim Palace Guards who were stationed around the room. Jibril's men weren't dressed as sailors anymore. They were wearing green camouflage battle uniforms. Each man was armed with a handgun that was holstered at his side and a rifle slung over his shoulder. They stood the same way Hawk had seen Sarah stand when she was readying herself for action.

They were trained commandos. Even if they'd been unarmed, Hawk knew he was no match physically for any of these men. That didn't stop him from wanting to smash his fist into the face of every one of them for the strain this was putting on Sarah.

But a confrontation at this stage would be fruitless. If he or Sarah showed any resistance, they would likely be bound and gagged again.

''This way, please.''

Hawk looked at the guard who had fetched them from their room. It was the crooked-nosed man named Ahmed. He and all the others were continuing their charade of civility despite their actions. They betrayed no emotion as they carried out their orders.

Sarah moved to follow Ahmed. Hawk reached for her hand but she angled herself so she was just out of his reach.

Hawk swallowed his frustration and fell into step beside her. He knew she preferred to have her hands free and to have space to move, but that wasn't the main reason she had pulled away. She didn't want him to touch her. She said it was over. She wanted to forget they had made love.

The hell of it was, he could see her point. They had to put their personal feelings aside and concentrate on surviving. He was no soldier, he couldn't shut off his emotions, but for her sake he could control his actions. He owed her that much, didn't he?

An image of Sarah tied up in the helicopter flashed into his mind. Hawk clenched his teeth. Would he ever get used to the rage?

Yet Sarah walked with dignity, just as she always did. She had her chin lifted and her back straight, meeting the guards' gazes squarely, betraying none of the fear Hawk knew was churning inside her.

Her inner strength continued to humble him. She was a woman in a million. And once they got home…

Once they were home, she would probably want to leave him again.

"Ah, good. I'm so pleased my guests have decided to join me." Jibril was lounging in the center of one of the room's long white couches. He was in full traditional dress today, the folds of his djellabah draped gracefully around him. The glass table in front of him held a silver coffee service but only one cup. There were no other couches or chairs nearby—obviously the charade of courtesy only went so far. Jibril didn't expect his "guests" to sit.

Ahmed guided Hawk and Sarah toward a spot several yards away from Jibril's couch and brought them to a halt. He took one pace back, resting his hand on the trigger of his gun.

"I trust you're enjoying my hospitality?" Jibril asked. "Is there anything you desire?"

"I demand that you release us," Hawk said.

Jibril shook his head. "After all the trouble you put me through to bring you here?"

"People will already be searching for us. Let us go now before it's too late."

Jibril laughed. "You are a fool, Hawkins."

Hawk didn't respond. He waited for Jibril to go on. He wanted him to gloat because that was the quickest way to get information. He wasn't disappointed.

"We're in international waters," Jibril said. "No one can board us legally without just cause. Even then, they would have difficulty getting past the *Faith's* defenses. Regardless, no one would suspect you were here since the *Faith* left Stockholm almost a full day before you did.''

Hawk waited again. Jibril was obviously enjoying demonstrating how clever he was. The mask of affability he'd used the last time they'd spoken in this room was completely gone. Jibril must have been storing up resentment for years.

''Furthermore, no one has been searching for you because no one is yet aware that you're missing.''

''Someone would have witnessed our abduction.''

''No, I'm afraid not. My men assured me the area where they acquired you was deserted. There were no witnesses. In addition, your luggage has been removed from your hotel room and disposed of, your bill has been settled and your credit card has been used to book a rental car.'' Jibril smirked. ''As a matter of fact, your credit cards will be leaving a trail throughout Europe.''

''It will never work,'' Hawk said.

''On the contrary, it works out perfectly. Everyone will assume the famous Dr. Lemay wished to escape the limelight in order to find privacy with his…how shall I put this politely?'' Jibril tilted his head and looked at Sarah. ''His latest conquest?''

Hawk felt Sarah touch his sleeve, but he didn't need her caution. He wasn't going to respond to Jibril's provocation. Besides, there was no point denying that he had a relationship with Sarah. From the moment they had arrived onboard until Sarah had awakened in their quarters, he'd made his concern for her plain.

''I'm pleased you have availed yourself of the soaps and lotions I provided, Captain Fox,'' Jibril said. ''And the comb. But those clothes are a sight. I must arrange to supply you with spare garments and have yours laundered.''

Sarah didn't respond to the goading. Hawk wasn't surprised. Although she had scrubbed herself clean and then tamed her hair into a braid after her soak in the bath, he knew she hadn't done it solely for the sake of her appearance. Her sense of self-worth went far deeper than that.

"Yes, you always did have an eye for beauty," Jibril went on, returning his gaze to Hawk. "That is fortunate for the lovely captain. It is your interest in her that is keeping her alive."

Hawk had suspected as much. Sarah hadn't been the target of whatever Jibril was planning, Hawk had. She was only here because of her connection to him. She had been put into harm's way—again—because of him. "You said you wanted me dead, Jibril. Why did you bring us here? Why keep either of us alive?"

"Don't you want to know why I hired Weltzer to kill you?"

"That's obvious. You wanted to stop my research."

"There are other more personal reasons I might want you dead, Hawkins."

"If this was because I once had Faith, your jealousy wouldn't have waited fourteen years, and you wouldn't have gone to the expense of hiring a hit man. You said yourself that you're a practical man."

Jibril got to his feet. His smile was gone, as was the indolent pose. "Yes, I am practical. Dieter Weltzer was an investment to guarantee the continuing prosperity of Moukim. Weltzer was to have eliminated you in such a way that no suspicion fell on me."

Hawk had had plenty of time to think about this during those endless two days while Sarah had been sedated. All the pieces fit. Jibril had as much motive as any of his OPEC associates. He would have known about Hawk's habits, so he would have advised Weltzer how to set up that first assassination attempt. When that had failed, it was possible Jibril had been planning to kill Hawk after having his men spirit him away from the reception on the first night of the conference, but Sarah had foiled that, too, just as she'd eliminated the risk the next day by notifying the embassy of Hawk's visit to the *Faith.*

Sarah had suspected Jibril immediately, but Hawk had let his personal feelings—and his plans for his work— blind him to the truth.

The regrets kept mounting. "How much wealth and power will be enough, Jibril?" he asked. "Will there ever be a point when you're satisfied?"

"When I have it all, Hawkins," he replied. "I told you before, in any competition there is room for only one winner. But you deceive yourself if you think this is not about the past. You yourself made it that way. You waited fourteen years for your revenge. Did you really think I would allow it?"

Revenge? That threw him. "What are you talking about?"

"Your research. You knew my country was rich in oil, so you devoted your life to finding an alternative." He snapped his fingers at the two nearest guards. They came forward to move the table with the coffee service aside, then took up positions on either side of him. "That was how you planned to defeat me," he said. "You wanted to destroy my wealth and my power. You chose your path because you wanted revenge. You hide behind your noble ideas of what fusion power could do for the world, but this has always been about the woman I won from you."

Hawk felt himself waver. No. Jibril couldn't be right, could he? Just how much influence did Hawk's past have on his life? "I began researching fusion power because I did my doctorate work on particle physics. It had nothing to do with you. It wasn't some personal vendetta."

Jibril continued as if Hawk hadn't spoken. "Then you had the impertinence to insult me with your offer to share. *Share*. Pah! You expected me to share your discoveries with my neighbors and then the world. You did not truly expect me to agree to that, did you, Hawkins? That would be a fool's bargain."

"You should have taken it," Hawk said. "The research you wanted to stop belongs to everyone now. The world's best physicists are working to complete it. Killing me won't prevent that, and you can't kill them all."

"Which brings us to the reason you are here." Jibril approached, his guards at his elbows. He stopped when he was still well out of reach and barked out a command in Arabic. More guards converged on Hawk and Sarah, their weapons drawn. Only then did Jibril move closer. "It appears you have involved me in another competition, Hawkins."

Hawk regarded the man he had once considered his friend. There was no trace of warmth in Jibril's dark eyes, just cold calculation. "What do you want, Jibril?"

"I want what you offered me before. Fusion power."

"I told you. It already belongs to everyone."

"It is only the promise that belongs to everyone, not the final key. You made this a race. I intend to use you to reach the finish line first."

"How?"

"You will complete your work before anyone else. Your power will give me power. By the time the rest of the world catches up to our technology, if it ever does, Moukim will already control their economies. There will be a new world order that my nation will dominate. We will be invincible."

It would be easier if Hawk could believe that Jibril was mad, but his scheme was all too plausible. It was true that

Hawk would be able to complete his research before other scientists could. He'd devoted his life to it so he had an advantage no one else had.

But this hoarding by one nation was exactly what Hawk had hoped to prevent. He moved his head from side to side. "Completing my research isn't that simple. I would need my notes and my computer for my theoretical work as well as time on a particle accelerator to run experiments. For the final stages I would need access to the equipment in my lab to build a prototype reactor."

"Our Royal Academy of Science has all the equipment and facilities you require. Preparations are already underway to provide you with exclusive access. By the time we arrive in Moukim, the arrangements will be complete. Moreover, all of your research to date is—How did you put it? Freely available on the Web sites of every major university? That was very obliging of you. My men have already transferred those files to the computer I have acquired for you. As you see, there is no reason you cannot complete your research while you remain my guest. In fact, now that the computer equipment has been delivered here to the *Faith*, you can resume your theoretical work tomorrow."

Hawk didn't respond. Jibril had thought it all through. The material, the equipment, the place to work, everything Hawk needed would be provided. There was only one element missing to ensure the scheme's success: Hawk's compliance.

Jibril's smile slashed through his beard. "Since you said you were still months away from a breakthrough, I believe you will wish to waste no time getting started." He moved his gaze to Sarah. "And this is where you come in. You will provide our Hawkins with his motivation."

Until now, Sarah had remained silent, but Hawk knew

she had taken in everything. She had probably figured out where this was leading before he had.

Sarah regarded Jibril unblinkingly. "You won't harm Hawk because you want him to work for you," she said. "But threatening me won't win his cooperation. As you said, I'm just his latest conquest. We mean nothing to each other. We had already said goodbye when your men took us."

"That makes no difference," Jibril said easily. "One of Hawkins's many flaws is he wants to view himself as a hero. Whether he is through with you or not, he will act the gentleman."

"You're projecting your own dishonesty on others," Sarah said. "You're incapable of seeing that Hawk is an honorable man. He has devoted his life to his work. No matter what happens to me, he won't permit a twisted bastard like you to profit from his genius."

Jibril's eyes widened. He snapped his fingers and gave another command. Four guards grasped Hawk's arms while Ahmed stepped forward to place the muzzle of his gun beneath Sarah's chin.

Hawk jerked against the guards' hold. "Let her go, Jibril. If you kill her I won't give you anything."

"Kill her? No, I won't kill her yet, even though she tries to provoke me." Jibril stared at Sarah, then looked pointedly at the place where the gun was pressed to her throat. "How does it feel to have our positions reversed? Did you think I would forgive the affront I suffered when you dared to assault me?"

Sarah sniffed. "I should have shot you when I had the chance."

"You will soon wish that you had. The penalty under Moukim law would have been far quicker and more merciful."

Hawk tasted bile in his throat. *Moukim* law?

Jibril drew himself up with a swish of his robes. "In my country, if someone puts their hand on a member of the royal family, the punishment is to cut off the hand. You touched me with your hands, your arms and your legs."

Oh, God. "No," Hawk rasped. *"No!"*

Jibril looked at Hawk. "As I said, I do not plan to kill Captain Fox. That would not serve my purpose. Instead, I plan to carry out her sentence. She will lose one part of her body for each week you take to complete your work."

The feelings that crashed over Hawk were too primitive to identify. Jibril's threat was so barbaric, it was unthinkable. Was he mad after all? How could a sane man contemplate such cruelty?

Hawk lunged forward. Four men held his arms, but the force of his fury dragged them with him. He managed to get within a yard of Jibril before his arms were wrenched back in their sockets and he was slammed facefirst to the floor.

Jibril hopped backward and waved his hand toward the guards. "Take them away. I believe my friend Hawkins has enough incentive to get started."

Sarah focused on the glass, concentrating on her grip. One finger at a time, she ensured her hold was solid. She could feel the cold from the water already seeping through the glass to her skin. If she waited much longer, the condensation would make the glass slippery. She was thirsty. She wanted a drink.

But she knew that if she tried to lift the glass, her hand would shake too badly to get the water to her mouth.

She yanked her hand back from the table and crossed

her arms, squeezing farther into the cushions of the white
armchair, hugging herself to keep the scream inside.

Without a word Hawk knelt in front of her chair, picked
up the glass and held it to her lips.

It took every ounce of Sarah's energy to fight her terror.
She had nothing left to fight him. She drank.

He waited until she had emptied the glass, then set it on
the table. "The bathroom is clear," he said. "Same as this
room. Jibril's men didn't leave anything behind while we
were out."

Hawk had checked for bugs the way she had taught him
as soon as they had been brought to their quarters. She
should have thought of that herself. It was her responsibility. Doing a sweep of a room was standard procedure
whenever the location had been left unguarded.

She pressed her lips together. There was a sob rising
with the scream, and she had to keep it down, too. She
would be no good to Hawk if she fell apart.

"Jibril's wrong, Sarah," Hawk said. "Your friends will
find us."

She thought about the men of Eagle Squadron. They
would be starting their training mission tomorrow. The
transport would already have left Fort Bragg. It might have
passed directly above this ship, for all she knew. She had
been eager to join them, to run away from Hawk and the
feelings he stirred…

But she couldn't run anywhere now. In a few weeks she
might not be able to walk.

"The Major told me about those men who consider
themselves your brothers," Hawk said. "If they were
blessed with even a fraction of your courage, they won't
let anything stop them."

Sarah remembered the tension on Redinger's face the
last time she had seen him. He'd asked her whether anyone

had approached Hawk about completing his work. Well, it seemed the Major had anticipated events correctly.

Only, instead of offering money, Jibril was trading pieces of Sarah's body.

She curled her hands into fists, tucking them against her ribs beneath her breasts. Which body part would they start with? Probably her hands. Severing a hand would cause the fewest medical complications. Individual fingers would be even better. Less loss of blood, no mobility issues, excellent likelihood of survival...

Oh God, oh God, oh God. The army was the only life she knew, but how could she be a soldier with no hands? How could she pull a trigger or drive a jeep or work a radio? She wouldn't even be able to salute her superiors properly. What would the general say to such a breach in protocol?

Sarah's teeth chattered. She knew very well what the general would say. The words were playing in her head in an endlessly repeating loop. *Do your duty like a good little soldier.*

The first time she'd heard those words she'd been four years old and had been standing beside her mother's grave. Clods of earth had been falling on the coffin, making horrible, hollow thudding sounds. She had wailed. The general had ordered her not to cry. He'd brushed the dirt off their palms and had shown her how to salute instead.

She had. She'd made him proud. All her life she'd done what she'd been taught, she'd buried the pain and kept the feelings inside just as he did, just as all the men did. That's why she understood the men of Eagle Squadron so well. She was as skilled as they were at locking the hurt inside her heart.

This time the general's words weren't helping. They

didn't make her want to straighten her spine or square her shoulders, they made her want to scream.

She clamped her jaw shut to stop the noise of her clattering teeth and breathed in deeply through her nose. She couldn't let anyone see her like this. She was ashamed of her weakness. As the general always said, nobody would love a weakling.

Hawk rose to his feet and crossed the room to take a blanket from the bed. He returned and spread it over her knees. "Try to get some rest."

She shook her head. "Not yet. We have to plan our strategy."

He folded the upper edge of the blanket around her shoulders, then braced his hands on the arms of her chair and leaned over her. "I know things don't look good right now, but once Interpol and Intelligence trace Weltzer to Jibril, Redinger will put together what happened. He'll figure out where to look. Your friends will find us," he said again. "I trust them."

She could feel his gaze on her face. She didn't want to meet it. She was too close to the edge. She knew that if she saw sympathy in his eyes, the thread of her control would snap.

It wasn't only her life at stake here, it was his, too. She *had* to hang on. "You're right, the odds of escaping on our own aren't good," she said. "Rescue is our only feasible option, but it could…take a while."

"Sarah, I won't let them hurt you."

"No matter what happens to me, you can't give Jibril what he wants."

"Sarah—"

"Think, Hawk. He's gone too far. He can't leave witnesses. He won't let you go free. The minute you complete your research and prove the fusion power technology works, your value to him will be gone. He'll execute you and…'' And whatever's left of me, she thought. ''He'll eliminate us both.''

''I know that.''

She could feel the warmth of his breath waft over her cheek. His scent surrounded her. It steadied her. ''All right,'' she said. ''It's good you understand. Then you'll have to stall for time. Pretend you're cooperating. No more confrontations.''

He didn't reply.

She lifted her gaze. She looked at the fresh bruise that had been added to his cheek when Jibril's men had thrown him to the floor. ''Hawk, what you did tonight was pointless. You shouldn't have gone for him.''

''I couldn't help it, Sarah. I wanted to kill him.''

He'd spoken softly. The mild tone held neither apology nor bravado. It was the quiet certainty of a man at his most dangerous.

She had no doubt that he would have killed Jibril if he'd been able to reach him. The look on Hawk's face as he'd thrown himself forward had been so deadly it had made her shiver. She didn't know how he'd had the strength to drag four of the largest Moukim palace guard with him.

But then, this wasn't the first time she had seen him fight for her. The night of Weltzer's attack, Hawk had acted just as fiercely. His ability hadn't come from training, it had come from instinct.

Her gaze moved over his jaw. He still looked dangerous. He also looked very…male. The shadow of his beard stubble deepened the lines beside his mouth and hardened the angles of his face. His shoulders were tensed, straining the fabric of his shirt. She could make out the swell of his flexed muscles beneath his sleeves. His collar hung open at his throat as he leaned over her. She could see inside his shirt to the dark hair that sprinkled the muscles on his chest…

Her breath hitched. Her lips parted. And she felt the precise moment when her fear transformed.

Sarah knew what was happening. This is what the psych training cautioned against. It was a natural reaction, the body trading one primitive emotion for another. The racing pulse, the rapid breathing, the sweating palms…

Fear or lust, the reactions were the same.

She tightened her fists, trying to fight the awareness that was washing over her, but the movement pushed her knuckles into her breasts. Her nipples hardened so swiftly she gasped.

She'd thought she'd understood the effects of hormones. She'd believed that was the main cause of her attraction to Hawk. But she'd never known anything like *this*.

Her mouth was dry. She moistened her lips. She moved her knuckles again and shuddered at the sensation that stabbed through her flesh.

"Sarah?"

She looked at his mouth. She remembered the way he'd used his tongue on her breast to stroke and flick and soothe. She thought of the scrape of his teeth, the caress of cool air as he blew on the moisture he'd left on her skin.

Yes, yes, it would be so easy. He was already so close. If she lifted her face she could bring her lips to his. She could lose herself in the power of his kiss. She would welcome his thrusts, his taste, the sounds he made.

He could give her what she wanted. He still wanted her, didn't he?

She moved her gaze back to his chest. The rhythm of his breathing was getting faster, the pace accelerating like hers. She lowered her gaze farther. He stood bent forward at the waist, his legs braced apart. His knuckles whitened where he gripped the arms of her chair. His long, strong, sensitive fingers were clenched on the upholstery.

She looked at his hips. His shirttail had pulled out of his belt on one side. She remembered the feel of fine wool rubbing against her bare thighs when she'd been so eager for him the first time that she hadn't waited for him to finish undressing....

Yes, oh, yes. She could see him swell. He did still want her. All she had to do was reach out and she would be able to trace the heavy length that pushed against the front of his pants. She took one hand from her breast. The blanket slid from her shoulders to her lap.

"Sarah, did you believe what you told Jibril?"

She began to extend her arm. What had she said? That they meant nothing to each other? "Hawk..."

"You said I was an honorable man."

"You are."

"Then you'll understand why I'm not going to let you touch me."

She stopped, her fingers less than an inch from his zipper. She bit her lip.

"Every fiber of my body wants to accept the invitation I see in your eyes. And you can see for yourself I want you to put your hand exactly where it's heading." His voice was hoarse. He released his grip on the chair and straightened up. "But I know you'd regret this, Sarah. I respect you too much to take advantage of you."

She snatched her hand back. She drew up her feet, wrapping her arms around her ankles, pressing her throbbing nipples to her thighs.

Damn the man, he'd done it again.

How did he know what she really wanted when she wouldn't even admit it to herself?

Oh, he was honorable, all right. She should be grateful for his restraint. She had too much pride for this. She wasn't herself. If they had sex now she would be using him. It would be meaningless, nothing but proximity and adrenaline...

But wasn't that what she'd claimed it had been the last time?

Yet the night they had spent together hadn't been meaningless. It had been special. He had filled needs that were more than merely physical....

If you'd only wanted sex, you would have had it before now.

She waited until her breathing had steadied before she spoke. "I'm sorry I came on to you, Hawk."

"I'm not. I think we needed to clear the air about this, too."

"This? You mean lust? I never denied we had that much between us."

"I'm not going to debate what we call it. Just because I agreed not to push you, that doesn't mean my desire for you has changed. I can't turn it off, no matter how much we tell ourselves we have to concentrate on surviving."

She didn't know what to say. She wanted to apologize again, but she wasn't sure what for this time. She tightened her grip on her legs. Her breasts ached. "I was out of line."

"You were being human. You feel better now, don't you?"

She realized she did. Her fear was once more under control. Too bad she had to stir up all these other feelings to do it. "I'm fine."

"You're an extraordinary woman, Sarah. I hope Jackson realized how fortunate he was to win your love."

"It's getting late. We should both try to get some rest."

He rubbed his face. His words were muffled by his hands. "Right. And you need your distance."

You need your distance, especially from the people you love.

Had he been right about that, too?

She dropped her forehead to her knees. "It was over between us before we got here, Hawk," she said. "We have to be able to think objectively. I thought you understood that. Our lives will depend on it."

He remained where he was for a while. She could feel his gaze. She could feel his tension. Finally he snatched the cushions from the chair beside hers and tossed them toward the door. "I'll sleep there. You can take the bed."

She glanced at the bed. She hadn't considered their sleeping arrangements. She hadn't thought that far ahead.

Hawk walked to the bathroom. He returned carrying more chair cushions. He arranged them in front of the door with the others to fashion a makeshift pallet.

His intentions were plain. He planned to spend the night on the floor. He had placed the cushions across the doorway the same way she used to position her cot to block the door of their hotel room, as if he intended to keep her from harm while he slept. The protective gesture was futile, yet it was very…Hawk.

More feelings stirred. Sarah rose from the chair. She turned out the lights, undressed and got into the bed. "Hawk?"

"What?"

There were too many thoughts whirling in her head. She would have to sort them out later. She settled for the simplest one. "You were right. I would have regretted it. Thank you."

He was silent for a while. "Sarah?"

"Yes?"

"Next time don't expect me to refuse."

Chapter 12

The lines on the screen were beginning to blur. Hawk pinched the bridge of his nose. At his motion, there was the creak of boot leather behind him. He fought to keep his expression impassive, but his frustration was pushing him close to the breaking point.

He had never worked with someone looking over his shoulder before. That had been one of the benefits of being able to fund his own research. He hadn't been pressured to publish his findings or to produce results. He hadn't been answerable to anyone other than his own conscience.

But for the past four days, everything he'd done had been scrutinized by Jibril's guards. At least two of them had positioned themselves behind him to watch each move he made. He didn't believe they understood what they were seeing—there was only a handful of scientists in the world who could. They were merely following orders.

Jibril obviously didn't trust Hawk to do as he said. It

wasn't enough that the bastard was keeping him a prisoner and threatening to mutilate an innocent woman.

Hawk closed his hand into a fist. He pressed it to his forehead, breathing hard through his nose, trying to retain control over his helpless anger. He wouldn't be any good to Sarah if he lost it.

Four days had gone by since Jibril's ultimatum. Only three were left. Then the first week would be up.

He didn't believe that Jibril was bluffing. It would be counterproductive to bluff. If Jibril let the first seven days pass with no penalty, Hawk would have no incentive to complete his work.

Were Redinger and Eagle Squadron on their way yet? Did they even know where to look? If help didn't arrive soon...

He moved his gaze to Sarah. She was seated on a metal chair on the other side of the plain wooden table that held the computer equipment. They were deep inside the hull of the ship—he could hear the throb of the engines through the far bulkhead. The furnishings on this level were utilitarian rather than luxurious. Hawk guessed that this particular room had been designed as a lunch room for the crew before Jibril had converted it to serve as an extension of their prison.

There were no portholes here. The room was bare, apart from the computer equipment, a wooden table that served as a desk and two metal chairs. The computer wasn't any desktop chain-store variety, it was state-of-the-art, with enough speed and memory to be the envy of any research lab. Acquiring it couldn't have been easy—this was probably the cause of the two-day delay before Jibril had revealed his intentions. It couldn't have been cheap, either, but Jibril would regard it as an investment, just like the cost of hiring Weltzer.

In addition to the guards who looked over Hawk's shoulder, two flanked the room's entrance, their weapons at the ready. Another pair waited in the corridor. Two more stood behind Sarah, watching her every move. She sat serenely. Although she kept her arms crossed and her hands tucked protectively beneath her elbows, her face was a mask of calm.

She wouldn't let them see her fear. She didn't like to let Hawk see it, either.

Yet she couldn't hide from him. She might have locked her terror into a compartment behind her sworn duty, but he knew it was always there. He caught glimpses of it at times when her fingers trembled or when her gaze turned inward, as if she were listening to commands only she could hear. The awareness that had started on a Stockholm sidewalk more than a week ago was strengthening with each hour that passed. She chewed her cheek when she was uncertain. She stiffened her back when she was trying to be brave. The gold flecks in her eyes sparked when she was angry and glowed when she was thoughtful.

There were more details, intimate ones, that only a lover should know. Hawk had absorbed every one of them. She brushed her hair before she went to sleep. She liked to tuck in the blanket at the foot of the bed. She started the night curled on her side, yet by dawn she was usually sprawled on her stomach, her fine blond hair spread on the pillow around her head like a halo. In the morning, before she was fully awake, her lips would slowly purse. Her lashes would flutter while her body stretched beneath the blanket. Sometimes she made a sound, part sigh and part groan, as if she wanted to cling to the shelter she found in her dreams.

Each morning he would sit by the door and watch her awaken. And each morning he thought about crossing the room, drawing the covers aside, lying down beside her and pulling her into his arms. Those were the worst times, when the equations he did in his head all night no longer worked and his control was worn thin. That was when he wondered why he was bothering to be noble. What difference would it make whether it was only lust? He and Sarah might never get off this ship alive. Why not relieve at least one source of the tension they were feeling?

Four times, he'd come so close. But then the ship would roll with a wave or heavy footsteps would sound in the corridor and Sarah awoke with her armor already firmly in place.

He hated that armor, but he knew her well enough by now to understand how much a part of her it was. She used it to shield her heart. She seemed to need it more than she needed him. So whatever it took, he would help her get through this, he would keep her safe. Even if that meant safe from him.

Hawk returned his gaze to the computer screen. Three days left. Only three. And he couldn't make sense of the numbers he saw. He swore.

"Dr. Lemay needs a break," Sarah said. "May we have some coffee, please?"

Hawk slammed his fist on the table beside the keyboard. "I don't need a break. I need new software."

Ahmed stepped forward. He was the guard who appeared to be the most fluent in English. He was also the one in command, so he had been the one to relay Hawk's requests to Jibril. "What is the problem?" he asked.

Hawk jerked his head at the screen. "I'm trying to run a modeling sequence, but the software on this unit doesn't have the mathematical capabilities I need."

"What program do you require?"

"It was custom-designed at Stanford for particle physics research. It's installed on the mainframe in my lab there."

"You will have to work with what is here."

"Do you want to explain to the prince why Fedor Yegdenovich develops fusion power for Russia first? He has the program. So does every serious physicist in the world."

Ahmed narrowed his eyes. "You work with what is here," he repeated.

"All I need is to link this computer to the one in my lab. I could download the program in minutes."

"No."

Hawk returned his fingers to the keyboard. "Here's the remote access code for the server and my password. Hook this unit up to your communications system and—"

"No, you are not permitted to establish a link."

"Dammit, you're wasting time. Let me talk to Jibril myself," Hawk said, reaching for the radio that was clipped to Ahmed's belt.

Instantly his elbows were seized and wrenched behind him. From the corner of his eye, he saw two other guards move in on Sarah.

Ahmed kept his gaze on Hawk as he unclipped the radio. He had a brief conversation in Arabic, then jammed the radio to the side of Hawk's head so the receiver was against his ear.

"I had been expecting this, Hawkins."

At the sound of Jibril's high-pitched voice, Hawk's vision filled with red. This was the first time he'd had any contact with the bastard since Jibril had uttered his obscene threat. He looked at Sarah and fought to control his temper. Whatever it took, he reminded himself. "Jibril, I need—"

"It's disappointing. I hadn't expected such a transparent attempt."

"Transparent?"

"What were you planning to do once you established your communication link, Hawkins? Send an e-mail message for help perhaps? Post information about your location on the Internet?"

"For God's sake, this isn't a trick. If you won't let me link to my own computer, then you download the files yourself. Or get the program from someone else." He paused. He took a steadying breath, then spoke through his teeth. "I'm admitting that you've won, Jibril. You always win, just as you won Faith. You've given me no choice but to do what you want. I'm begging you. Let me do it."

Sarah sat cross-legged in the center of the bed, drawing the gold-plated brush through her hair. The ritual usually soothed her, but it didn't tonight. She was worried. Until now, Hawk had been holding up well, but she could see that the strain was getting to him. The outburst this afternoon was uncharacteristic—she knew he usually could exert much more self-control.

He hadn't spoken more than ten words since they had been escorted back to their quarters after Hawk's "work" session. They had gone through the routine of checking for surveillance devices, just as they did each time they left their room, but his movements had been abrupt and edgy.

He'd asked the guards to allow him to jog around the deck after their dinner, but naturally permission had been denied. Ahmed and his men weren't taking any chances. Although no land was visible through the portholes on this side of the ship, Sarah could tell by the change in the air that the *Faith* must be in the Mediterranean by now. Going into the water here wouldn't necessarily be suicidal as it would be in the North Atlantic. That was why the guards were keeping their weapons drawn and their formation tight during the daily walk from this room to the window-less box where Hawk was expected to work. They were barely giving them space to move. They wouldn't allow Hawk the freedom to run.

So instead of jogging to work off his tension, Hawk had stripped down to his boxer shorts and was on the floor, apparently going for the world's record for sit-ups.

Sarah remembered the last time she'd seen him exercise like this. The determination in his eyes was the same as it had been that afternoon in the hotel gym. Was the reason for it the same, too? Was he trying to get his feelings under control?

I'm admitting that you've won, Jibril. You always win, just as you won Faith.

Hawk was so focused on his work—and Sarah was try-ing so hard to stay calm—sometimes she forgot how com-plicated this ordeal must be for him. He'd sounded so...defeated.

She lowered the brush to her lap. She should have seen this coming. She knew Hawk tended to hold himself re-sponsible for their situation, but just how deep did his guilt go? "Hawk, you know what's happening isn't personal, don't you?"

He curled forward, his abs contracting into a perfect six-pack. He replied on the way back down. "You've made that very clear, Sarah. That's why I sleep on the floor."

"I don't mean about us," she said quickly. "I meant the whole situation."

"Better explain that to me."

"Jibril's doing this for the power he hopes to gain, not because of you."

He did two more reps, breathing deliberately with each

one. "I'm the one who's supposed to give him that power."

"Yes, the fusion energy. That's what he wants. This isn't really about your past. If that Russian scientist, Yegdenovich, had been the closest one to making the breakthrough, he would be here now, not you."

"Fedor wouldn't sell out his country."

"You're missing the point. I've seen men like Jibril in action before. He's a petty despot who uses any means available to get what he wants. This isn't about the history you and he share, it's about his greed."

Hawk stopped, draping one arm across his forehead as he lay on his back. He breathed deeply for a minute, staring at the ceiling. "Sometimes I wonder. Maybe I did choose to research fusion energy out of a desire for revenge."

"No. I don't believe that."

"What if I brought this nightmare on us myself because deep in my subconscious I did want to ruin Jibril?"

"He said those things because he was viewing you through his own warped motivations."

"You have to admit, it would have been a subtle way to get even. Cheap, renewable energy would destroy the economy of Moukim."

"Sure, but if you'd wanted revenge, then why would you have gone to the trouble of trying to bargain with Jibril to introduce fusion energy gradually?"

"That wasn't one of my brighter ideas." He turned over, flattened his palms against the floor and started on a series of push-ups.

She watched the muscles bunch across his shoulders. She ached to run her hands over his back to smooth out his tension. She dropped the brush on the pillow behind her, braced her hands on the mattress and leaned forward.

"Hawk, it's not in your nature to be so devious. That's not how you are. You're a good man."

He looked at her sideways, his jaw hard. "I'm not a saint, Sarah. Would you mind sitting up?"

She glanced down at herself. She and Hawk had been given some spare clothes a few days ago, but only the basic necessities. The white T-shirt she used for sleeping had likely been borrowed from a member of the ship's crew. It was far too large for her. The V-neckline was gaping loosely over her bare breasts.

She straightened up and tugged the neckline into place. Sitting cross-legged wasn't such a good idea, either, she thought, bringing her thighs together and shifting her legs to one side.

Hawk moved his gaze back to the floor and continued his push-ups.

Sarah tried to remember what she'd wanted to say. "Did you ever blame Jibril for what happened to Faith?"

He paused with his arms extended, his body poised above the floor. "No. Faith's death was an accident. There was a heavy rainstorm. The roads were slippery and visibility was poor."

"What about for the way she left you? Do you blame him for that?"

He lowered himself slowly, then pushed up again. "No. It was Faith's decision."

"So you had no reason to seek revenge. I don't think you blame Faith, either. Last week Jibril was the one who made a crack about not being able to trust women, but you've never said a word against her."

He sat back on his heels and rubbed his chin. He remained silent.

"I know why you won't criticize her," Sarah said. "Besides being loyal to her because you loved her, you hold yourself responsible for the mistake. You think your judgment was off.''

''It was.'' He looked at her. ''Faith said what we had wasn't real.''

It was too familiar, Sarah thought. In his words she heard an echo of the things they'd said to each other. Had she been right? Did Hawk's determination to hang on to her stem from the way he had lost Faith?

''I see what you're thinking,'' he said. ''Don't.''

''Hawk—''

''I was only twenty-one when I decided to marry Faith. I made a mistake. It wasn't her fault or Jibril's. I accepted that and learned from my experience. I'm not confusing you with her. You're two completely different people.'' He uncoiled from his crouch, straightening to his full height. His boxers slipped down a few inches. He hitched them up to rest at his hipbones. ''I realize now I couldn't have really known Faith. That's why I wanted the chance to know you, Sarah.''

''I'm not that complicated.''

''I disagree, but that's a whole different topic.'' He crossed his arms and leaned back against the door. ''Where's all this coming from, anyway? Why the sudden interest in my past?''

''I'm concerned about you. I see how hard it is for you to sit at the computer each day and pretend to do the work you used to love. This is tangled up with so many important things in your life, I can't imagine how awful that must be.''

''The only important thing in my life right now is keeping you from harm. I'm doing whatever I have to.''

''But you don't have to let Jibril push your buttons.'' She slid across the mattress so that she could swing her feet over the edge. ''The point I was trying to make was that our situation isn't about your past. You don't have to feel responsible for it. All Jibril's talk about competitions and winning was meant to mess with your head. He wants your work. It isn't personal.''

He raised his eyebrows. ''Now I get it. Is this about my tantrum this afternoon?''

''It was more than a tantrum, Hawk. You seemed frantic over your work.''

''I was telling the truth. Without the software I need, I can't make any progress.''

''But you're not supposed to make any progress, remember?''

He pushed away from the door. He did a circuit of the room. ''I know we already discussed this, Sarah. But I'm not sure how much Jibril knows.''

''What do you mean?''

''I needed to keep up the farce. I wanted him to believe I'm cooperating because he's beaten me.''

''You were very convincing.''

''I had to be. I'm sorry if I caused you concern.''

She turned her head to keep him in sight as he paced the floor. ''When I saw you grab for Ahmed's radio, I was afraid the stress had gotten too much for you. From what I heard him tell Jibril before he let you speak, he thought you had cracked, too.''

He walked to the bed and stopped in front of her. ''Close, but not yet.''

Sarah caught a whiff of soap and warm man. Hawk's skin was damp from his exercise. It gleamed beneath its dusting of dark hair. The veins on his arms were swollen, throbbing against his hardened muscles. He'd been allowed the use of a razor to shave that morning, but the beginning of his beard was already shadowing his jaw.

She thought about the first time she'd kissed him. He'd been hot and damp from a workout then, too.

She pressed her lips together, yet again trying to remember what she wanted to say. "Okay. That's good. So far you've done a great job stalling for time, but I realize it must be wearing on your nerves."

He returned the perusal she had just given him. "There are a lot of things wearing on my nerves, Sarah."

She wanted to ask him to put on more clothes. How the hell was she supposed to keep her train of thought when he was strutting around in nothing but his boxers?

He exhaled hard. The mattress dipped as he sat on the bed beside her. "All I care about is your safety. I'll do whatever it takes to get you out of danger."

"Is that why you demanded that software?"

"Yes."

She could feel the heat of his bare thigh only inches away from her knee. She struggled to keep her mind on what he was saying. "You didn't really believe you could trick Jibril into letting you link to the Internet, did you?"

"No. He might be criminally insane but he's not stupid. He wouldn't give me the opportunity to send a message. I'm hoping my performance was convincing enough for him to send the message himself."

"I don't understand."

"I know how important winning is to Jibril. I mentioned Faith to him because I was pushing his buttons, not the other way around. I wanted him to take the bait."

"What bait?"

"The software I mentioned is very specific to the mathematical modeling needed for fusion research. Only someone with years of study in the field of particle physics would have any use for it. The instant Jibril tries to obtain the program, whether he does it through the computer in my lab or from the techs who developed it, he's going to signal my whereabouts to anyone who might be looking.''

For a moment Sarah couldn't breathe. After so many days of simply enduring the wait and preparing herself for whatever horror might come, the spurt of hope took her by surprise. She grabbed his knee. ''Oh, Hawk. You sent up a flare.''

''Yes.'' He looked at her hand. His thigh hardened. He moved his gaze to her mouth. ''You're smiling.''

Was she? Yes, she could feel the pressure in her cheeks. It had been so long since she'd had anything to smile about, she couldn't remember the last time…

Oh, she remembered it now. It had been after the last time she and Hawk had made love. She'd been feeling smug and sated and they'd joked about doing it again….

Her smile wavered. The way she felt now couldn't compare to the afterglow of sex, but compared to the past few days, it was wonderful. ''That was brilliant, Hawk.''

''Jibril will have raised some flags when he had his people download my research and when he acquired the computer equipment. Whether Weltzer was traced to him or not, he must already be a suspect in my disappearance. This should help to pinpoint my location, as long as someone knows enough to follow the trail.''

''They will,'' she said. ''You'd be surprised what my colleagues in Intelligence can do when they want to track someone down. Even if Redinger believed I had taken the full five-day leave he'd offered, six have gone by now since I spoke with him, so someone would definitely be looking for us.''

''What leave?''

''It's not important.'' Sarah got to her knees on the mattress and clasped his shoulders. She grinned and gave him a shake. ''This won't only show the team where we are, it will give them the grounds they need to raid this ship. Hawk, you're a genius.''

He smiled. "Technically, yes, I am.''

It was his smile that did it. One of his dimples folded right through the fading bruise on his cheek. Laugh lines crinkled into the weariness around his eyes. Sarah leaned forward and planted a quick kiss on his mouth. "Okay, since there's a chance the team is on its way, we'd better get busy,'' she said. "Our first priority is finding a way to signal our exact location within the vessel. It has to be simple. We could put a lamp in front of a porthole—''

Hawk clamped one hand over the back of her neck.

"Do you have a better idea?'' she asked.

He held her in place and returned the kiss. It wasn't quick like the one she had given him. It was slow and thorough, wrapping around her senses like a lazy sunrise, as if they had all the time in the world.

Sarah shuddered. But they didn't have time. She shouldn't do this. They had to make a plan. They had to find a way to aid in their escape and—

He tilted his head, his nose rubbing hers as he ran his tongue over the seam of her lips. He coaxed her gently and slipped inside.

Sarah's hands clenched on his shoulders, then slid downward over his arms. She fitted her palms over his biceps, feeling the throb of his pulse in his veins and the slick heat of his skin. Her knees nudged his thigh. She opened her mouth to him, drawing in his taste. For long, stolen minutes she took the sweet pleasure he gave her.

It was just a kiss, only a kiss. She didn't invite more, and Hawk didn't push. He didn't move his hand from her nape; he didn't press her down on the bed. Beneath her fingers she could feel the muscles of his arms tremble with his effort at control, yet the moment she started to ease away, he lifted his head.

He rubbed his thumb over her lower lip and carried the moisture to his mouth. He closed his eyes, his chest heaving. "I'll set up the lamp."

Sarah swallowed against a sudden lump in her throat. He was picking up the conversation where they had left off. She knew how much he wanted her, but he was doing what she'd asked.

She would rather forget her duty and kiss him again.

Oh, it would be so easy to fall in love with a man like Hawk...

She rolled off the bed. Hazel. Jackson's eyes were hazel. His smile was...boyish. Yes, that was it. He had dimples beside his mouth.

No, it was Hawk who had dimples.

She blinked hard. Jackson was the perfect soldier, everything a man should be. He was honorable, loyal and courageous and it had taken four men to haul him down....

No, that had been Hawk, too.

Jackson understood her. He respected her opinions and listened to more than her words, so he knew when to hold her and when to let her go....

Damn, even that was Hawk.

Why was she fighting this so hard? She worked in Intelligence. She wasn't an idiot. She was skilled at gathering information and putting together the pieces of a puzzle.

Of course, what she felt for Hawk was more than lust or a crush or an infatuation. That was obvious by now.

So why was she so desperate to deny the feelings that were growing in her heart? Why was she trying to convince herself that Hawk wasn't the right man?

The answer was simple. Because when she was with him, she turned into the wrong woman.

Chapter 13

It took one more day for Jibril to take the bait, but the special program Hawk had requested was on the computer by the morning of the sixth day. Hawk didn't try to hide his relief when he discovered it—the reaction would be expected. He set to work immediately, doing nothing to tip off the guards to his strategy.

It was Sarah's own reaction that worried her. She was having a hard time maintaining her game face. Although for the remainder of the day she sat in her designated chair across the table from Hawk, just as she had for the past five days, she kept catching herself leaning toward him.

In a way, the hope was more painful than the waiting. It was tempting her to look beyond the next minute, the next hour, the first deadline. What if they really did escape? What then?

As Hawk had once said, even soldiers went home eventually.

The apartment Sarah rented in Fayetteville near the base

was a lovely place. It took up the entire second floor of a
stately Victorian three-story. It came complete with a
rounded turret room and a beautiful view of her landlady's
rose garden. Sarah hadn't spent much effort decorating the
apartment, since she wasn't often there, and she had no
house plants or pets for the same reason. Still, it was comfortable.

She and Jackson would have had a house of their own
once they were married. She didn't know whether they
would have had a garden or pets, though. They'd never
discussed it. With the demands of their separate careers,
they wouldn't have been there often, either. Was that why
she'd never pictured going home to him?

She had awakened to the sight of Hawk every day for
more than a week now. She was so accustomed to him she
could feel his presence. His scent flavored the air she
breathed. His voice strummed her senses. She could picture him in the turret room at night with the starlight
streaking his hair silver. She could imagine him among her
landlady's roses in the morning, his long fingers stroking
the dewdrops from the petals. She could even imagine the
glint in his eyes as he pilfered a flower to lay on her pillow.

What would have happened if she'd admitted to Jackson
that she really did like flowers? Would he have brought
her some, even though they weren't practical?

Had the general given her mother flowers? She couldn't
remember seeing any in the house, so he probably hadn't.
He and Jackson were a lot alike. That's why they had
gotten along so well—Jackson had been like the son he'd
always wanted. The general had been bursting with pride
when she and Jackson had announced their engagement.
He'd kissed her on the cheek and had said, "Well done,
soldier."

The memory used to make her smile. It didn't now. It

was almost as if she'd said yes to Jackson just to please her father. There had to have been more to it than that. She'd loved Jackson deeply. He'd been a good man. He'd made her happy.

But had he ever challenged her? Had he pushed her to be honest? Had he seen beyond the surface to the woman who was trying so hard to be someone he could love?

Maybe Jackson had never really known her. That wasn't his fault. She had kept him at a distance. She'd shown him only the woman everyone expected her to be. When had that started? On their first date? When they had met? She suspected the pattern of her life had begun long before that.

What if she'd told her father that sometimes she'd wanted to cry instead of saluting? The idea had never entered her head—after her mother's death, Sarah had been so terrified of losing another parent, she had thought only of molding herself into someone her father could love. He was an officer, a prominent general, so his attention was always focused on the soldiers under his command. The only time she earned his attention or his praise was when she acted just like his men. Tough. Strong. In charge.

Still, she thrived on her career in Delta Force and couldn't imagine doing anything else. It wasn't an act— she *was* tough, strong and in charge when she had to be. She enjoyed the excitement of each new mission and the satisfaction of stretching her mental and physical abilities to the limit. What had begun as a way to win approval had become the best part of her life. She had no regrets about that.

Yet while Hawk respected her dedication to her career, he had always seen that there was more to her than what she could do. He'd seen *her*. With Hawk, she didn't need to prove anything.

It made her wonder. If she'd given her father a chance, if she hadn't tried so hard, if she hadn't allowed the emotional distance between them to grow, would he have loved her anyway?

And what about Jackson? Why couldn't she think of him as Kyle? How different would their relationship have been if she had insisted that he look her in the eye when he said goodbye?

"Son of a…"

At Hawk's low murmur, Sarah brought her thoughts back to the present. He wasn't looking at her; he was staring at the computer monitor. She didn't think it was a ploy the way it had been before. His face was drained of color, as if he'd just been punched. He moved his head from side to side, his gaze never leaving the screen.

The guards behind him took a step closer. At the sound of their footsteps, Hawk pressed his lips together and hunched over the keyboard. He typed rapidly for a few minutes, his fingers a blur on the keys. Then he leaned back in his chair and looked at Sarah.

He had regained control of his expression, but he couldn't hide the hardness in his gaze.

She felt her blood begin to pound. What was it? Had he seen something? A message in the new program? It was possible Redinger and the team had been one step ahead of them. Could they have slipped a coded signal into the software that Jibril had had downloaded?

Whatever Hawk had seen, it didn't appear to be good.

She glanced at the guards behind Hawk. They didn't seem any more or any less attentive than usual. If they had noticed anything on the screen, they hadn't understood it.

As always, she and Hawk didn't speak until they had checked their quarters at the end of the day. But this time, Hawk wasn't satisfied with one sweep. He went over the rooms twice. He was so meticulous Sarah wanted to scream with impatience. When he started on the third sweep, she grabbed his hand, led him to the bathroom and opened the faucets on the bathtub.

She sat on the edge of the marble tub and gestured behind her. "Even if we missed something, the sound of the running water will mask our conversation."

He nodded. "All right. Thanks."

"What happened? What did you find?"

He dragged one of the armchairs next to the tub. He sat on the arm and put his head close to hers. "I found a mistake."

"In the new program?"

"No. The fault isn't in the program I requested, it's in the data. I had been staring at it all week but hadn't realized what I was seeing. It's the reason why the numbers weren't making sense."

"I don't understand. I thought you got a message."

"Message? How?"

"In the software. I thought—" She waved her hand. "Never mind. What are you talking about?"

"I had assumed all the matrix elements of the short-range pairing interactions were equal. I used that approximation so I could integrate the equations—"

"Hawk, nuclear physics isn't one of the languages I'm fluent in."

"Sorry. I'm still trying to grasp it myself. I'll never know why I didn't see it before. Maybe the stress of this situation is forcing me to look at everything from a different viewpoint." He sat back and raked his fingers through his hair, then rested his clasped hands between his knees. Water continued to rush from the faucet, sending wisps of steam into the air. "It was an intuitive leap. I had a change in perspective."

"And?"

"What it boils down to is there's an error in one of the premises of my work."

"Okay. There's a problem in your research data, is that what you're saying?"

"Not exactly. It's a flaw in my reasoning. An incorrect assumption. Everything that followed it led to a dead end."

It was the strain in his voice more than his words that she understood. She laid her palm over his clasped hands. "Go on."

"The files I uploaded to the Internet last week contain this flaw. Unless someone knows where to look and recognizes it, the information will lead nowhere."

Her grip on his hands tightened. "Oh, no. Are you sure?"

"I spent the whole day running modeling sequences to verify my new hypothesis. I'm sure."

"I'm sorry, Hawk. I understand how important your work is. This must be a horrible blow."

"It's not the research that concerns me, it's our lives."

She drew in her breath as the import of his words finally registered. "If the research you made public is flawed, then this race to be the first to achieve fusion power—"

"The race is a figment of Jibril's paranoid imagination. No one who downloaded my work is any closer to a breakthrough than they were a week ago because my research will send them in the wrong direction."

"Oh, God." She glanced around the room. "Now I understand why you wanted to be certain we weren't overheard. If Jibril learns about this, then he'll have no more reason to keep either of us alive. He'll know that fusion power is impossible."

"It's not impossible, Sarah."

"What? But you said your research was no good."

"I said I found the flaw." He paused. "I also found the solution."

"The solution?"

"It's what was stopping my progress. Once I saw where the problem was, I modified the incorrect assumption, and the rest of the reasoning cascaded into place. My work wasn't worthless, it just needed to be approached from a different direction."

"Are you saying…" She had to shake her head. "I must have misunderstood. It sounds as if you made a breakthrough."

"You could call it that. I would still need to run tests on a particle accelerator to prove my theory would work in practice, but it all fits. I can feel it. It's the key I've been looking for for years."

"Oh, Hawk! That's incredible. That's—" She stopped. The water that splashed into the tub behind her began to gurgle in the drain, echoing the sudden emptiness she felt.

Hawk should have been celebrating. This was the moment he'd worked toward his entire career. His dream of fusion power could become a reality.

Instead, it was only deepening the nightmare.

This was why he'd looked so bleak this afternoon. It wasn't because he'd found a mistake, it was because he'd found the solution.

He knew as well as she did what this meant.

She clamped her hands over the edge of the bathtub. Despite the steam that warmed the air, the marble was like ice beneath her fingers. It wasn't fair. Why now? "Did you erase your work?"

"Not yet. I encrypted it."

"Hawk, you have to destroy it completely."

He didn't respond.

She brought her face to his and lowered her voice. "You

can't let Jibril get possession of it. Giving him the discovery will only advance our execution."

"He won't kill us until I can prove the theory works. Giving it to him now could buy you more time."

She pushed her fingertips under her thighs. Time. Yes. There was only one day left before Jibril began to carry out her sentence. For a cowardly instant she wanted to give in… "No," she said. "We had agreed on this. You were only supposed to stall."

"I wasn't deliberately looking for the answer. It just happened. I can use it to bargain."

"Do you really believe a man like Jibril would keep his word?"

He rubbed his face, then stood and walked across the room. He paced restlessly between the sinks and the doorway, his strides stiff, his body rigid.

"You can't let the bastard have this power," Sarah said. "You heard how he plans to use it."

He stopped in front of her. "I would gladly give my life if I thought it would save yours."

She felt a shiver of foreboding at the calm certainty in his tone. "Don't say that."

"You were willing to do the same for me."

"That was different. It was a controlled risk. It was my job."

"And it was my work that put you at risk. I was a fool. I once thought achieving my ambition was all that mattered, but when I saw those equations fall into place on the screen today, I wasn't thinking about the benefits fusion energy could bring to the world. I was sorry I'd ever started it."

"You'll be able to duplicate it when we get out of here, won't you?"

"I don't know. The equations are complex, so there's no guarantee I'll remember every factor."

"Hawk, I'm sorry."

"It doesn't matter to me anymore. You do." He pried loose her grip from the tub and pulled her to her feet. He brought her hands to his lips. He kissed her fingers, lingering over each one in turn. He kissed her palms and the heels of her hands. "Jibril's men won't hurt you. I swear." He pressed her hands to his chest. "Not one precious part of you."

She spread her fingers, focusing on the sight of Hawk's large hands enclosing hers. The horror she felt at the prospect of being maimed was always there, lurking beneath the surface, waiting to snare her. One more day. There might be less time than that if Jibril decided he'd be better off executing them immediately.

A tremor shook her arm.

"Sarah, you have to think positive."

"Right. We'll be rescued."

He moved her hands over his heart. "Yes."

"Even though the *Faith* is a floating fortress," she said. "And Ahmed and his men aren't going to roll over."

"Your team must have faced worse odds than that."

"Right. They have. And Eagle Squadron always takes care of its own." She inhaled shakily. "But this is the last time I believe the Major when he calls a mission easy."

"Sarah, I don't have the words to express how sorry I am for involving you in this. If I could have foreseen at the start where it would all lead…" His mouth moved into the ghost of a smile. "No, I can't honestly say I would have sent you away. There has never seemed to be anything logical about my feelings for you."

Or mine for you, she thought.

If this had been last week, Sarah would have found an

excuse to pull away by now. He was getting too close. She was feeling too exposed.

But he wasn't the only one seeing things from a new perspective. Was this what he meant by an intuitive leap? She eased her hands from his. Instead of leaving, she framed his face between her palms. "Hawk, I know we should be reassessing our options and coming up with a contingency plan in the light of what you learned to-day..."

"But?"

"But what would you do if I told you that I was afraid?"

A muscle in his jaw twitched against her thumb. Other than that he kept himself completely motionless. "If you told me you were afraid, I would ask you if you would let me hold you."

"Would you think I was weak?"

His gaze moved over her face. "Never, Sarah. I would feel honored by your trust."

She touched her index fingers to the laugh lines beside his eyes. "And if we were standing on a street corner and I said it wasn't only the cold wind that was making my eyes water..."

"I would do my best to keep you warm." He stroked her hair. "And I would admire you for your strength to stand up to whatever storm was causing your tears."

"But would you expect me to be strong?"

"I only expect you to be Sarah."

The reply was so typical of Hawk's insight, she caught her breath on a sob. "Hawk," she whispered. "I can't do this alone anymore. I am scared."

He didn't ask. He reached behind her to shut off the bathtub faucets, then slipped one hand behind her back, the other beneath her knees and lifted her into his arms.

Sarah felt something crumble inside her. There was a moment of panic—the habits of a lifetime were hard to break—but then Hawk brushed his lips against her forehead and Sarah felt the first of her tears carve a path down her cheek.

Hawk swept it away with the tip of his tongue. His tenderness didn't make her feel weak, it made her feel… cherished. The heat and strength of his body surrounded her. His embrace was more comforting than sexual, yet it was more intimate than anything she'd experienced before. She didn't want distance. This was what real closeness was about. She looped her arms around his neck as she dried her cheek on his shoulder.

He carried her to the bedroom and over to the portholes. Two tables were stacked on top of each other beneath one. A lamp burned on top of them, its bulb positioned against the glass. The sight of their meager attempt at a signal made Sarah shiver, but Hawk pulled her more tightly to his chest. "Look out there, Sarah," he said, stopping in front of a different porthole. He braced his feet apart, holding her gently while his body swayed to counteract the movement of the ship. "It's a world of infinite possibilities. We have to believe we're going to make it out of here somehow."

She looked at the darkness, but all she could see was their reflection.

Another piece of her armor crumbled. The sight of Hawk's face aligned with hers, his gaze strong and steady as he focused on the unknown, seemed completely…right.

Sarah wasn't sure when she realized for certain that she loved him. The knowledge had been there for some time, but she hadn't wanted to admit what she was seeing. She wasn't deliberately looking for the answer. Sometime between one heartbeat and the next, it simply happened.

Why now? she thought. They might not live past to-morrow. It was a cruel twist of timing, like the break-through in Hawk's research. This should have been a cause for celebration, too. Instead, she was achingly conscious of how fragile—and how fleeting—it all could be.

She would never be able to go back in time and call Jackson "Kyle." She might not have the chance to plant a garden of her own or bring a bouquet of fresh roses into her own house. At least she could spend her remaining time with Hawk without regrets, couldn't she?

She slid out of his embrace to stand in front of him and locked her hands behind his waist. "Hawk, whatever happens tomorrow, I want you to know I don't blame you."

He kissed her forehead.

"You're a good man. If life was fair…"

His breath tickled her temple. "If life was fair, we'd still be in my hotel room in Stockholm, living off room service and telling the world to go to hell."

Her eyes misted again. Could it have been as easy as he made it sound?

"What's the first thing you're going to do when you get home, Sarah?"

That depends on how much of me is left, she thought. She pushed the thought away. He was trying to think pos-itive, so she would, too. There were changes she wanted to make. Where could she start? "I'm going to get a cat."

"A cat? Why?"

"When the general and I lived in Germany, we had a gray tabby cat who came with the house. We left him behind when we moved, but I always wanted another one. I never told him that. When I get home, I'm going to go down to the animal shelter and adopt one."

"That sounds like a good idea." He eased his fingers through her hair. "What else?"

"Remember that blue dress I wore to the reception?"

"How could I forget?"

"I didn't buy that only because I needed it for the re-connaissance mission. I bought it because it was gorgeous. As shallow as that is, I liked the way it made me feel, and I liked the way it made your eyes darken when you looked at me. It's the same as my lace underwear. I'm going to buy more clothes like that when I get home."

"I look forward to seeing you wear them."

She had an image of herself in the blue dress. But it had an empty sleeve. She splayed her hands on Hawk's back and spoke quickly. "What kind of music do you like, Hawk?"

"Beethoven or Schubert when I'm working. The Stones when I'm driving. What about you?"

"I like Harry Connick, Jr. And Diana Krall. I always wanted to learn to play the piano when I was a kid. I never told my father that, either. When I get home…" Her fingers clenched. There might not be any point taking piano lessons. So much wasted time. So many regrets. Was she going to add another one to the list? She turned her face to Hawk's chest.

Should she tell him she loved him? He was already dealing with enough grief. He was trying so hard to protect her. What would it do to him if she lost a hand tomorrow? He would be devastated. He'd hold himself responsible. He might even pity her…. No, she wouldn't do that to him. "Did you know I lied to you?"

"What? When?"

"That afternoon on the bridge. Before we were taken. I said the sex wasn't that good."

He drew back his head to look at her. His eyes gleamed.

Had she thought the embrace wasn't sexual? Oh, yes, the awareness was always there. It took only one glance for it to surface. She felt her body soften. "The sex was more than good," she said. "It was awesome."

His lips curved into a slow and lusciously sexy smile. He grasped her waist, his thumbs stroking along her midriff to the underside of her breasts. "Awesome. I like that."

She lowered her hands to his buttocks and squeezed gently. "I liked it, too."

"With everything else that's happened, I never got the chance to tell you…"

"Tell me what, Hawk?"

He paused. His thumbs whispered higher. "How much I needed you that night."

Even through her clothes, his touch made her sway. "I think I knew. That's why I stayed."

He pressed his knee to her thighs. "Was that the only reason?"

"No." She eased her feet apart and leaned closer, feeling his thigh ride up between her legs. "Hawk, I need you tonight. Let's make love again."

"Sarah—"

"You said you wouldn't refuse." She moved her hands to his chest and undid the top button of his shirt. She stretched up to lick the hollow at the base of his throat. "It's not like the last time. I'm scared, but I know what I'm doing. I'm not going to regret this."

"Are you sure?"

She stepped back, pulled off her sweater and dropped it to the floor. Looking him straight in the eye, she peeled off the rest of her clothes and smiled. "What do you think?"

For a breathless instant, Hawk didn't move. He stood and stared, his body trembling. Then he reached out and cupped her breasts in his hands. "Sarah, I don't really want to think anymore."

She finished unbuttoning his shirt and tugged it out of his pants. "Good. I don't really want to talk anymore, either."

He ended their conversation the same way he'd ended one once before. He leaned forward and sucked her nipple into his mouth.

Sarah fisted her hands in his shirt as a bolt of pure delight shot through her. She arched more firmly into his kiss, yanking his shirt over his shoulders. It caught at his elbows so she left it there and opened the front of his pants. He shuddered as she ran her nails down his hardness. When she closed her fingers around him, he squeezed her breasts and closed his teeth around her.

Moist heat rushed between her legs. For lost, blissful minutes she took what he gave her and returned all she could until her knees no longer held her. She hooked her foot behind his calf and grabbed his shoulder in her free hand, lifting herself up to him.

Hawk caught her by the waist, pressed her back to the wall between the portholes and pushed himself inside her.

It was like the first time, and yet it was different. The urgency was the same. Sarah clasped his hips with her thighs and rode his thrusts, her body rippling around him in wave after shimmering wave. Yet the pleasure came from a source deeper than the friction of their joined bodies.

Hawk kicked free of his pants and carried her to the bed. He came down on top of her, slick and still hard between her thighs. They slid together again, finding the angle, falling into the rhythm as easily as old lovers, their kisses flavored with need and yearning. The world contracted, leaving no room for fear or the unknown of to-morrow.

They had talked about going home. Sarah realized that in her heart she already was.

She wrapped her arms around Hawk's back and felt the tremors of his release send her soaring through her own.

There was a muffled clang. The bed shook. It wasn't from anything they were doing.

Hawk lifted his head. He looked around.

It took Sarah a critical second to switch gears. She lay on her back, trying to catch her breath. The clang, the vibrations, it was like…a concussion grenade. She grasped Hawk's shoulders and looked past him toward the door. She strained to listen over the pounding of her pulse….

No, it wasn't her pulse.

It was gunfire.

Oh, God. Was it possible? Could it really be happening?

Hawk sat up, pulling her with him. ''Sarah, do you hear it?''

She listened to the gunfire. Jibril's men carried Kalash-nikovs, but those shots sounded like they had come from an M4 assault rifle, one of the weapons used by…

She got to her knees and grabbed his hand. ''Hawk, they're here! Eagle Squadron's here!''

Chapter 14

Sarah jumped off the bed. Her senses expanded to the hyperawareness of battle. Time didn't slow, it screamed past. She had to absorb it all at once.

The gunfire came from overhead and was drawing closer. The team must have arrived by air. A parachute drop? Quick descent from a helicopter? There was another bang, this one from the direction of the corridor. More shots, close enough for her to distinguish the whine of ricocheting bullets.

She struggled to assess the clues in the sounds, but her expanded senses also caught Hawk's scent, and the warm imprint of his chest that lingered on her breasts....

Her pulse raced. She couldn't fight it. She didn't even try. She knew she couldn't push her feelings aside and be objective. This was as personal as it got.

Yet she didn't feel as if her emotions were blocking her abilities; they were enhancing them. The team was here. Suddenly there was a chance for Hawk and for her and for the love she'd just discovered. She wanted that chance so badly she was shaking.

She yanked on her clothes, then ran to put her ear to the door.

Hawk got dressed and came up behind her. He didn't touch her—he knew she liked room to move—yet she felt his presence as vividly as she heard the crack of the high-caliber weapon on the other side of the door. A voice called out orders in Arabic. Sarah caught Hawk's hand and pulled him to the floor. "We'd better stay low," she said, flattening herself out. "I know these walls are thick, but the high-caliber rounds might pierce—"

Hawk slid on top of her back, the same way he had the last time they'd been under fire.

She didn't protest. She knew it was no use. If she had the weight and strength to get her way, she'd be doing the same thing for him.

The gunfire was getting closer. The very fact that she could hear gunfire meant the rescue wasn't going to be neat. On most missions, the teams from Eagle Squadron were good enough to get in and get out before anyone knew they had arrived. They preferred to use stealth rather than firepower. When they did engage the enemy, it was usually a short fight. This was already going on longer than it should have.

She moved her arm along the floor until she could reach Hawk's hand. He kissed her ear and laced his fingers with hers.

It was so close it was painful. After so many days of barely daring to hope, it was torture to know her friends might be only a few yards away. Had they realized Jibril had manned the ship with Moukim palace guards? Gathering intelligence for a mission was usually her job. She could only pray someone else had cared enough to do it right.

And what were the defenses Jibril had boasted about? He'd mentioned bullet-proof glass, a triple hull and a superstructure built to tank specs. What other surprises did the *Faith* hold?

There was a sudden, vicious exchange of fire from the far end of the corridor, followed by a sharp pop. There was an ominous lull.

She thought about the tactics the team might use to neutralize resistance in a small space. When firepower didn't work, they would lob in a canister of...

"Gas." Sarah drew in her breath. She tasted a faint, sour tang. "Hawk, they're using gas!"

Before she could give him instructions, Hawk had pushed himself off her and was sprinting to the bathroom. She followed and grabbed towels as he soaked them down. They stuffed the wet towels across the crack under the door while they held two more to their faces.

"The gas isn't toxic," she said. "It would just knock us out, but we'd be more help if we could walk on our own when they get here."

He looked at her over the towel he held to his nose. "Is there anything else we can do?"

"No."

"So we wait?"

"For now. We'll give them five minutes. The gas loses its potency fast. If they don't clear the corridor by then..."

Hawk pressed his head to hers and waited. The faint background drone of the *Faith's* engines cut off. The ship began to roll with the swells.

Something heavy hit the door. There was a burst of gunfire directly outside. Hawk yanked Sarah to the floor and spread-eagled himself over her back once more.

Another thud. A muffled voice called out. This time, the words were in English. "Captain Fox?"

It was crazy to feel tears. Sarah had been on enough missions to know this didn't mean they were home free yet, but the moment she heard the familiar voice, a sob of relief clogged her throat. She couldn't say a word. It was her friend Rafe Marek.

Hawk lifted his head. "In here."

"We're going to blow the lock in five," Rafe called.

Sarah and Hawk dove for cover behind the bed. Five seconds later there was a flashing pop. The door swung inward through a cloud of smoke.

Two tall commandos in full battle gear materialized through the smoke. Their faces were covered with gas masks. Grenades hung from their belts. Each man had a knife strapped to his calf, a sidearm at his thigh and an assault rifle in his hands. They were a pair of walking arsenals, but Sarah knew they didn't need the help of weapons to make them deadly.

There was a sharp whistle from the corridor. At the signal, the larger man pulled his gas mask aside and let it dangle from his helmet. A grim, twisting network of scars gouged the entire right side of his face. He moved forward, his vibrant blue gaze fierce with concern. "Captain, are you all right?"

She wiped her eyes and got to her knees. "No problem, Rafe. We're both fine."

Rafe held out his hand, but Hawk was already back on his feet, helping Sarah up. Sarah leaned into Hawk for a moment, waiting for her pulse to steady. She smoothed his hair, her fingers trembling. She was aching to kiss him, but she had a feeling that once she started, she wouldn't be able to stop.

Hawk understood. Of course he would understand. She

was back on duty now. He rested his hands at her waist and gave her a smile.

Oh, how she loved this man.

Rafe activated the transmitter that was attached to the radio gear on his helmet. "We've got them both, Major. They're unharmed."

The second commando unfastened his mask. Sarah wasn't surprised to see it was Flynn O'Toole—if Rafe was around, Flynn wouldn't be far away. The two men were as different in appearance as they were in temperament, but they had watched each other's backs on every mission Sarah could remember.

A crooked grin lit up Flynn's startlingly handsome face. "Evenin', Captain Fox." He tipped his head toward the lamp in front of the porthole. "Your buddies back at the Funny Platoon are going to bust a gut when I tell them about that beacon."

She hiccuped on a laugh. Leave it to Flynn to come up with some irreverent comment. "It worked, didn't it?"

"Yes, ma'am. It showed us which door to choose." He drew his pistol and offered it to her. "But it was a good thing you left a cyberspace bread crumb trail for us to follow here."

She pulled away from Hawk in order to take the gun from Flynn. She ejected the magazine to check how many rounds were left, then shoved it back into place with the heel of her hand. "The cyberspace trail was Dr. Lemay's idea," she said

"Right." Flynn's smile disappeared as he turned his gaze on Hawk. "The Major told us about you, Lemay. We need to have a talk on the ride home."

"Yeah," Rafe said. "Count on it."

Hawk put his hand on Sarah's shoulder. He was almost the same height as the other men. He met their stares over her head, his expression as sober as theirs. "I look forward to it, gentlemen."

Despite the scattered gunfire she could still hear overhead, Sarah had a sudden urge to laugh. She knew what Rafe and Flynn were doing. They were giving notice they planned to interrogate Hawk because of what Redinger must have told them, and she would bet they wouldn't be as subtle about it as the Major had been.

But then, she hadn't been too subtle about checking out Glenna and Abbie when she'd seen how Rafe and Flynn had felt about them.

Eagle Squadron took care of its own in more ways than one.

"What's between Hawk and myself is our business, Flynn," she said. She squeezed Hawk's hand as she turned to Rafe. "The testosterone fest will have to wait. What's our current situation, Sergeant Marek?"

Rafe glanced briefly at the way she was touching Hawk, then dug into a pocket on his thigh. He came up with a magazine that would fit Flynn's pistol and tossed it to Sarah.

She realized it was no accident that she had to release Hawk's hand in order to catch it.

"Norton and Lang are covering the exit to the deck," Rafe said. "The Major and Gonzales have the main force of Jibril's men pinned down on the bridge. The servants and ship's crew are contained in the galley."

She slipped the extra ammunition into her pants pocket. "What's our escape plan?"

"We've got a chopper holding a mile to port," Flynn said, his tone all business. "It'll come in on our signal. Chief Esposito rigged charges to blow the helicopter pad on the aft deck to cover our retreat."

"Time frame?"

"Eight minutes."

"We need to get below first." She glanced at Hawk. "There's a computer we have to destroy."

He nodded once to indicate he understood. They couldn't risk leaving his work for Jibril's people to find, whether it was encrypted or not.

"The chief can do it," Rafe said. "Give me the location and I'll relay the info."

Sarah quickly described the location of the computer equipment Hawk had used. Rafe repeated the information into his microphone to Esposito and started for the door. "He's on his way. Let's move out."

"What about Jibril?" Hawk asked.

"The prince is holed up on the bridge with his men," Flynn replied, putting a fresh magazine in his rifle as he moved after Rafe. "Shouldn't give us any problem."

"You're not just going to leave him here, are you?" Hawk asked.

"This is strictly a rescue mission," Rafe said. "He's the crown prince of Moukim. We can't touch him." He checked the corridor, then stepped outside with a fluid, twisting movement, his gun directed toward the staircase to the deck. Several guards lay motionless on the floor, their ankles bound and their wrists fastened together behind their backs with plastic bundling ties.

Flynn followed Rafe into the corridor, his weapon pointed in the opposite direction. He gestured for Hawk and Sarah to join him. "Prince Jibril covered his tracks too well, Lemay. Apart from your testimony, there would be no smoking gun so we don't have the authority to take him."

"He was going to cut off Sarah's hands," Hawk said.

Rafe and Flynn stopped where they were. They both looked at Sarah.

She scowled, clasping her borrowed pistol more firmly. "It's the penalty under Moukim law for the way I assaulted him at the conference last week. Let it go. It's got nothing to do with the mission."

Rafe turned to Hawk. "Give me a summary."

"It was going to start tomorrow. One body part a week until I gave him fusion power."

Rafe activated his transmitter again. He repeated what Sarah and Hawk had told him. His voice roughened. "Major? Requesting permission to kill the son of a bitch."

Hawk and Flynn ran across the deck toward the stern of the *Faith* behind Rafe and Sarah. The air was filled with the sound of waves slapping against the hull and the staccato pops of gunfire from the men who were covering their retreat. On their left was the bulky silhouette of Jibril's helicopter where it was tied down on its pad. The helicopter platform was elevated, extending partially over the stern so it provided cover on one side. Rafe led them around a lifeboat that hung from a davit beside the port railing and dropped into a crouch behind it. Sarah fell to one knee and steadied her gun on the other knee, her attention on the deck behind them.

"Four minutes," Flynn said, crouching behind Hawk. "The chopper's on its way. It'll be hugging the wave tops behind the stern. When it comes up over the railing, dive inside and roll to the right to grab for the next man. There won't be much time."

"Sarah goes first," Hawk said over his shoulder.

"We wouldn't do it any other way."

Hawk heard the resolve in Flynn's voice and knew he could count on him. These men were every bit as protective of Sarah as the Major had claimed.

Redinger had denied the team permission to go after

Jibril. He'd agreed with Sarah. Their objective wasn't to bring Jibril to justice, it was to get off the *Faith* in one piece. Rafe and Flynn didn't like leaving unfinished business any more than Hawk did, but the Major was right. As much as Hawk would prefer to see Jibril pay for his cruelty to Sarah and for the men who had died because of Weltzer, his priority was still Sarah's safety. The sooner they accomplished their escape, the safer she would be.

The dark forms of the rest of the team converged on the stern from various points around the deck, the muzzles of their weapons flashing as they continued to fire behind them. Redinger was the last to arrive. He placed himself at the far end of the group, gave them a thumbs-up and turned to watch the water. No lights were visible, but the stuttering hum of a helicopter was rapidly approaching.

Hawk hooked one hand in the back of the waistband of Sarah's pants, preparing to toss her into the helicopter as soon as it arrived. She threw him a look over her shoulder, part exasperation and part something else he couldn't interpret.

Rafe and Flynn maneuvered themselves in front of Hawk on either side of Sarah and each grabbed one of her arms. Apparently they had the same thing in mind as Hawk. Sarah opened her mouth to say something then, but her words were drowned out by a sudden thudding boom.

Lights flared to life along the upper edge of the bridge, flooding the deck with a white glare. Car-size plates of metal in the superstructure swung open, exposing two pairs of long-barreled weapons. There was another boom. A shell rocketed over the deck to burn a trail through the darkness.

"The bastard has artillery," Flynn said. "We don't have the ordnance to take that out."

Another panel opened to reveal an unmanned machine

gun that was mounted high on a circular metal base. It swiveled toward them. A line of sparks shot up from the deck between the helicopter pad and the back of the lifeboat less than a yard away from the team.

"These must be what Jibril meant by the *Faith's* defenses," Sarah said. "He must have been waiting until he could pin us all down before he used them."

As quickly as it had begun, the gunfire ceased. The point had been made. A voice cut through the sudden silence. *"Throw down your weapons!"* The words were amplified by a loudspeaker, but Jibril's high-pitched, Oxford-tinged tone was instantly recognizable. *"Surrender and you will not be harmed."*

"Yeah, right," Flynn said. "Tell us another one."

"This is all a terrible misunderstanding," Jibril continued.

"I've heard that before," Sarah muttered.

"Allow my guests to remain with me and the rest of you are free to leave. You have ten seconds to decide."

"Three minutes until the charges blow," Rafe said. "That will give us the cover we need to board the chopper. We have to stall."

"Seven seconds…six…"

Hawk didn't need more than half a second to make his decision. He took a deep breath and released his grip on Sarah's waistband. "Hang on to her, Rafe," he said, rising to his feet. "You'll have your three minutes."

"Hawk," Sarah, cried. "Oh, my God! No!"

"Three…two…"

"Don't shoot!" Hawk shouted. He raised his hands over his head, stepped away from the group and strode forward.

"Ah, Hawkins. I'm pleased you elected to join me."

Hawk could hear a scuffle behind him and Sarah's muttered curses. Her voice cut off suddenly, as if someone had put their hand over her mouth. He didn't look back. He was confident she wouldn't be able to break free of her large and determined friends.

Flynn had said the explosives were under the helicopter pad. Hawk glanced at the raised platform on his right. The charges would have been positioned so that the team wouldn't be harmed when they went off. That meant the force of the blast would be directed away from the stern, likely toward the front and the sides. He wondered how accurate Chief Esposito's timing was.

"But what about your lovely…incentive," Jibril said. *"I am still waiting for her."*

Hawk walked past the lifeboat so he would have a clear path to the railing at the side of the ship. He was now in line with the front of the helicopter pad. He squinted against the floodlights that shone in his eyes and cupped his hands around his mouth. "You don't need her, Jibril," he shouted. "I have what you want. I discovered the key today. I can give you fusion power."

The loudspeaker fell silent. Hawk could hear the men behind him shifting. He tried to keep track of the time in his head, but it was dragging by in nightmare slow motion. He knew Jibril had no intention of letting Sarah and her team go free. He could only hope that as long as he kept Jibril talking, the palace guards wouldn't open fire.

The mahogany doors that led into the upper part of the ship swung open. At least twenty heavily armed guards burst through and fanned out along the deck. Hawk heard the clicks of weapons being readied behind him. He was right in the middle. If there was gunfire, he would be caught between both sides and be dead within seconds. He was counting on Jibril's greed to keep him alive.

A blur of white appeared at the doors. It was Jibril himself. Hawk felt his pulse kick. He hadn't expected the prince to swallow his act that well.

Twelve more guards fell into position around Jibril, forming a human wall to shield him as he advanced, although he had probably deduced the men from Eagle Squadron wouldn't be allowed to harm him. Otherwise, he wouldn't have appeared, no matter how many guards he hid behind. He gathered his djellabah around him and moved with his characteristic smooth glide despite the slow roll of the deck. He halted when he was still several yards from Hawk. "If you lie," he called out. "I will kill all of you."

Hawk lowered his hands. "I never lie, Jibril. I do have the key to fusion power. Ask your guards. They were watching me when I found it."

There was an exchange of words between Jibril and the guard on his right before Jibril and his human shield came two paces closer. With the floodlights behind him, his face was in shadow, yet his dark eyes appeared lit from within. "The technology will be mine and mine alone."

"Fly me to Moukim tonight," Hawk said. "I'll begin running the tests as soon as we arrive. You'll have a prototype reactor by next month."

"You see? I win again, Hawkins."

"Yes." How long now? One minute? Half a minute? "You always win, just as you won Faith."

Jibril laughed. There was a manic edge to the sound. "Yes, I won Faith. It was only a matter of finding the right incentive then, too."

Hawk's muscles were bunching with the urge to move but he forced himself to remain motionless. Didn't Jibril hear the approaching helicopter? Or did he plan to wait for it to get closer before he gave the order to destroy it?

Hawk felt a bead of sweat trickle down his temple. He had to keep Jibril talking. "You mean your money?"

"No, Hawkins. Nothing so crass. You were the incentive that time. I used the same tactic with Faith that I did with you."

Twenty seconds? Fifteen? "I don't understand."

Jibril took a quick step forward. His guards hastened to resume their formation. "No, you never did understand that I was the true genius. What a shame. It was so pathetically easy." He laughed again. "Would you like to know, Hawkins?"

He hoped the team could get Sarah into the helicopter first. Yet with so many of the palace guards positioned on the deck, would the explosion provide enough cover? "Know what, Jibril?"

"How I did it. I convinced Faith that if she married you she would be a widow by the end of the day. To keep you alive, she was willing to do anything."

Hawk's entire consciousness was focused on counting off three minutes. His thoughts were filled with the people whose lives depended on him. This wasn't about his past. It wasn't personal.

But it was. Dammit, the past had never been over. Jibril's words lanced through his heart, rupturing the wound that Hawk had believed was long healed.

Time stopped as the buried pain came pouring out. Faith had left him at the altar. She had agreed to marry Jibril. She had done it because...

Because she'd thought she was saving Hawk's life.

In the space of a heartbeat, everything crystallized. It fit. Finally it made sense. The love Hawk and Faith had shared had been real after all. Jibril had recognized that love and had used it. He'd twisted it.

All these years Hawk hadn't seen the truth. He hadn't

trusted his feelings. He'd hidden behind his logic, but he could have listened to his heart all along.

It was all so gloriously simple.

Jibril waved his hand toward Hawk and gave a curt order in Arabic to his guards.

Before the guards could react, a whistle split the air. Hawk snapped out of his daze and dove for the brass railing at the edge of the deck. A blinding flash reflected in the metal. Thunder erupted around him. He was already on his way over the side when the force of the blast caught him, flinging him upward and away from the hull.

He had only an instant to glimpse the scene behind him, but every detail seared into his brain. The platform at the stern of the ship tilted forward on billows of flame. The helicopter that had been resting on it split apart as its fuel ignited, raining deadly chunks of metal decking and burning wreckage on the palace guards. In the center of the guards, a tall, slender figure was cowering on his knees, his robes alight, his face contorted in a scream.

And in the glare on the edge of the destruction, a group of men tossed a small blond woman through the open door of the helicopter that rose above the corner of the deck.

Hawk was smiling when the first piece of debris hit him.

Chapter 15

"How is he?"

Sarah wiped her eyes on her sleeve and glanced over her shoulder. "No change, Rafe."

Rafe moved into the room to stand at the foot of the hospital bed. He and Flynn had been the first ones out of the helicopter when they'd spotted Hawk in the water. Rafe's uniform had dried during the flight to the carrier, but his boots were still damp enough to make wet sounds as he walked. "Norton said he probably got a concussion from the blast."

"Yes, I remember." Sergeant Norton was the team's medic. He'd started working on Hawk the moment they'd winched him onboard the helicopter. There hadn't been much he could do, other than start an IV and control the bleeding.

All Sarah had been able to do was pray.

She tried to block the memory, but the image of that scene rose yet again in her mind. Hawk's sodden clothes

had been charred and torn. His right side had been a mess
of bruises and blistered skin from being caught so close to
the explosion. Blood had seeped from his ears and his nose
and poured from a gash at his hairline, mixing with the
seawater to form a macabre veil over his face. He'd been
so still, for one horrifying instant she'd imagined the worst
until Norton had assured her Hawk's heart was still beat-
ing.

Sarah dragged her chair closer to the bed. The blood
had been cleaned up and his burns and abrasions had been
dressed, but Hawk still hadn't moved. If he had a simple
concussion, he should have shown signs of coming around
by now, shouldn't he? She touched her fingertips to the
bandage that was wrapped around Hawk's skull. Something big, probably a piece of metal, had struck him before
he'd hit the water. It had taken eighteen stitches to close
the wound. This was the injury that concerned the doctors
the most.

She glanced at the array of medical equipment that mon-
itored Hawk's vitals. The facilities on this aircraft carrier
were as good as any hospital. The ship was part of the
navy's Mediterranean fleet. It had been on routine maneu-
vers when the team had arranged to launch their raid on
the *Faith* from here. The medics had been prepared for
them to return with casualties.

But apart from Hawk, no one on the team was injured.
Thanks to him, they had escaped certain death without a
scratch.

And their deaths had been certain. Sarah had heard the
final order that Jibril had given just before the charges had
gone off. Take Hawkins and kill the rest.

They had been trapped. If Hawk's quick thinking hadn't
bought them time, the *Faith's* artillery could have taken
out the chopper. The machine guns that had been trained

on the team could have cut them to shreds. Hawk had understood the situation instantly and had placed himself between them and the guns.

I would gladly give my life if I thought it would save yours.

She didn't bother trying to stop the tears this time. They rolled down her cheeks and fell on the sleeve of Hawk's hospital gown. As she watched the dark circles grow on the pale-blue cotton, she thought about the other things that Jibril had said. He'd boasted about Faith. He'd mocked their love.

Sarah should be ashamed to feel pleased that the bastard had suffered before he'd died.

The fire hadn't spread past the *Faith's* deck, so the innocent servants and ship's crew who had been hiding in the galley hadn't been hurt. While the guards who had survived had declined the Navy's offer of help for their wounded, the diplomats had worked fast. One of Jibril's cousins, the next in line for Moukim's throne, had been eager to smooth over the incident, so he was already publicly claiming his predecessor had perished in a tragic helicopter accident.

"The men drew straws," Rafe said. "I get to sit with Lemay if you want to catch some sleep."

She shook her head. "Thanks, but I'm not leaving until I talk to the doctor. He said they'll have the test results any minute."

"Do you remember what you told me when Glenna was in the hospital a few months ago?"

Had it only been a few months? It seemed longer. So much had happened. "What was it?"

"You said it was going to work out, that Glenna and I were two of the lucky ones."

"Yes, I did say that. It turned out you were."

"You have to believe that you will be too, Sarah. Lemay won't give up."

"Damn right, he won't." She stroked Hawk's knuckles, careful not to disturb the IV needle in the back of his hand. "He's going to pull through this, and when he does, I'm going to kick his butt from here to Bragg for trying to be such a goddamn hero—" She pressed her lips together, fighting to keep the sob inside.

Rafe cleared his throat. "Yeah."

Crepe soles squeaked on the floor. Sarah looked up as the doctor entered the room. He went to the monitors first, then turned to examine Hawk. His movements had the briskness that only came from years of experience. His white hair and the deep creases that underlined his face spoke of experience, too.

Was that why he wasn't meeting Sarah's gaze? She rose to her feet. "What's Dr. Lemay's condition?" she asked.

When the doctor finally looked at Sarah, she almost wished he hadn't. He couldn't hide the sympathy in his gaze. "His condition appears to be stable."

All right. At least it wasn't worse. "When will he wake up?"

"It's hard to say."

"That wasn't an answer," Rafe said.

"I'm sorry. I don't have one." The doctor glanced at Rafe, then back at Sarah. "The scans showed no damage to Dr. Lemay's internal organs, which is good news, but he has a serious skull fracture and there is still a significant amount of swelling on his brain. We're hoping this will subside without surgical intervention, yet even then there's no guarantee."

Dread knotted Sarah's lungs. She didn't want to ask, but she knew she had to. "No guarantee of what? He's going to live, isn't he?"

"Yes, he'll live, but I've seen head trauma like this before. In most cases as severe as this…"

She saw the truth on his face. Oh, God, she was wrong. She didn't want to know.

"It would be best if you try to prepare yourself," the doctor continued. "There's a strong possibility of brain damage."

She looked at Hawk. His eyes were closed. She pictured the sharp glint of intellect behind his blue gaze. She curled her fingers around the metal rail at the side of the bed. "No." She shook her head. "No. That can't happen. Don't you know who this man is?"

"Yes, Captain Fox, I'm aware—"

"This is Hawkins Lemay. He's a Nobel laureate. He's a gifted scientist and a certified genius. He's got so many degrees he can string half the alphabet after his name."

"I'm sorry. I wish—"

"He might not wear a uniform, but he's the most courageous, honorable man I've ever known. He was willing to sacrifice everything he'd worked for to keep people from dying. He was willing to give his life for me…." Her throat closed. She strode around the bed and caught the doctor by the front of his lab coat. "You said it's only a possibility."

"Yes. A strong—"

"I don't give a damn what the odds are." She gave the doctor a hard shake. "He's going to be fine. You hear me?"

A firm hand settled on her shoulder. "Sarah," Rafe said. "Maybe we'd better wait outside."

She whirled on him. "I won't give up on Hawk. No matter what happens and no matter how long it takes."

Another man entered the room. It was Major Redinger.

"Captain Fox," he said. "Sergeant Marek is right. We should let the doctor do his job."

The sight of her C.O. should have snapped her to attention. Her father's voice echoed through her memory but she ignored it. She knew what she was. She was a woman in love. "I won't leave Hawk, sir."

"Neither will we," Redinger said. He looked at the doctor. "How soon can he be moved?"

The metal tray dropped to the floor, wobbled back and forth with an echoing clang, then finally lay still. Footsteps squeaked across the room. There was a muttered curse, a soft scrape, then the footsteps retreated. A whispering slide, like a door swinging shut, then silence...except for a steady beep and music that played softly from somewhere behind him.

Hawk opened his eyes. He was flat on his back. The ceiling was white. He saw a soft-looking pouch hanging from a hard, shiny pole. A tube came out of the pouch. He moved his gaze down the tube and saw that it disappeared beneath a strip of white tape inside his elbow.

There was a connection to the facts. It floated just out of his reach, like one of those things when it was cold and there were colors.... A leaf. Yes, that's what it was like. A leaf in a breeze, spiraling in one direction then tumbling in another.

Hawk closed his eyes and tried to figure it out, but his mind felt sluggish. He was in bed. He wasn't tired exactly. He felt the way he did when he stayed up all night to work out an interesting equation and then fell asleep with his head on his desk. The music was familiar. He struggled to find the pattern to the melody... Beethoven. The ninth symphony. Yes. He listened to that when he worked, but he couldn't be in his lab, could he?

His ribs itched. So did the place where the tape covered his elbow. And his forehead. It itched, too. He lifted his arm. He heard the…plastic—yes, that was what it was called—the plastic tube thump softly against the metal support. He brought his fingers to his head and scratched.

There was a ridge of tender, lumpy skin on his forehead. He traced it to his scalp and discovered a strip where his hair felt short and bristly. He inhaled carefully. The air smelled like boiled cotton and disinfectant….

The facts suddenly congealed. The beeping sound accelerated. This was a hospital room. There must have been an accident. He blinked, braced his elbows against the bed and tried to sit up.

The door whispered open again. A tall man in a green-and-brown camouflage uniform stood in the doorway. He was talking over his shoulder to someone outside, apologizing for being late for his shift and saying he was going to change the CD to something that rocked. He turned his head toward Hawk and stopped dead.

More facts fell into place as the man's name clicked in Hawk's brain. Flynn O'Toole. Sarah's friend… *Sarah!* "Where…"

Flynn grabbed the door frame and leaned outside. "Get the doctor! Lemay's awake."

Hawk coughed. His throat was dry. He tried again. "Where?"

"You're in the base hospital," Flynn said, striding to the bed. "Fort Bragg. We brought you home with us."

He must be saying it wrong, Hawk thought. He had to try harder to make Flynn understand. "Where…is…Sarah?"

"On her way." Flynn glanced at the clock on the wall, then grinned at Hawk. "Oh, man, your timing couldn't be better. I won the pool."

* * *

Sarah couldn't help it. She ran. One of the nurses smiled and called out as she reached the junction of the corridors and turned the corner past the nurses' station, but Sarah didn't stop. She couldn't get there soon enough.

He's awake. The word had spread through the team faster than speed dial. Sarah had been on one of the target ranges in the Delta Force compound on the other side of the base when the news had reached her. She was grateful no one had gotten in her way when she'd left.

A group was already gathered in the hall outside Hawk's door. Rafe was laughing as Norton counted out a handful of bills and handed them to Flynn—the men had placed bets on when Hawk would wake up.

Esposito was the first to spot her. His gold tooth glinted from his grin as he called to the other men, "The captain's here."

The men of Eagle Squadron turned to face her. The past few weeks had been the longest in Sarah's life, yet her friends had been there through every minute. She wanted to pause and thank them for their time and their support. She wanted to hug every one of these commandos and tell them they were the best brothers anyone could have.

But Sarah didn't want to wait another second. Hawk was awake. She hoped they would understand.

They did. As one, the men straightened up and snapped their hands to their foreheads in a salute.

It was a moment she knew she would always treasure, one of those blinks in time when everything in her life seemed perfectly right.

She didn't have to choose whether to cry or to salute. She did both.

"...still need therapy and further testing. We won't

know the extent of the damage for a while, but your initial responses do look promising.''

Sarah recognized the voice that came through the open doorway. It was Dr. Owens, the specialist the Major had convinced to take over Hawk's case.

''We'll set up a therapy schedule with the staff here,'' Redinger said. ''We'll provide accommodation on the base for you so you can continue with it after you're released from the hospital.''

''First…I need…to see…Sarah.''

Her heart leaped at the sound of Hawk's voice. He spoke slowly, as if each word was an effort, but the deep Southern-tinged tone was the same, and sweeter to her than any music. The soles of her boots skidded on the floor as she caught the door frame to stop her momentum and pivoted into the room.

At first the Major and the doctor blocked her view of the bed. They turned at the sound of her entrance. They probably said something, but she didn't hear. She brushed past them.

Hawk wasn't lying on the bed as he had been all the other times she'd seen him here. He was sitting on the edge of it. His broad shoulders stretched the cotton hospital gown he wore, his hair stood up in tufts around his scar where it was beginning to grow back and he was looking straight at her.

She didn't need to wait for the results of the doctor's tests. This was what she'd prayed for. Hawk's gaze was bright and completely lucid. ''Hawk,'' she breathed.

He smiled and held out his arms.

Sarah didn't remember crossing the room. The next thing she knew, she had stepped between Hawk's knees, put her arms around him and was enveloped in his embrace. She felt his breath on her hair, his hands on her back, and she felt as if she'd come home.

She had so much to say, she didn't know where to start.

Almost three weeks had passed for her since the escape from the *Faith,* but only a few minutes had passed for Hawk. Sarah had had more than enough time to sort through her feelings. She'd spent so many nights sitting by Hawk's bedside, stroking his hand, telling him she loved him, she had almost forgotten that he couldn't have heard her.

The team knew how she felt. So did the staff at the hospital. Even her father knew. He was still in Washington, but she had made a point of calling him to give him regular updates on Hawk's condition. The general hadn't changed—he still hoped for a match with a military man for his little girl—but he was handling the disappointment well, probably because even his pals at the Pentagon had heard about Hawk's heroism.

There was a rustle of movement behind her. "Captain Fox," Dr. Owens said. "Excuse me, I haven't finished my examination."

She didn't move away. She only pulled back enough to look at Hawk's face. "How are you feeling?"

He cupped her cheek in his palm. "Good."

"Am I hurting you?"

He caught a lock of her hair and rubbed it between his fingers, then brought it to his nose and inhaled. "Never."

She moved her hand to his chest. The wires that had hooked him up to the monitors were gone. So was the IV tube. His burns and abrasions had healed well while he'd been unconscious. The regular physical therapy he'd received had kept his muscle tone strong. The doctor had said that Hawk's excellent physical condition prior to the explosion helped contribute to his recovery. Sarah could feel for herself that his strength had returned.

She brushed her fingers over the healing line on his forehead and followed it to his scalp. "What about this? Does it hurt?"

"It itches." He paused. "Inside, too. It feels thick. When I think...I scratch it."

"That's an excellent analogy, Dr. Lemay," Dr. Owens said, moving to the foot of the bed beside them. "The damage is like a healing scab. The more mental stimulation you have, the faster your brain will establish alternate pathways."

Hawk rolled his eyes toward the doctor. "My head might be...slow. Everything else...works...fine."

"Yes, it's really quite remarkable." He made a note in the chart he held. "Major Redinger, I have to thank you for bringing Dr. Lemay's case to my attention. I have some colleagues who are also doing research in this field and would be extremely interested in following his progress."

Hawk returned his gaze to Sarah. The lines at the corners of his eyes crinkled with humor. "Damn...scientists," he muttered.

Her lips trembled with a laugh, but she knew if she let it out it would likely emerge as a sob. She clasped his waist and pressed closer to the bed between his thighs.

"Captain Fox?"

She replied to the Major without taking her gaze off Hawk. "Yes, sir?"

"It starts at 1700 hours."

"Thank you, Major." She saw Hawk raise one eyebrow. She would explain later about the long-overdue leave she had negotiated. She rubbed her fingers along his hips. "One more thing, Major?"

"Yes, Captain?"

"Is it possible for Dr. Owens to continue his discussion with you somewhere else?"

"I believe that can be arranged."

"Thank you, sir."

"Excuse me, Captain," the doctor said. "As I mentioned before, I need to—"

"Dr. Owens," Sarah said. "Would it set back Dr. Lemay's recovery if I kissed him?"

"Well, no. Any stimulation he could get would actually be quite beneficial."

Hawk had grasped the back of her head and pressed his lips to hers before the doctor had finished speaking. Hoots of encouragement sounded from the men in the hallway. Sarah was dimly aware of the sound of Redinger's voice as he ushered Dr. Owens out of the room, then the soft whoosh of the closing door.

Hawk's touch felt the same. So did his taste. But his kiss was different. She had always loved the way he kissed. Whether he was being fierce or gentle, whether it was fast or slow, she had always felt his total absorption. This time it was more than that. He kissed her as if they were fitting together, like two halves of the same whole.

Or was the difference in her? The sense of rightness she'd felt when she'd stepped into his embrace was only growing stronger. She hadn't known what to expect when she'd walked into this room today, but she'd known in her heart that whatever she'd found wouldn't have changed her love for him.

Hawk trailed kisses across her cheek to her ear, then rubbed her earlobe between his teeth.

Sarah gasped at the tickle of awareness that shot through her. She drew back to look at him. Just how much stimulation could they risk?

He slid farther back on the narrow bed and tugged her

toward him. She grinned, climbed onto the bed and swung her legs across his lap. There was no lock on the door, but she intended to get as close as the situation allowed. He looped his arms around her shoulders, pressing his forehead to hers. He held her in silence for a while before he spoke again. "So much I want...to say, Sarah. So glad you're...safe."

"We all owe you our lives."

"Glad it worked. Jibril..." He swallowed hard. "Faith killed him."

Sarah had a twinge of uneasiness. His thoughts couldn't be as clear as she'd thought. "No, Hawk. He threatened to kill you, but—"

"I mean the ship," he said. "The *Faith*. Pieces of the ship. From the explosion."

Sarah realized there was nothing wrong with his reasoning. He'd just seen the facts from a different angle. "That's true. I guess you could say *Faith* killed him. Kind of a fitting irony."

"I loved her."

She clasped his head and nodded. She had to remind herself again that only a few minutes had passed for him since those last terrible moments. Jibril's revelations would still be fresh in his mind. So would the wound from them. "Yes. I know. I'm so sorry, Hawk."

"I love you."

She stilled. Was it due to his struggle with words? Had he meant what he'd said? She waited.

"Don't need my...brain to know that," he said. He took her fingers and tapped them over his heart. "Love you in here, Sarah."

It was too much. Having Hawk back, having him healthy, was all she'd dared ask for. To be gifted with his love as well...

She tipped his head forward to brush a kiss over his healing scar, then hung on to his shoulders and smiled into his eyes. "I love you, too."

His gaze grew brighter. "Wish I was...better."

"I only expect you to be Hawk."

Epilogue

"We need a bigger bathtub."

Sarah laughed. She'd always considered the old-fashioned claw-footed bathtub in her apartment to be enormous, but not when a six-foot-two, 198-pound man was sharing it with her. She leaned over the edge to retrieve the soap. More water sloshed onto the floor. "Oops."

Hawk hooked his arm in front of her waist and hauled her back into the tub. He brushed aside a mound of bubbles, then kissed the nape of her neck. "Either that, or you'll have to stop moving around so much."

"Mmm." Sarah looked at where his knees angled above the water on either side of her. Moisture trickled down his thigh, flattening the dark hair against his skin, gleaming over a temptingly taut curve of muscle. He'd started jogging again last week as soon as the doctor had cleared him to resume his normal activities.

Of course, there were some activities he'd resumed long before that. As a matter of fact, the day he'd been released from the hospital they had barely made it through the apartment door before they'd recommenced one of them. She let the soap thud to the bottom of the tub and dragged her fingernail along his thigh. "Okay, I can try not to move, but I'm not so sure about you."

"Aha." He turned his hand to cup her breast. "You know I can't resist a challenge."

"Just one of the things I love about you, Hawk."

"I can't begin to list the things I love about you, Sarah." He sat forward, resting his chin on her shoulder as he lifted his hand. The upper curve of her breast appeared above the surface of the water. "But if pressed, I suppose I could name one."

"Only one?"

He moved his other hand and did the same for her other breast. "Maybe two." He slicked his fingertips over her nipples. "Fascinating. Here's three and four. This could take a while."

Sarah curled her hand around his leg. They had made love before they'd gotten out of bed that morning, but the familiar tingles were starting again. "You'd better count faster, darling. Your session with Dr. Owens starts in less than an hour."

"I'm not going today. We decided to cut back the sessions to once a week."

"Hawk, that's wonderful."

"I believe the word he used was 'regrettable.'" Hawk scooped a handful of bubbles over her shoulder. "He says my progress is throwing off the data for his research project. I don't fit his projections. He still hasn't figured out that you're the real reason for my recovery."

"Mmm. Therapeutic sex," she murmured. "It might catch on."

"It's love, Sarah. It always was."

"You're right about that." She twisted her head to give him a kiss. "Do you know when I probably started falling in love with you?"

"No, when?"

"When you drew me that bath the night before Weltzer's attack."

"Don't remind me. I thought I'd go insane listening to you naked."

"How can you listen to someone naked?"

He dipped his hand into the water and slowly stroked her arm. The sound of his wet palm sliding over her skin was as sensuous as wet silk.

"I see your point."

"Sarah, do you want to call it a draw?"

"What?"

"In about five seconds, I'm not only going to move, I'm going to send the rest of this bath water pouring through the landlady's ceiling."

They managed to leave most of the water behind as they got out of the tub. Sarah had just reached for a towel when a sharp knocking sounded on the apartment door.

Hawk took the towel from her hands and started drying her off. "Expecting someone?"

She lifted her arms to make it easier for him. "No, I..." She muttered a curse. "I completely forgot. Glenna and Abbie wanted to go over the wedding plans before I head to the base today. They're early."

Hawk groaned. "Why can't we elope?"

"We already agreed to make it a group ceremony. The whole team is looking forward to it."

He leaned down to lick a drop of water from the small of her back. "I can see why they'd like it. It's starting to resemble a military campaign."

"Well, Glenna is a professional event planner. She tends to think big."

"Rafe and Flynn agree with me. They're not that happy about waiting."

"Mmm. That changes things. If those two decide on eloping, they'll probably hijack the wedding."

Hawk turned her around, brushing his lips across her hip to her stomach. He kissed away the water that lingered in her navel. "Personally, I'd prefer a short ceremony and a long honeymoon."

"Mmm. Hold that thought. I have to answer the door."

There was another round of knocking, followed by a sharp meow and a string of sour notes. Sarah snatched the towel back from Hawk and wrapped it around herself as she padded through the living room. The white kitten she had adopted was bounding across the keyboard of the piano Hawk had surprised her with the week before. "Keep up the practice, Rosie," Sarah said to the kitten. "At least you sound better than I do." She unlocked the door and swung it wide. "Sorry to keep you waiting, Glenna…"

It wasn't Rafe's bride-to-be who stood on the threshold, it was Major Redinger.

"Excuse me, Captain," he said. "I don't mean to intrude."

Sarah wasn't embarrassed by her lack of clothing—this was her home, after all. But she was puzzled to see the Major here. "Sir?"

"I learned at the hospital that Dr. Lemay no longer needs regular therapy."

"Yes, that's true."

"In that case, there's something I need to discuss with him. I assume he's here?"

She showed the Major to the living room sofa and went to get dressed. By the time she had fixed her hair and put on her uniform, Hawk and Redinger were already deep in discussion.

"Were you bluffing when you told Prince Jibril that you had found the key to fusion power?" the Major asked.

"No, it wasn't a bluff. I had recognized an error in my research that afternoon, which led me to the discovery of how to correct it."

"Dr. Owens says your recovery has progressed to the point where you could soon resume your work."

Hawk paused. "The work was destroyed before we left the *Faith.*"

"That was my idea, sir," Sarah said, walking forward. "It was the only way we could guarantee it wouldn't fall into the wrong hands."

"Yes, that was unfortunate."

"It was the only choice," Hawk said. He looked at Sarah. "I would do it all again if I had to."

Sarah moved beside the arm of Hawk's chair and rested her hand on his shoulder. She could feel the tension in his muscles through his shirt. She squeezed gently. "What's this about, Major?"

"I've been asked to approach Dr. Lemay with another offer."

Hawk remained silent.

"The Defense Department is still very interested in working with you on an exclusive basis," Redinger said. "Particularly since the information you gave to the public was flawed."

Hawk leaned forward suddenly, his gaze hard. "What I told you just now can go no farther. I don't want another Weltzer."

"I understand."

"I don't think you do," Hawk said. "Otherwise, you wouldn't have come to me with this offer. Jibril is dead,

but there are still many others who would want to stop me
from succeeding. If it became known that the work I published was flawed and I agreed to work exclusively for our
government, I would be back where I started. I would be
making myself the target of another assassin.''

"We would provide security—"

"I might have been willing to gamble *my* life for an
idea, but I will not gamble with my fiancée's.'' Hawk had
spoken quietly, but the calm resolve in his tone echoed
through the room. He got to his feet, signaling an end to
the discussion. "If and when I decide to resume my research, it won't be done in secrecy, Major.''

Redinger stood. He straightened his uniform. "Does this
mean you do plan to continue?"

Hawk moved to Sarah and put his arm around her waist.
He drew her firmly to his side. "Someday, when I've regained my full mental capabilities, yes, I do plan to continue. But right now, I'm focusing on getting well and
getting married.''

"Congratulations, by the way.''

"Thank you.''

Redinger turned his gaze to Sarah. He looked at her for
a long moment, as if debating what he was going to say.
Finally his mouth moved into one of his rare smiles. "It
looks as if I made the right decision after all.''

"I'm not sure I understand you, sir.''

"Last month, when I sent you to Stockholm, I never did
tell you the full extent of your mission objectives.''

"My mission…'' She frowned. "I was to protect
Hawk.''

"If the mission had been simply to protect him, I
wouldn't have been asked to send a woman who was still
recovering from an injury. You were chosen because of
your gender and your intelligence-gathering skills.''

The arm Hawk held around her waist tightened. Sarah stared at the Major. She remembered the distance she'd sensed in Redinger during their telephone conversations and the discomfort she'd noticed when they'd met at the hotel. With everything else that had happened, she had pushed her earlier suspicions to the back of her mind.

Tell me the truth, Captain Fox. What's the real reason you're here?

"Oh, my God. Are you saying…" She took a deep breath. "You really did want me to spy on Hawk?"

"Those were my orders. We had to keep track of who might approach Dr. Lemay at the conference and any other offers he might receive."

Sarah's head reeled. This was precisely what Hawk had said. "Why didn't you tell me?"

Redinger looked at Hawk. "Ask him. I believe he knows."

Hawk nodded. "Yes, I know. It's just as you said. Sarah could never be forced into doing anything she didn't want to do."

"Exactly. I did what I was asked by sending her, but I thought it best not to put Captain Fox in a position where she had to choose between her honor and her orders." He picked up his coat and walked to the door. "It's… interesting how it all worked out, isn't it?"

The instant the Major was gone, Hawk started to chuckle. Sarah pulled away from him and paced across the room. "I can't believe this. It isn't fair."

Hawk's chuckle turned to a laugh. "What isn't fair?"

She came back and caught the front of his shirt. "You were right after all! My God. I hadn't seen it, but you had it figured out from the start."

He had a hard time catching his breath, he was laughing so hard. "Well, I am a genius."

"Okay, genius." She stepped closer, pressed her hips to his and gave his shirt a sharp tug. Three buttons flew off and bounced on the floor. She undid two more and splayed her hands over his chest. "See if you can figure this out."

Still laughing, he scooped her off her feet and carried her to their bedroom.

Sarah smiled. His brain certainly worked fine.

And so did everything else.

*   *   *   *   *

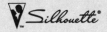

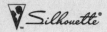

✂

Your opinion is important to us! Please take a few moments to share your thoughts with us about your experiences with Harlequin and Silhouette books. Your comments will be very useful in ensuring that we deliver books you love to read. *Please take a few minutes to complete the questionnaire, then send it to us at the address below.*

Send your completed questionnaires to:
Harlequin/Silhouette Reader Survey, P.O. Box 9046, Buffalo, NY 14269-9046

---

1. As you may know, there are many different lines under the Harlequin and Silhouette brands. Each of the lines is listed below. Please check the box that most represents your reading habit for each line.

Line	Currently read this line	Do not read this line	Not sure if I read this line
Harlequin American Romance	❏	❏	❏
Harlequin Duets	❏	❏	❏
Harlequin Romance	❏	❏	❏
Harlequin Historicals	❏	❏	❏
Harlequin Superromance	❏	❏	❏
Harlequin Intrigue	❏	❏	❏
Harlequin Presents	❏	❏	❏
Harlequin Temptation	❏	❏	❏
Harlequin Blaze	❏	❏	❏
Silhouette Special Edition	❏	❏	❏
Silhouette Romance	❏	❏	❏
Silhouette Intimate Moments	❏	❏	❏
Silhouette Desire	❏	❏	❏

2. Which of the following best describes why you bought *this book?* One answer only, please.

the picture on the cover	❏	the title	❏
the author	❏	the line is one I read often	❏
part of a miniseries	❏	saw an ad in another book	❏
saw an ad in a magazine/newsletter	❏	a friend told me about it	❏
I borrowed/was given this book	❏	other: _____	❏

3. Where did you buy *this book?* One answer only, please.

at Barnes & Noble	❏	at a grocery store	❏
at Waldenbooks	❏	at a drugstore	❏
at Borders	❏	on eHarlequin.com Web site	❏
at another bookstore	❏	from another Web site	❏
at Wal-Mart	❏	Harlequin/Silhouette Reader	❏
at Target	❏	Service/through the mail	
at Kmart	❏	used books from anywhere	❏
at another department store or mass merchandiser	❏	I borrowed/was given this book	❏

4. On average, how many Harlequin and Silhouette books do you buy at one time?

I buy _____ books at one time ❏
I rarely buy a book ❏

MRQ403SIM-1A

5. How many times per month do you shop for any *Harlequin and/or Silhouette* books?
One answer only, please.

1 or more times a week	❏	a few times per year	❏
1 to 3 times per month	❏	less often than once a year	❏
1 to 2 times every 3 months	❏	never	❏

6. When you think of your ideal heroine, which *one* statement describes her the best?
One answer only, please.

She's a woman who is strong-willed	❏	She's a desirable woman	❏
She's a woman who is needed by others	❏	She's a powerful woman	❏
She's a woman who is taken care of	❏	She's a passionate woman	❏
She's an adventurous woman		She's a sensitive woman	❏

7. The following statements describe types or genres of books that you may be
interested in reading. Pick *up to 2 types* of books that you are most interested in.

I like to read about truly romantic relationships	❏
I like to read stories that are sexy romances	❏
I like to read romantic comedies	❏
I like to read a romantic mystery/suspense	❏
I like to read about romantic adventures	❏
I like to read romance stories that involve family	❏
I like to read about a romance in times or places that I have never seen	❏
Other: _____	❏

*The following questions help us to group your answers with those readers who are
similar to you. Your answers will remain confidential.*

8. Please record your year of birth below.
19 ____

9. What is your marital status?
single ❏   married ❏   common-law ❏   widowed ❏
divorced/separated ❏

10. Do you have children 18 years of age or younger currently living at home?
yes ❏   no ❏

11. Which of the following best describes your employment status?
employed full-time or part-time ❏   homemaker ❏   student ❏
retired ❏   unemployed ❏

12. Do you have access to the Internet from either home or work?
yes ❏   no ❏

13. Have you ever visited eHarlequin.com?
yes ❏   no ❏

14. What state do you live in?
_____

15. Are you a member of Harlequin/Silhouette Reader Service?
yes ❏   Account # _____   no ❏   MRQ403SIM-1B

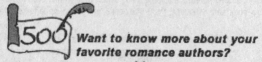

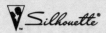

 Silhouette®

COMING NEXT MONTH